PENGUIN  CLASSICS

PENGUIN SELECTED ENGLISH POETS
GENERAL EDITOR: CHRISTOPHER RICKS

SIR PHILIP SIDNEY: SELECTED POEMS

SIR PHILIP SIDNEY was born at Penshurst Place in 1554, the eldest son of Sir Henry Sidney, thrice lord deputy of Ireland. He was educated at Shrewsbury School, at the same time as his friend and biographer Fulke Greville, and at Christ Church, Oxford, but left without taking a degree. From 1572 to 1575 he travelled to Europe, visiting Paris, Germany, Austria and Italy. On his return he became a courtier to Queen Elizabeth I but retired to Wilton, the home of his sister, Countess of Pembroke, after a quarrel with the Earl of Oxford. There he wrote *Arcadia*, although this version was later re-written. He was knighted in 1583 and the same year married Frances, the daughter of Francis Walsingham. In 1585 he was appointed Governor of Flushing, an appointment which prevented him from sailing to the West Indies with Ralegh and Drake. In September 1586 he led an attack on a Spanish convoy and was mortally wounded. He died twenty-six days later and was buried with great ceremony in St Paul's Cathedral. Sidney's major works are *The Lady of May*, *Arcadia*, *An Apology for Poetry* and *Astrophil and Stella*, none of which were published in his lifetime.

CATHERINE BATES was educated at Oxford, where she took a first in English, and was awarded the Violet Vaughan-Morgan and the Shelley-Mills University Prizes. She was a Fellow of Balliol College, Oxford, and from 1990 has been a Fellow of Peterhouse, Cambridge. She is the author of *The Rhetoric of Courtship in Elizabethan Language and Literature* (1992).

Sir Philip Sidney
Selected Poems

EDITED WITH AN INTRODUCTION AND NOTES
BY CATHERINE BATES

PENGUIN BOOKS

PENGUIN BOOKS

Published by the Penguin Group
Penguin Books Ltd, 27 Wrights Lane, London w8 5tz
Penguin Books USA Inc., 375 Hudson Street, New York, New York 10014, USA
Penguin Books Australia Ltd, Ringwood, Victoria, Australia
Penguin Books Canada Ltd, 10 Alcorn Avenue, Toronto, Ontario, Canada m4v 3b2
Penguin Books (NZ) Ltd, 182–190 Wairau Road, Auckland 10, New Zealand

Penguin Books Ltd, Registered Offices: Harmondsworth, Middlesex, England

First published 1994
10 9 8 7 6 5 4 3 2 1

Filmset in 10/11.5 pt Monotype Ehrhardt by
Datix International Limited, Bungay, Suffolk
Printed in England by Clays Ltd, St Ives plc

Contents

Introduction   xiii
Further Reading   xix
Table of Dates   xxi

Poems from *The Lady of May*

i To one whose state is raised over all   3
ii Come, *Espilus*, come now declare thy skill   3
iii *Silvanus* long in love, and long in vain   4

Poems from the *Old Arcadia*

The First Book or Act
I.i Thy elder care shall from thy careful face   9
I.ii Transformed in show, but more transformed in
   mind   9
I.iii What length of verse can serve brave *Mopsa*'s good to
   show   10
I.iv Come shepherd's weeds, become your master's
   mind   10
I.v Now thanked be the great god *Pan*   11

The First Eclogues
I.1 Come, *Dorus*, come, let songs thy sorrows signify   12
I.2 Fortune, Nature, Love, long have contended about
   me   17
I.3 If mine eyes can speak to do hearty errand   18
I.4 Lady, reserved by the heav'ns to do pastors' company
   honour   19

The Second Book or Act

II.i In vain, mine eyes, you labour to amend 27

II.ii Let not old age disgrace my high desire 27

II.iii Since so mine eyes are subject to your sight 28

II.iv My sheep are thoughts, which I both guide and serve 28

II.v Ye living powers enclosed in stately shrine 29

II.vi My words, in hope to blaze my steadfast mind 29

II.vii Loved I am, and yet complain of love 30

II.viii Over these brooks trusting to ease mine eyes 30

II.ix With two strange fires of equal heat possessed 31

II.x Feed on my sheep; my charge, my comfort, feed 31

II.xi Leave off my sheep: it is no time to feed 32

II.xii A hateful cure with hate to heal 33

II.xiii *Apollo* great, whose beams the greater world do light 33

The Second Eclogues

II.1 *Dorus*, tell me, where is thy wonted motion 34

II.2 Fair rocks, goodly rivers, sweet woods, when shall I see peace? 37

II.3 My Muse what ails this ardour 40

II.4 Reason, tell me thy mind, if here be reason 42

II.5 O sweet woods, the delight of solitariness! 43

The Third Book or Act

III.i Sweet glove, the witness of my secret bliss 45

III.ii The merchant man, whom gain doth teach the sea 45

III.iii The merchant man, whom many seas have taught 46

III.iv *Phoebus* farewell, a sweeter saint I serve 47

III.v Since that the stormy rage of passions dark 47

III.vi Hark, plaintful ghosts! Infernal furies, hark 48

III.vii How is my sun, whose beams are shining bright 49

III.viii My true love hath my heart, and I have his 49

III.ix O words which fall like summer dew on me 50

III.x Do not disdain, O straight upraised pine 51

III.xi You goodly pines, which still with brave ascent   51
III.xii Like diverse flowers, whose diverse beauties
    serve   52
III.xiii All what you are still one, his own to find   52
III.xiv Lock up, fair lids, the treasures of my heart   53
III.xv Why dost thou haste away   53
III.xvi O stealing time, the subject of delay   54
III.xvii My lute, within thyself thy tunes enclose   55
III.xviii When two suns do appear   55
III.xix *Aurora*, now thou show'st thy blushing light   56
III.xx Beauty hath force to catch the human sight   56
III.xxi Get hence foul grief, the canker of the mind   57
III.xxii Virtue, beauty, and speech, did strike, wound,
    charm   57
III.xxiii The love which is imprinted in my soul   58
III.xxiv What tongue can her perfections tell   59

The Third Eclogues
III.1 Let mother earth now deck herself in flowers   64
III.2 As I my little flock on *Ister* bank   67

The Fourth Book or Act
IV.i O night, the ease of care, the pledge of pleasure   72
IV.ii Since wailing is a bud of causeful sorrow   72

The Fourth Eclogues
IV.1 Ye goat-herd gods, that love the grassy
    mountains   74
IV.2 I joy in grief, and do detest all joys   76
IV.3 Now was our heav'nly vault deprived of the
    light   79
IV.4 Unto the caitiff wretch whom long affliction
    holdeth   84

The Fifth Book or Act
V.i Since Nature's works be good, and death doth
    serve   88

Poems from *Certain Sonnets*

i Since, shunning pain, I ease can never find   91
ii When Love, puffed up with rage of high disdain   91
iii The scourge of life, and death's extreme disgrace   92
iv Thou Pain, the only guest of loathed constraint   92
v You better sure shall live, not evermore   93
vi Like as the dove which seeled-up doth fly   93
vii Oft have I mused, but now at length I find   94
viii Thou blind man's mark, thou fool's self-chosen
     snare   94
ix Leave me, O Love, which reachest but to dust   95

Astrophil and Stella

1 Loving in truth, and fain in verse my love to show   99
2 Not at first sight, nor with a dribbed shot   99
3 Let dainty wits cry on the sisters nine   100
4 Virtue, alas, now let me take some rest   100
5 It is most true, that eyes are formed to serve   101
6 Some lovers speak, when they their Muses
     entertain   101
7 When Nature made her chief work, *Stella*'s eyes   102
8 Love, born in *Greece*, of late fled from his native place   102
9 Queen Virtue's court, which some call *Stella*'s face   103
10 Reason, in faith thou art well served, that still   104
11 In truth, O Love, with what a boyish kind   104
12 *Cupid*, because thou shin'st in *Stella*'s eyes   105
13 *Phoebus* was judge between *Jove*, *Mars*, and Love   105
14 Alas, have I not pain enough, my friend   106
15 You that do search for every purling spring   106
16 In nature apt to like when I did see   107
17 His mother dear *Cupid* offended late   107
18 With what sharp checks I in myself am shent   108
19 On *Cupid*'s bow how are my heart-strings bent   108
20 Fly, fly, my friends, I have my death-wound, fly   109
21 Your words my friend (right healthful caustics)
     blame   109

22 In highest way of heav'n the sun did ride   110
23 The curious wits, seeing dull pensiveness   110
24 Rich fools there be, whose base and filthy heart   111
25 The wisest scholar of the wight most wise   111
26 Though dusty wits dare scorn astrology   112
27 Because I oft, in dark abstracted guise   112
28 You that with allegory's curious frame   113
29 Like some weak lords, neighboured by mighty
    kings   113
30 Whether the Turkish new moon minded be   114
31 With how sad steps, O Moon, thou climb'st the
    skies   114
32 *Morpheus*, the lively son of deadly sleep   115
33 I might, unhappy word, O me, I might   115
34 Come, let me write. 'And to what end?'   116
35 What may words say, or what may words not say   116
36 *Stella*, whence doth this new assault arise   117
37 My mouth doth water, and my breast doth swell   117
38 This night, while sleep begins with heavy wings   118
39 Come sleep, O sleep, the certain knot of peace   118
40 As good to write as for to lie and groan   119
41 Having this day my horse, my hand, my lance   119
42 O eyes, which do the spheres of beauty move   120
43 Fair eyes, sweet lips, dear heart, that foolish I   120
44 My words I know do well set forth my mind   121
45 *Stella* oft sees the very face of woe   121
46 I cursed thee oft, I pity now thy case   122
47 What, have I thus betrayed my liberty?   122
48 Soul's joy, bend not those morning stars from me   123
49 I on my horse, and Love on me doth try   123
50 *Stella*, the fullness of my thoughts of thee   124
51 Pardon mine ears; both I and they do pray   124
52 A strife is grown between Virtue and Love   125
53 In martial sports I had my cunning tried   125
54 Because I breathe not love to every one   126
55 Muses, I oft invoked your holy aid   126
56 Fie, school of Patience, fie; your lesson is   127
57 Woe, having made with many fights his own   127
58 Doubt there hath been, when with his golden
    chain   128

59 Dear, why make you more of a dog than me?   128
60 When my good angel guides me to the place   129
61 Oft with true sighs, oft with uncalled tears   129
62 Late tired with woe, e'en ready for to pine   130
63 O grammar rules, O now your virtues show   130
i First Song   131
64 No more, my dear, no more these counsels try   132
65 Love, by sure proof I may call thee unkind   132
66 And do I see some cause a hope to feed   133
67 Hope, art thou true, or dost thou flatter me?   133
68 *Stella*, the only planet of my light   134
69 O joy, too high for my low style to show   134
70 My Muse may well grudge at my heav'nly joy   135
71 Who will in fairest book of Nature know   135
72 Desire, though thou my old companion art   136
ii Second Song   136
73 Love still a boy, and oft a wanton is   137
74 I never drank of *Aganippe* well   138
75 Of all the kings that ever here did reign   138
76 She comes, and straight therewith her shining twins do
     move   139
77 Those looks, whose beams be joy, whose motion is
     delight   139
78 O how the pleasant airs of true love be   140
79 Sweet kiss, thy sweets I fain would sweetly indite   141
80 Sweet swelling lip, well mayst thou swell in pride   141
81 O kiss, which dost those ruddy gems impart   142
82 Nymph of the garden where all beauties be   142
83 Good brother *Philip*, I have borne you long   143
iii Third Song   143
84 Highway, since you my chief *Parnassus* be   144
85 I see the house; my heart thyself contain   144
iv Fourth Song   145
86 Alas, whence came this change of looks?   147
v Fifth Song   147
vi Sixth Song   150
vii Seventh Song   152
viii Eighth Song   153
ix Ninth Song   156

87 When I was forced from *Stella* ever dear   157
88 Out, traitor absence: dar'st thou counsel me   158
89 Now that of absence the most irksome night   158
90 *Stella*, think not that I by verse seek fame   159
91 *Stella*, while now by honour's cruel might   159
92 Be your words made (good sir) of Indian ware   160
x Tenth Song   160
93 O fate, O fault, O curse, child of my bliss   162
94 Grief, find the words, for thou hast made my
    brain   162
95 Yet sighs, dear sighs, indeed true friends you are   163
96 Thought, with good cause thou lik'st so well the night   163
97 *Dian*, that fain would cheer her friend the Night   164
98 Ah bed, the field where joy's peace some do see   164
99 When far-spent night persuades each mortal eye   165
100 O tears, no tears, but rain from beauty's skies   165
101 *Stella* is sick, and in that sick-bed lies   166
102 Where be those roses gone, which sweetened so our
    eyes?   166
103 O happy *Thames*, that didst my *Stella* bear   167
104 Envious wits, what hath been mine offence   167
xi Eleventh Song   168
105 Unhappy sight, and hath she vanished by   169
106 O absent presence, *Stella* is not here   170
107 *Stella*, since thou so right a princess art   170
108 When sorrow (using mine own fire's might)   171

Poems from *The Psalms of David*

Psalm XII *Salvum me fac*   175
Psalm XXII *Deus Deus meus*   176
Psalm XXIII *Dominus regit me*   179
Psalm XXVIII *Ad te Domine clamabo*   180
Psalm XXXV *Judica Domine*   182

Notes   185
Index of First Lines   215

Introduction

Sidney's writings present textual problems on three inter-related fronts. In the first place, Sidney frequently revised and reorganized his material, making for obvious difficulties in establishing a final, authoritative text – difficulties which particularly attend the *Arcadia* poems, since his rewriting of this major work was left unfinished when he died. Secondly, while many of Sidney's texts circulated in manuscript, not one of them was published during his lifetime. Written, as they were, during a period of transition between a largely manuscript culture and the age of the printed book, Sidney's texts are unusually vulnerable to the vagaries of scribal corruption and interpolation. Lastly, the principles governing the editing of Sidney's texts have themselves been a matter of dispute over the years, as modern editors continue to debate the special problems posed by a many-versioned *oeuvre*.

The present text relies heavily on the work of Sidney's Oxford editors, and aims to give a readable, modernized and representative selection of Sidney's verse which takes full account of current editorial thinking, as well as of recent manuscript finds. This is the place to pay tribute to the work of W. A. Ringler, Jean Robertson, Jan van Dorsten, Katherine Duncan-Jones and Victor Skretkowicz in establishing Sidney's text, and to direct the reader who seeks full reference and a complete text to their Oxford editions (see Further Reading, p. xix).

The Lady of May

There are two substantive texts of Sidney's entertainment: the version first published at the end of the 1598 *Arcadia* (*98*), and the considerably more careless version to be found in the Helmingham Hall manuscript (Hm). I follow both Ringler (*Poems*, pp. 3–5, 361–3) and van Dorsten and Duncan-Jones (*Miscellaneous*

Prose, pp. 13–32), who adopt *98* as copy-text, but follow the latter in adopting the reading of Hm at *LM* iii, line 13: *joyful I* (not *98*'s 'joyfully'), and at *LM* iii, line 17: *woeful I* (not *98*'s 'woefully').[1] I depart from van Dorsten and Duncan-Jones, however, to preserve the following *98* reading: *LM* i, line 12: *my* (not 'mine'). The present selection includes all the poems contained within *The Lady of May*.

The *Old Arcadia*

Editing poems from the *Old Arcadia* presents more of a problem. Sidney composed his text between 1578 and 1580 while staying with his sister, the Countess of Pembroke, at her house in Wilton, the work 'being done in loose sheets of paper, most of it in your presence, the rest by sheets sent unto you as fast as they were done', as he wrote in his dedication of the text to her (quoted in Robertson, p. 3). Over the next few years, Sidney made small changes to his text on at least five different occasions, before radically recasting his narrative into the form that eventually became the unfinished *New Arcadia*. First published in 1590 (*90*), this incomplete text was then reprinted in 1593 (*93*) with the final three books of the *Old Arcadia* added on to the end.

The complexity of the *Arcadia*'s textual history inevitably creates problems in the establishment of a critical text – problems that are exemplified by Ringler's editorial policy. In his edition of the *Poems*, Ringler entitles this group as 'Poems from the *Old Arcadia*', and gives the sequence and nomenclature of the *Old Arcadia* text. Yet (with the exception of those poems which appear only in *Old Arcadia* manuscripts: *OA* II.x, xi; III.i, ii, iii) he chooses as his copy-text the *New Arcadia* (*90*, *93*) on the grounds that it contains 'Sidney's latest revisions' (p. 380). Since several of the *Old Arcadia* poems are rearranged and ascribed to different characters in the *New Arcadia*, Ringler's policy makes for a degree of confusion, and necessitates lengthy explanatory notes. Moreover, poems that are homogeneous to the *Old Arcadia* narrative often have a quite different function in the *New*, above all the Eclogues, which were rearranged in *90*, and again in *93*. Indeed, it remains uncertain how Sidney intended to distribute the Eclogues in his revised version of the *Arcadia*, and whether he meant to include them at all. In a prefatory note, Fulke Greville and Matthew Gwinne (the editors of *90*) explain that Sidney had postponed revision of the Eclogues 'till the work had been finished' (quoted in Skretkowicz, p. lvi), and therefore take responsibility for the reordering of the pastoral interludes themselves.

Since the sequence and attribution of poems in the *New Arcadia* are so different from those of the *Old* and so fraught with attendant editorial problems, the aim of the present text is to clarify the issue by giving, as stipulated, poems from the *Old Arcadia*. This means the version of the poems as Sidney wrote and revised them for the final version of the *Old Arcadia*, before he embarked on the wholesale rewriting of the text as the *New Arcadia*. The present text is therefore based not on Ringler but on Robertson, whose edition aims to give 'a clean, readable text of the latest version available of Sidney's *Old Arcadia*' (p. lxvi). Like Robertson, I have recorded the most significant of Sidney's later revisions in the Notes. Where appropriate, I have also taken into consideration variants from the Ottley manuscript (O).[2] Apart from incidentals, I depart from Robertson's excellent text only to make the following changes: *OA* II.viii, line 11: *makes* (the reading of three manuscripts; the singular form is required by 'The sound'); *OA* III.i, line 5: *do* (O only; the plural form is required by 'mine eyes'); *OA* III.ii, line 8: *wat'ry* (Sidney's usage elsewhere – e.g. *OA* I.1, lines 151–2; *OA* II.viii, line 5; *Astrophil and Stella* 82, line 3 – and the majority of *OA* manuscripts support Ringler's thesis that the alternative 'watered' arose from a d/e error in Sidney's transcript); *OA* III.1, line 28: *which in* (correcting Robertson's transposition, 'in which').

In order to reproduce both the intrigues of Sidney's plot and the variety of his verse-forms, the present selection includes all those poems embedded within the prose narrative of the *Old Arcadia*, together with those Eclogues (over half) spoken by the principal characters of the action.

Certain Sonnets

Ringler adopts *98* as his copy-text, the most complete and most accurate of the substantive witnesses to the *Certain Sonnets*, and notes that 'there are no textual problems of any complexity' (p. 425). The Ottley manuscript supports Ringler's emendation at *CS* vi, line 7: *neither*, but contains nothing else to modify his original view that there is 'no evidence of authorial revisions in any of the poems' (p. 425).[3] Germaine Warkentin speculates that the sequence of the *Certain Sonnets* in the Bodleian manuscript (Bo), which is different from that in *98* and the Clifford manuscript (Cl), records 'a revision made on principles which were leading [Sidney] by a process of experimentation towards the variety of organization, fluidity of design, and narrative strength of *Astrophil and Stella*'.[4] The evidence remains inconclusive, however, and the present selection follows Ringler's text, departing from it only to make the following changes: *CS* v, line 2: *sea's* (reverting to *98*'s 'seas', but as a genitive not a plural; 'sea's rage' is a more satisfactory rendering of Horace's 'procellas' than Ringler's 'Sea rage'); *CS* vi, line 4: *doth* (O only; grammatically correct); *CS* viii, line 8: *shouldst* (O only; grammatically correct). The present selection includes nine of the thirty-two sonnets and verse translations that go to make up the *Certain Sonnets*.

Astrophil and Stella

Sidney's sequence of 108 sonnets and eleven songs (given here in its entirety) probably took shape between 1581 and 1582. *98* is the most complete text and serves as the copy-text for Ringler whose edition represents 'the first attempt at a truly critical reconstruction' of Sidney's original holograph (p. 457). Ringler's emendations (including the functional line indentations which differ from *98*'s standardized pattern) have the support of one or more substantive texts in virtually all cases. Nothing of any significance has emerged to justify a wholesale revision of Ringler's text, and the latter therefore forms the basis for the present edition.[5] Apart from incidentals, I depart from Ringler in only the following cases: *AS* 27, line 8: *do* (correcting Ringler's typographical error, 'to'); *AS* 77, line 7: *past-praise* (not *98*'s 'passe-praise': Stella's skin is beyond compare – past praise – and therefore justifies the reading of the second Quarto (Q2) here. Sidney was fond of such compounds: see also 'past-comfort sorrow', *New Arcadia*, ed. Skretkowicz, p. 343); *AS* iv, line 40: *let me first* (the *98* reading, metrically preferable to Ringler's emended 'first let me').

The Psalms of David

Sidney's translation of the Psalms – thought to be a late work – was left unfinished at the time of his death, and was subsequently revised and completed by his sister, the Countess of Pembroke. The revised version of the Psalms has been edited by J. C. A. Rathmell, but Ringler's remains the only edition which seeks to 'present Sidney's own version freed from the revisions later made by his sister' (p. 500), and thus forms the basis of the present edition.[6] This selection includes five of the forty-three Psalms translated by Sidney.

Spelling has been modernized throughout this edition, although old grammatical forms (e.g. shouldst, ware, spake), and certain archaic words (e.g. franzy, couthe, foen) have been retained where required by the register or the rhyme (these have been glossed in the Notes). I have followed Robertson (p. lxix) in using 'evil' and 'ill' according to modern practice, except where rhyme or scansion demand the less usual form. Punctuation has been modernized throughout, and elisions indicated where necessary. Certain personifications have been capitalized where appropriate (eg. Love, Muse), and italics are reserved for proper names.

Notes

[1] An emendation later endorsed by Ringler: see W. A. Ringler, 'The Text of *The Poems of Sidney* Twenty-five Years After', in M. J. B. Allen, D. Baker-Smith, A. F. Kinney and M. M.

Sullivan, eds., *Sir Philip Sidney's Achievements* (New York, 1990), pp. 129–44 (p. 131).

[2] Peter Beal, 'Poems by Sir Philip Sidney: The Ottley Manuscript', *The Library* 33 (1978), pp. 284–95.

[3] A view supported by Jean Robertson, 'A Note on "Poems by Sir Philip Sidney: The Ottley Manuscript"', *The Library* 2 (1980), pp. 202–5.

[4] Germaine Warkentin, 'Sidney's *Certain Sonnets*: Speculations on the Evolution of the Text', *The Library* 2 (1980), pp. 430–44 (p. 441).

[5] See Ringler, 'The Text of *The Poems of Sidney* Twenty-five Years After', p. 135. On the text of *Astrophil and Stella*, see: Priscilla Bawcutt, 'A Crux in *Astrophil and Stella*, Sonnet 21', *Notes and Queries* 29 (1982), pp. 406–8; Jean Robertson's conjectural discovery of a lost song in her review of Ruth Hughey, ed., *The Arundel Harington Manuscript of Tudor Poetry*, in *Review of English Studies* 13 (1962), pp. 403–6; and H. R. Woudhuysen, '*Astrophel and Stella* 75: A "New" Text', *Review of English Studies* 37 (1986), pp. 388–92.

[6] J. C. A. Rathmell, ed., *The Psalms of Sir Philip Sidney and the Countess of Pembroke* (New York, 1963).

Further Reading

Editions

W. A. Ringler, ed., *The Poems of Sir Philip Sidney* (Oxford, 1962).

Jean Robertson, ed., *The Countess of Pembroke's Arcadia* (*The Old Arcadia*) (Oxford, 1973).

Victor Skretkowicz, ed., *The Countess of Pembroke's Arcadia* (*The New Arcadia*) (Oxford, 1987).

Jan van Dorsten and Katherine Duncan-Jones, eds., *The Miscellaneous Prose of Sir Philip Sidney* (Oxford, 1973).

Geoffrey Shepherd, ed., *An Apology for Poetry* (Manchester, 1973).

Biographies

John Buxton, *Sir Philip Sidney and the English Renaissance* (London, 1954).

Katherine Duncan-Jones, *Sir Philip Sidney: Courtier Poet* (London, 1991).

J. M. Osborn, *Young Philip Sidney, 1572–77* (New Haven, CT, 1972).

Criticism

M. J. B. Allen, D. Baker-Smith, A. F. Kinney and M. M. Sullivan, eds., *Sir Philip Sidney's Achievements* (New York, 1990).

Dorothy Connell, *Sir Philip Sidney: The Maker's Mind* (Oxford, 1977).

S. K. Heninger, *Sidney and Spenser: The Poet as Maker* (University Park, PA, 1989)

David Kalstone, *Sidney's Poetry: Contexts and Interpretations* (Cambridge, MA, 1965).

Dennis Kay, ed., *Sir Philip Sidney: An Anthology of Modern Criticism* (Oxford, 1987).

Arthur F. Kinney, ed., *Sidney in Retrospect: Selections from English Literary Renaissance* (Amherst, MA, 1988).

Michael McCanles, *The Text of Sidney's Arcadian World* (Durham, NC, 1989).

R. L. Montgomery, *Symmetry and Sense: The Poetry of Sir Philip Sidney* (Austin, TX, 1961).

J. G. Nichols, *The Poetry of Sir Philip Sidney: An Interpretation in the Context of his Life and Times* (Liverpool, 1974).

Neil L. Rudenstein, *Sidney's Poetic Development* (Cambridge, MA, 1967).

G. F. Waller and M. D. Moore, eds., *Sir Philip Sidney and the Interpretation of Renaissance Culture* (London, 1984).

More specific suggestions for further reading are in the Notes.

Table of Dates

1554   Born at Penshurst, Kent, 30 November.

1564   Enters Shrewsbury School.

1568   At Christ Church, Oxford.

1572   Departs for continental tour in the train of the Earl of Lincoln. Witnesses the Massacre of St Bartholomew's Day in Paris, 24 August. Spends winter in Frankfurt; meets Hubert Languet.

1573   Continues expedition, visiting Heidelberg, Strasbourg, Basle, Bratislava, Vienna and Venice.

1574   Studies in Padua; visits Venice, Genoa and Florence. Travels to Vienna in August; brief trip to Poland; winter in Vienna.

1575   Visits Brno, Prague, Dresden, Frankfurt, Heidelberg and Antwerp, returning to England in May. Attends royal entertainment at Kenilworth Castle in July.

1576   In Ireland with his father, Sir Henry Sidney, July–September.

1577   Ambassador to the Imperial Court at Prague, February–June. On returning to England, defends his father's policy in Ireland in the 'Discourse on Irish Affairs'.

1578   (or 1579?) writes *The Lady of May*. Begins the *Old Arcadia* at Wilton while staying with his sister, the Countess of Pembroke.

1579   Writes to Queen Elizabeth advising her against the Alençon match, November or December.

1580   Probably completes the *Old Arcadia*. Perhaps begins *An Apology for Poetry*.

1581   Takes seat in Parliament. Takes part in tournaments at court in May. Perhaps begins *Astrophil and Stella*. Hubert Languet dies. Penelope Devereux ('Stella') marries Lord Rich, 1 November.

1582   Escorts Alençon back to the Netherlands. Perhaps finishes *Astrophil and Stella*.

1583   Knighted. Marries Frances, daughter of Sir Francis Walsingham, 21 September.

1584   Begins wholesale revision of the *Arcadia*. Writes *Defence of the Earl of Leicester*.

1585   Perhaps begins his translation of Philippe Duplessis-Mornay's *De la vérité de la religion Chrestienne* (1581); perhaps embarks on the metaphrase of the Psalms, and on a translation of Guillaume Salluste du Bartas's *La Semaine ou création du monde* (1578). Plans voyage to the West Indies with Sir Francis Drake. Appointed Governor of Flushing; arrives in the Netherlands in November.

1586   Wounded in a skirmish at Zutphen, 22 September; dies at Arnhem, 17 October.

1587   Buried at St Paul's, 16 February. Arthur Golding completes Sidney's translation of Duplessis-Mornay, and publishes it as *The Trueness of the Christian Religion*.

1590   The *New Arcadia* published.

1591   *Astrophil and Stella* published.

1593   The *New Arcadia* with Books III–V of the *Old Arcadia* published.

1595   *An Apology for Poetry* (*The Defence of Poesy*) published.

1598   Publication of the *Arcadia*, *Certain Sonnets*, *Apology for Poetry*, *Astrophil and Stella* and *The Lady of May*.

Poems from *The Lady of May*

i [The Suitor]

To one whose state is raised over all,
Whose face doth oft the bravest sort enchant,
Whose mind is such, as wisest minds appal,
Who in one self these diverse gifts can plant;
5   How dare I, wretch, seek there my woes to rest,
      Where ears be burnt, eyes dazzled, hearts oppressed?

Your state is great, your greatness is our shield,
Your face hurts oft, but still it doth delight,
Your mind is wise, your wisdom makes you mild;
10 Such planted gifts enrich e'en beggars' sight:
      So dare I, wretch, my bashful fear subdue,
      And feed mine ears, mine eyes, my heart in you.

ii [Therion and Espilus]

Therion. Come, *Espilus*, come now declare thy skill;
      Show how thou canst deserve so brave desire;
      Warm well thy wits, if thou wilt win her will,
      For water cold did never promise fire:
5   Great sure is she, on whom our hopes do live;
          Greater is she who must the judgement give.

Espilus. Tune up, my voice, a higher note I yield;
      To high conceits the song must needs be high,
      More high than stars, more firm than flinty field
10   Are all my thoughts, in which I live or die:
          Sweet soul, to whom I vowed am a slave,
          Let not wild woods so great a treasure have.

Therion. The highest note comes oft from basest mind,
As shallow brooks do yield the greatest sound;
15   Seek other thoughts thy life or death to find;
Thy stars be fall'n, ploughed is thy flinty ground:
    Sweet soul, let not a wretch that serveth sheep
    Among his flock so sweet a treasure keep.

Espilus. Two thousand sheep I have as white as milk,
20   Though not so white as is thy lovely face;
The pasture rich, the wool as soft as silk,
All this I give, let me possess thy grace:
    But still take heed, lest thou thyself submit
    To one that hath no wealth, and wants his wit.

25   *Therion.* Two thousand deer in wildest woods I have;
Them can I take, but you I cannot hold;
He is not poor who can his freedom save,
Bound but to you, no wealth but you I would:
    But take this beast, if beasts you fear to miss,
30   For of his beasts the greatest beast he is.

Espilus. Judge you, to whom all beauty's force is lent.
Therion. Judge you of love, to whom all love is bent.

iii [*Espilus and Therion*]

Espilus. *Silvanus* long in love, and long in vain,
At length obtained the point of his desire,
When being asked, now that he did obtain
His wished weal, what more he could require:
5   'Nothing,' said he, 'for most I joy in this,
    That goddess mine my blessed being sees.'

Therion. When wanton *Pan*, deceived with lion's skin,
Came to the bed where wound for kiss he got,
To woe and shame the wretch did enter in,
10   Till this he took, for comfort of his lot:
    'Poor *Pan*,' he said, 'although thou beaten be,
    It is no shame, since *Hercules* was he.'

Espilus. Thus joyful I in chosen tunes rejoice,
That such a one is witness of my heart,
15   Whose clearest eyes I bliss, and sweetest voice,
That see my good, and judgeth my desert.

Therion. Thus woeful I in woe this salve do find,
My foul mishap came yet from fairest mind.

Poems from the *Old Arcadia*

The First Book or Act

I.i [The Delphic Oracle]

Thy elder care shall from thy careful face
By princely mean be stol'n and yet not lost;
Thy younger shall with Nature's bliss embrace
An uncouth love, which Nature hateth most.
5 Thou with thy wife adult'ry shalt commit,
And in thy throne a foreign state shall sit.
All this on thee this fatal year shall hit.

I.ii [Cleophila]

Transformed in show, but more transformed in mind,
I cease to strive, with double conquest foiled;
For (woe is me) my powers all I find
With outward force and inward treason spoiled.

5 For from without came to mine eyes the blow
Whereto mine inward thoughts did faintly yield;
Both these conspired poor reason's overthrow;
False in myself, thus have I lost the field.

And thus mine eyes are placed still in one sight,
10 And thus my thoughts can think but one thing still;
Thus reason to his servants gives his right;
Thus is my power transformed to your will.
      What marvel, then, I take a woman's hue,
      Since what I see, think, know, is all but you?

I.iii [*Alethes*]

What length of verse can serve brave *Mopsa*'s good
    to show,
Whose virtues strange, and beauties such, as no man them
    may know?
Thus shrewdly burdened then, how can my Muse escape?
The gods must help and precious things must serve to
    show her shape.

5   Like great god *Saturn* fair, and like fair *Venus* chaste;
As smooth as *Pan*, as *Juno* mild, like goddess *Iris* fast;
With *Cupid* she foresees, and goes god *Vulcan*'s pace;
And for a taste of all these gifts, she borrows *Momus*' grace.
Her forehead jacinth-like, her cheeks of opal hue,
Her twinkling eyes bedecked with pearl, her lips of sapphire
10   blue;
Her hair pure crapal-stone, her mouth O heav'nly wide,
Her skin like burnished gold, her hands like silver ore
    untried.
As for those parts unknown, which hidden sure are
    best,
Happy be they which will believe, and never seek the
    rest.

I.iv [*Dorus*]

Come shepherd's weeds, become your master's mind:
Yield outward show, what inward change he tries:
Nor be abashed, since such a guest you find,
Whose strongest hope in your weak comfort lies.

5   Come shepherd's weeds, attend my woeful cries:
Disuse yourselves from sweet *Menalcas*' voice:
For other be those tunes which sorrow ties
From those clear notes which freely may rejoice.
    Then pour out plaint, and in one word say this:
10   Helpless his plaint who spoils himself of bliss.

I.v [Dametas]

Now thanked be the great god *Pan*
That thus preserves my loved life:
Thanked be I that keep a man
Who ended hath this fearful strife:
5   So if my man must praises have,
      What then must I that keep the knave?

For as the moon the eye doth please
With gentle beams not hurting sight,
Yet hath sir sun the greatest praise
10   Because from him doth come her light:
      So if my man must praises have,
      What then must I that keep the knave?

The First Eclogues

I.1 [Lalus and Dorus]

Lalus.   Come, *Dorus*, come, let songs thy sorrows signify;
    And if, for want of use, thy mind ashamed is,
    That very shame with love's high title dignify.
No style is held for base where love well named is:
5   Each ear sucks up the words a true love scattereth,
    And plain speech oft than quaint phrase better framed
    is.

Dorus.   Nightingales seldom sing, the pie still chattereth;
    The wood cries most before it throughly kindled be;
    Deadly wounds inward bleed, each slight sore
    mattereth;
10 Hardly they herd which by good hunters singled be;
    Shallow brooks murmur most, deep silent slide away;
    Nor true love loves his loves with others mingled be.

Lalus.   If thou wilt not be seen, thy face go hide away;
    Be none of us, or else maintain our fashion:
15   Who frowns at others' feasts doth better bide away.
But if thou hast a love, in that love's passion,
    I challenge thee, by show of her perfection,
    Which of us two deserveth most compassion.

Dorus.   Thy challenge great, but greater my protection:
20   Sing, then, and see (for now thou hast inflamed me)
    Thy health too mean a match for my infection.
No, though the heav'ns for high attempt have blamed
    me,
    Yet high is my attempt. O Muse, historify
    Her praise, whose praise to learn your skill hath
    framed me.

Lalus.   Muse, hold your peace; but thou, my god *Pan*,
25   glorify
          My *Kala*'s gifts, who with all good gifts filled is.
          Thy pipe, O *Pan*, shall help, though I sing sorrily.
       A heap of sweets she is, where nothing spilled is,
          Who, though she be no bee, yet full of honey is;
30   A lily field, with plough of rose, which tilled is;
       Mild as a lamb, more dainty than a cony is;
          Her eyes my eyesight is, her conversation
          More glad to me than to a miser money is.
       What coy account she makes of estimation!
35   How nice to touch, how all her speeches peised be!
          A nymph thus turned, but mended in translation.

Dorus.   Such *Kala* is: but ah, my fancies raised be
          In one whose name to name were high presumption,
          Since virtues all to make her title pleased be.
40   O happy gods, which by inward assumption
          Enjoy her soul, in body's fair possession,
          And keep it joined, fearing your seat's consumption;
       How oft with rain of tears skies make confession,
          Their dwellers rapt with sight of her perfection,
45   From heav'nly throne to her heav'n use digression.
       Of best things then what world can yield confection
          To liken her? Deck yours with your comparison:
          She is herself of best things the collection.

Lalus.   How oft my doleful sire cried to me, 'Tarry, son,'
50   When first he spied my love? How oft he said to me,
          'Thou art no soldier fit for *Cupid*'s garrison.
       My son, keep this that my long toil hath laid to me:
          Love well thine own; methinks wool's whiteness
             passeth all;
          I never found long love such wealth hath paid to
             me.'
55   This wind he spent; but when my *Kala* glasseth all
          My sight in her fair limbs, I then assure myself,
          Not rotten sheep, but high crowns she surpasseth all.
       Can I be poor, that her gold hair procure myself?

Want I white wool, whose eyes her white skin
    garnished?
60   Till I get her, shall I to keep inure myself?

Dorus.   How oft, when Reason saw love of her harnished
    With armour of my heart, he cried, 'O vanity,
    To set a pearl in steel so meanly varnished!
    Look to thyself; reach not beyond humanity:
    Her mind, beams, state, far from thy weak wings
65   banished;
    And love which lover hurts is inhumanity.'
    Thus Reason said; but she came, Reason vanished;
    Her eyes so mast'ring me that such objection
    Seemed but to spoil the food of thoughts long
        famished.
70   Her peerless height my mind to high erection
    Draws up; and if, hope failing, end life's pleasure,
    Of fairer death how can I make election?

Lalus.   Once my well-waiting eyes espied my treasure,
    With sleeves turned up, loose hair, and breasts
        enlarged,
75   Her father's corn (moving her fair limbs) measure.
    'O,' cried I, 'of so mean work be discharged;
    Measure my case, how by thy beauty's filling
    With seed of woes my heart brim-full is charged.
    Thy father bids thee save, and chides for spilling:
    Save then my soul, spill not my thoughts well
80   heaped;
    No lovely praise was ever got with killing.'
    These bold words she did hear, this fruit I reaped:
    That she, whose look alone might make me blessed,
    Did smile on me, and then away she leaped.

85   *Dorus.*   Once, O sweet once, I saw, with dread oppressed,
    Her whom I dread: so that with prostrate lying
    Her length the earth in love's chief clothing dressed.
    I saw that richesse fall, and fell a-crying:
    'Let not dead earth enjoy so dear a cover,
90   But deck therewith my soul for your sake dying.

Lay all your fear upon your fearful lover;
    Shine eyes on me, that both our lives be guarded,
    So I your sight, you shall yourselves recover.'
I cried, and was with open rays rewarded;

95
    But straight they fled, summoned by cruel honour,
    Honour, the cause desert is not regarded.

Lalus.   This maid, thus made for joys, O *Pan*, bemoan
        her,
    That without love she spends her years of love:
    So fair a field would well become an owner.

100
And if enchantment can a hard heart move,
    Teach me what circle may acquaint her sprite,
    Affection's charms in my behalf to prove.
The circle is my round-about-her sight;
    The power I will invoke dwells in her eyes;

105
    My charm should be she haunt me day and night.

Dorus.   Far other care, O Muse, my sorrow tries,
    Bent to such one, in whom, myself must say,
    Nothing can mend one point that in her lies.
What circle, then, in so rare force bears sway,

110
    Whose sprite all sprites can spoil, raise, damn, or save?
    No charm holds her, but well possess she may;
Possess she doth, and makes my soul her slave,
    My eyes the bands, my thoughts the fatal knot:
    No thralls like them that inward bondage have.

115 *Lalus.*   *Kala*, at length, conclude my ling'ring lot:
    Disdain me not, although I be not fair.
    Who is an heir of many hundred sheep
    Doth beauties keep, which never sun can burn,
    Nor storms do turn: fairness serves oft to wealth.

120
    Yet all my health I place in your goodwill,
    Which if you will (O do) bestow on me,
    Such as you see, such still you shall me find,
    Constant and kind. My sheep your food shall breed,
    Their wool your weed; I will you music yield

125
    In flow'ry field; and as the day begins

With twenty gins we will the small birds take,
And pastimes make, as Nature things hath made.
But when in shade we meet of myrtle boughs
Then love allows our pleasures to enrich,
130   The thought of which doth pass all worldly pelf.

Dorus.   Lady, yourself, whom neither name I dare,
And titles are but spots to such a worth,
Hear plaints come forth from dungeon of my mind:
The noblest kind rejects not others' woes.
135   I have no shows of wealth: my wealth is you,
My beauty's hue your beams, my health your deeds;
My mind for weeds your virtue's liv'ry wears;
My food is tears; my tunes waymenting yield;
Despair my field; the flowers spirit's wars;
140   My day new cares; my gins my daily sight,
In which do light small birds of thoughts o'erthrown;
My pastimes none; time passeth on my fall;
Nature made all, but me of dolours made;
I find no shade but where my sun doth burn;
145   No place to turn: without, within it fries;
Nor help by life or death who living dies.

Lalus.   But if my *Kala* this my suit denies,
Which so much reason bears,
Let crows pick out mine eyes which too much saw.
150   If she still hate love's law,
My earthy mould doth melt in wat'ry tears.

Dorus.   My earthy mould doth melt in wat'ry tears,
And they again resolve
To air of sighs, sighs to the heart's fire turn,
155   Which doth to ashes burn;
Thus doth my life within itself dissolve.

Lalus.   Thus doth my life within itself dissolve,
That I grow like the beast
Which bears the bit a weaker force doth guide,
160   Yet patient must abide;
Such weight it hath which once is full possessed.

Dorus. Such weight it hath which once is full possessed
　　　That I become a vision,
　　　Which hath in other's head his only being,
165　　And lives in fancy's seeing.
　　　O wretched state of man in self-division!

Lalus. O wretched state of man in self-division!
　　　　O well thou say'st! A feeling declaration
　　　　Thy tongue hath made of *Cupid*'s deep incision.
170　　But now hoarse voice doth fail this occupation,
　　　　And others long to tell their loves' condition:
　　　　Of singing thou hast got the reputation.

Dorus. Of singing thou hast got the reputation,
　　　Good *Lalus* mine: I yield to thy ability;
175　　My heart doth seek another estimation.
　　　But ah, my Muse, I would thou hadst facility
　　　To work my goddess so by thy invention
　　　On me to cast those eyes, where shine nobility:
Seen and unknown; heard, but without attention.

I:2 [Dorus]

Fortune, Nature, Love, long have contended about me,
　　　Which should most miseries cast on a worm that I am.
Fortune thus gan say: 'Misery and misfortune is all one,
　　　And of misfortune, Fortune hath only the gift.
5　With strong foes on land, on seas with contrary tempests,
　　　Still do I cross this wretch, what so he taketh in hand.'
'Tush, tush,' said Nature, 'this is all but a trifle; a man's
　　　　self
　　　Gives haps or mishaps, e'en as he ord'reth his heart.
But so his humour I frame, in a mould of choler adusted,
10　　That the delights of life shall be to him dolorous.'
Love smiled, and thus said: 'Want joined to desire is
　　　　unhappy.
　　　But if he naught do desire, what can *Heraclitus* ail?

None but I works by desire; by desire have I kindled in his
  soul
 Infernal agonies unto a beauty divine,
Where thou, poor Nature, left'st all thy due glory to
15   Fortune.
 Her virtue is sovereign, Fortune a vassal of hers.'
Nature abashed went back; Fortune blushed, yet she replied
  thus:
 'And e'en in that love shall I reserve him a spite.'
Thus, thus, alas! woeful in nature, unhappy by fortune,
20 But most wretched I am now love awakes my desire.

I.3 [Cleophila]

If mine eyes can speak to do hearty errand,
Or mine eyes' language she do hap to judge of,
So that eyes' message be of her received,
   Hope, we do live yet.

5 But if eyes fail then, when I most do need them,
Or if eyes' language be not unto her known,
So that eyes' message do return rejected,
   Hope, we do both die.

Yet dying, and dead, do we sing her honour;
10 So become our tombs monuments of her praise;
So becomes our loss the triumph of her gain;
   Hers be the glory.

If the senseless spheres do yet hold a music,
If the swan's sweet voice be not heard but at death,
15 If the mute timber when it hath the life lost,
   Yieldeth a lute's tune,

Are then human minds privileged so meanly
As that hateful death can abridge them of power
With the voice of truth to record to all worlds
20   That we be her spoils?

Thus not ending, ends the due praise of her praise;
Fleshly veil consumes, but a soul hath his life,
Which is held in love; love it is that hath joined
    Life to this our soul.

25   But if eyes can speak to do hearty errand,
Or mine eyes' language she do hap to judge of,
So that eyes' message be of her received,
    Hope, we do live yet.

I.4 [Dorus and Cleophila]

Dorus.   Lady, reserved by the heav'ns to do pastors'
    company honour,
Joining your sweet voice to the rural Muse of a desert,
Here you fully do find this strange operation of Love,
How to the woods Love runs as well as rides to the palace,
5   Neither he bears reverence to a prince nor pity to beggar,
But (like a point in midst of a circle) is still of a nearness,
All to a lesson he draws, nor hills nor caves can avoid him.

Cleophila.   Worthy shepherd, by my song to myself all
    favour is happened,
That to the sacred Muse my annoys somewhat be revealed,
Sacred Muse, who in one contains what nine do in all
10   them.
But, O happy be you, which safe from fiery reflection
Of *Phoebus'* violence in shade of stately cypress tree,
Or pleasant myrtle, may teach th'unfortunate *Echo*
In these woods to resound the renowned name of a
    goddess.
15   Happy be you that may to the saint, your only Idea,
(Although simply attired) your manly affection utter.
Happy be those mishaps which, justly proportion holding,
Give right sound to the ears, and enter aright to the
        judgement;
But wretched be the souls which, veiled in a contrary
        subject,

How much more we do love, so the less our loves be
20   believed.
What skill serveth a sore of a wrong infirmity judged?
What can justice avail to a man that tells not his own case?
You, though fears do abash, in you still possible hopes be:
Nature against we do seem to rebel, seem fools in a vain
       suit.
But so unheard, condemned, kept thence we do seek to
25   abide in,
Self-lost and wand'ring, banished that place we do come
       from,
What mean is there, alas, we can hope our loss to recover?
What place is there left we may hope our woes to
       recomfort?
Unto the heav'ns? Our wings be too short; th'earth thinks
       us a burden;
Air, we do still with sighs increase; to the fire? We do want
30   none;
And yet his outward heat our tears would quench, but an
       inward
Fire no liquor can cool: *Neptune*'s seat would be dried up
       there.
Happy shepherd, with thanks to the gods still think to be
       thankful,
That to thy advancement their wisdoms have thee abased.

Dorus.   Unto the gods with a thankful heart all thanks I
35   do render,
That to my advancement their wisdoms have me abased.
But yet, alas! O but yet, alas! our haps be but hard haps,
Which must frame contempt to the fittest purchase of
       honour.
Well may a pastor plain, but alas his plaints be not
       esteemed.
Silly shepherd's poor pipe, when his harsh sound testifies
40   our woes,
Into the fair looker-on, pastime, not passion, enters.
And to the woods or brooks, who do make such dreary
       recital

What be the pangs they bear, and whence those pangs be
      derived,
Pleased to receive that name by rebounding answer of
      Echo,
45 And hope thereby to ease their inward horrible anguish;
Then shall those things ease their inward horrible anguish
When trees dance to the pipe, and swift streams stay by the
      music,
Or when an echo begins unmoved to sing them a love song.
Say then what vantage we do get by the trade of a pastor
(Since no estates be so base, but Love vouchsafeth his
50   arrow,
Since no refuge doth serve from wounds we do carry about
      us,
Since outward pleasures be but halting helps to decayed
      souls),
Save that daily we may discern what fire we do burn in?
Far more happy be you, whose greatness gets a free access,
55 Whose fair bodily gifts are framed most lovely to each eye.
Virtue you have; of virtue you have left proofs to the whole
      world,
And virtue is grateful with beauty and richesse adorned;
Neither doubt you a whit, time will your passion utter.
Hardly remains fire hid where skill is bent to the hiding;
But in a mind that would his flames should not be
60   repressed,
Nature worketh enough with a small help for the revealing.
Give therefore to the Muse great praise in whose very
      likeness
You do approach to the fruit your only desires be to
      gather.

Cleophila.   First shall fertile grounds not yield increase of
      a good seed;
First the rivers shall cease to repay their floods to the
65   ocean;
First may a trusty greyhound transform himself to a tiger;
First shall virtue be vice, and beauty be counted a blemish,
Ere that I leave with song of praise her praise to solemnize,

Her praise, whence to the world all praise had his only
    beginning;
70 But yet well I do find each man most wise in his own case.
None can speak of a wound with skill, if he have not a
    wound felt.
Great to thee my estate seems, thy estate is blest by my
    judgement:
And yet neither of us great or blest deemeth his own self.
For yet (weigh this, alas!) great is not great to a greater.
75 What judge you doth a hillock show by the lofty *Olympus*?
Such this small greatness doth seem compared to the
    greatest.
When cedars to the ground be oppressed by the weight of
    an emmet,
Or when a rich ruby's just price be the worth of a walnut,
Or to the sun for wonders seem small sparks of a candle,
80 Then by my high cedar, rich ruby, and only shining sun,
Virtue, richesse, beauties of mine shall great be reputed.
O no, no, hardy shepherd, worth can never enter a title
Where proofs justly do teach, thus matched, such worth to
    be naught worth.
Let not a puppet abuse thy sprite; kings' crowns do not
    help them
From the cruel headache, nor shoes of gold do the gout
85   heal,
And precious couches full oft are shaked with a fever.
If then a bodily evil in a bodily gloss be not hidden,
Shall such morning dews be an ease to the heat of a love's
    fire?

Dorus. O glitt'ring miseries of man, if this be the fortune
90 Of those Fortune lulls, so small rest rests in a kingdom.
What marvel though a prince transform himself to a pastor,
Come from marble bowers, many times the gay harbour of
    anguish,
Unto a silly cabin, though weak, yet stronger against woes?
Now by thy words I begin, most famous lady, to gather
95 Comfort into my soul. I do find, I do find what a blessing
Is chanced to my life, that from such muddy abundance

Of carking agonies (to estates which still be adherent)
Destiny keeps me aloof. For if all thy estate to thy virtue
Joined, by thy beauty adorned, be no means these griefs to
    abolish;
100 If neither by that help thou canst climb up to thy fancy,
Nor yet, fancy so dressed, do receive more plausible
    hearing;
Then do I think, indeed, that better it is to be private
In sorrow's torments than, tied to the pomps of a palace,
Nurse inward maladies, which have not scope to be
    breathed out,
105 But perforce digest all bitter juices of horror
In silence, from a man's own self with company robbed.
Better yet do I live, that though by my thoughts I be
    plunged
Into my life's bondage, yet may disburden a passion
(Oppressed with ruinous conceits) by the help of an outcry;
110 Not limited to a whisp'ring note, the lament of a courtier,
But sometimes to the woods, sometimes to the heavens, do
    decipher,
With bold clamour unheard, unmarked, what I seek, what
    I suffer.
And when I meet these trees, in the earth's fair livery
    clothed,
Ease I do feel (such ease as falls to one wholly diseased)
115 For that I find in them part of my estate represented.
Laurel shows what I seek; by the myrrh is showed how I
    seek it;
Olive paints me the peace that I must aspire to by
    conquest;
Myrtle makes my request; my request is crowned with a
    willow;
Cypress promiseth help, but a help where comes no
    recomfort;
Sweet juniper saith this: though I burn, yet I burn in a
120   sweet fire;
Yew doth make me bethink what kind of bow the boy
    holdeth

Which shoots strongly without any noise, and deadly
    without smart;
Fir trees great and green, fixed on a high hill but a barren,
Like to my noble thoughts, still new, well placed, to me
    fruitless;
125 Fig that yields most pleasant fruit, his shadow is hurtful:
Thus be her gifts most sweet, thus more danger to be near
    her.
But in a palm, when I mark how he doth rise under a
    burden,
And may I not (say I then) get up though griefs be so
    weighty?
Pine is a mast to a ship; to my ship shall hope for a mast
    serve?
Pine is high, hope is as high; sharp-leaved, sharp yet be my
130   hope's buds.
Elm embraced by a vine, embracing fancy reviveth.
Poplar changeth his hue from a rising sun to a setting:
Thus to my sun do I yield, such looks her beams do afford
    me.
Old aged oak cut down, of new works serves to the
    building:
So my desires, by my fear cut down, be the frames of her
135   honour.
Ash makes spears which shields do resist: her force no
    repulse takes;
Palms do rejoice to be joined by the match of a male to a
    female,
And shall sensive things be so senseless as to resist sense?
Thus be my thoughts dispersed; thus thinking nurseth a
    thinking;
Thus both trees and each thing else be the books of a
140   fancy.
But to the cedar, queen of woods, when I lift my beteared
    eyes,
Then do I shape to myself that form which reigns so
    within me,
And think there she do dwell and hear what plaints I do
    utter:

When that noble top doth nod, I believe she salutes me;
When by the wind it maketh a noise, I do think she doth
145   answer.
Then kneeling to the ground, oft thus do I speak to that
      image:
'Only jewel, O only jewel, which only deservest
That men's hearts be thy seat and endless fame be thy
      servant,
O descend for a while from this great height to behold me;
But naught else do behold (else is naught worth the
150   beholding)
Save what a work by thyself is wrought; and since I am
      altered
Thus by thy work, disdain not that which is by thyself
      done.
In mean caves oft treasure abides; to an hostry a king
      comes;
And so behind foul clouds full oft fair stars do lie hidden.'

155 *Cleophila.*   Hardy shepherd, such as thy merits, such may
      be her insight
Justly to grant thy reward, such envy I bear to thy fortune.
But to myself, what wish can I make for a salve to my
      sorrows,
Whom both Nature seems to debar from means to be
      helped,
And if a mean were found, Fortune th'whole course of it
      hinders.
Thus plagued, how can I frame to my sore any hope of
160   amendment?
Whence may I show to my mind any light of a possible
      escape?
Bound, and bound by so noble bands as loath to be
      unbound,
Gaoler I am to myself, prison and prisoner to mine own
      self.
Yet be my hopes thus placed, here fixed lives my
      recomfort,
165 That that dear diamond, where wisdom holdeth a sure seat,

Whose force had such force so to transform, nay to reform
    me,
Will at length perceive these flames by her beams to be
        kindled,
And will pity the wound festered so strangely within me.
O be it so: grant such an event, O gods, that event give!
170 And for a sure sacrifice I do daily oblation offer
Of my own heart, where thoughts be the temple, sight is an
        altar.
But cease, worthy shepherd, now cease we to weary the
        hearers
With moanful melodies, for enough our griefs be revealed
If by the parties meant our meanings rightly be marked;
175 And sorrows do require some respite unto the senses.

The Second Book or Act

II.i [Cleophila]

In vain, mine eyes, you labour to amend
    With flowing tears your fault of hasty sight;
Since to my heart her shape you so did send
    That her I see, though you did lose your light.

5   In vain, my heart, now you with sight are burned,
    With sighs you seek to cool your hot desire;
Since sighs (into mine inward furnace turned)
    For bellows serve to kindle more the fire.

Reason, in vain (now you have lost my heart)
10   My head you seek, as to your strongest fort;
Since there mine eyes have played so false a part
    That to your strength your foes have sure resort.
        And since in vain I find were all my strife,
        To this strange death I vainly yield my life.

II.ii [Basilius]

Let not old age disgrace my high desire,
    O heav'nly soul in human shape contained.
Old wood inflamed doth yield the bravest fire,
    When younger doth in smoke his virtue spend.

5   Ne let white hairs (which on my face do grow)
    Seem to your eyes of a disgraceful hue;
Since whiteness doth present the sweetest show,
    Which makes all eyes do honour unto you.

Old age is wise and full of constant truth;
10   Old age well stayed from ranging humour lives;
Old age hath known whatever was in youth;
        Old age o'ercome, the greater honour gives.
                And to old age since you yourself aspire,
                Let not old age disgrace my high desire.

II.iii [Dorus]

Since so mine eyes are subject to your sight,
That in your sight they fixed have my brain;
Since so my heart is filled with that light,
That only light doth all my life maintain;

5   Since in sweet you all goods so richly reign,
That where you are no wished good can want;
Since so your living image lives in me,
That in myself yourself true love doth plant;
        How can you him unworthy then decree,
10   In whose chief part your worths implanted be?

II.iv [Dorus]

My sheep are thoughts, which I both guide and serve;
Their pasture is fair hills of fruitless love;
On barren sweets they feed, and feeding starve;
I wail their lot, but will not other prove.
5   My sheephook is wanhope, which all upholds;
My weeds, desire, cut out in endless folds.
        What wool my sheep shall bear, while thus they live,
        In you it is, you must the judgement give.

II.v [Philoclea]

Ye living powers enclosed in stately shrine
Of growing trees, ye rural gods that wield
Your sceptres here, if to your ears divine
A voice may come which troubled soul doth yield,
5   This vow receive, this vow O gods maintain:
       My virgin life no spotted thought shall stain.

Thou purest stone, whose pureness doth present
My purest mind; whose temper hard doth show
My tempered heart; by thee my promise sent
10   Unto myself let after-livers know.
       No fancy mine, nor others' wrong suspect
       Make me, O virtuous Shame, thy laws neglect.

O Chastity, the chief of heav'nly lights,
Which makes us most immortal shape to wear,
15   Hold thou my heart, establish thou my sprites;
To only thee my constant course I bear.
       Till spotless soul unto thy bosom fly,
       Such life to lead, such death I vow to die.

II.vi [Philoclea]

My words, in hope to blaze my steadfast mind,
This marble chose, as of like temper known:
But lo, my words defaced, my fancies blind,
Blots to the stone, shame to myself I find;
5   And witness am, how ill agree in one,
       A woman's hand with constant marble stone.

My words full weak, the marble full of might;
My words in store, the marble all alone;
My words black ink, the marble kindly white;
10   My words unseen, the marble still in sight,
       May witness bear, how ill agree in one,
       A woman's hand with constant marble stone.

II. vii [Cleophila]

Loved I am, and yet complain of love;
As loving not, accused, in love I die.
When pity most I crave, I cruel prove;
Still seeking love, love found as much I fly.

5   Burnt in myself, I muse at others' fire;
What I call wrong, I do the same, and more;
Barred of my will, I have beyond desire;
I wail for want, and yet am choked with store.

This is thy work, thou god for ever blind;
10   Though thousands old, a boy entitled still.
Thus children do the silly birds they find
With stroking hurt, and too much cramming kill.
      Yet thus much love, O Love, I crave of thee:
      Let me be loved, or else not loved be.

II. viii [Cleophila]

Over these brooks trusting to ease mine eyes
(Mine eyes e'en great in labour with their tears),
I laid my face (my face wherein there lies
Clusters of clouds which no sun ever clears).
5   In wat'ry glass my watered eyes I see:
      Sorrows ill eased, where sorrows painted be.

My thoughts, imprisoned in my secret woes,
With flamy breath do issue oft in sound;
The sound to this strange air no sooner goes
10   But that it doth with echo's force rebound
      And makes me hear the plaints I would refrain:
      Thus outward helps my inward griefs maintain.

Now in this sand I would discharge my mind,
And cast from me part of my burd'nous cares;
15   But in the sands my pains foretold I find,
And see therein how well the writer fares.
            Since stream, air, sand, mine eyes and ears conspire:
            What hope to quench where each thing blows the
                fire?

II.ix [Gynecia]

With two strange fires of equal heat possessed,
The one of love, the other jealousy,
Both still do work, in neither find I rest;
For both, alas, their strengths together tie;
5   The one aloft doth hold the other high.
            Love wakes the jealous eye lest thence it moves;
            The jealous eye, the more it looks, it loves.

These fires increase, in these I daily burn;
They feed on me, and with my wings do fly;
10   My lively joys to doleful ashes turn;
Their flames mount up, my powers prostrate lie;
They live in force, I quite consumed die.
            One wonder yet far passeth my conceit:
            The fuel small, how be the fires so great?

II.x [Dorus]

Feed on my sheep; my charge, my comfort, feed;
With sun's approach your pasture fertile grows,
O only sun that such a fruit can breed.

Feed on my sheep, your fair sweet feeding flows,
5   Each flow'r, each herb, doth to your service yield,
O blessed sun whence all this blessing goes.

Feed on my sheep, possess your fruitful field,
No wolves dare howl, no murrain can prevail,
And from the storms our sweetest sun will shield.

10   Feed on my sheep, sorrow hath stricken sail,
Enjoy my joys, as you did taste my pain,
While our sun shines no cloudy griefs assail.
      Feed on my sheep, your native joys maintain,
      Your wool is rich; no tongue can tell my gain.

II. xi [Philisides]

Leave off my sheep: it is no time to feed,
My sun is gone, your pasture barren grows,
O cruel sun, thy hate this harm doth breed.

Leave off my sheep, my show'r of tears o'erflows,
5   Your sweetest flow'rs, your herbs, no service yield,
My sun, alas, from me for ever goes.

Leave off my sheep, my sighs burn up your field,
My plaints call wolves, my plagues in you prevail,
My sun is gone, from storms what shall us shield?

10   Leave off my sheep, sorrow hath hoised sail,
Wail in my woes, taste of your master's pain,
My sun is gone, now cloudy griefs assail.
      Leave leaving not my mourning to maintain,
      You bear no wool, and loss is all my gain.

II.xii [Dametas]

A hateful cure with hate to heal;
A bloody help with blood to save;
A foolish thing with fools to deal;
Let him be bobbed that bobs will have.
5   But who by means of wisdom high
      Hath saved his charge? It is e'en I.

Let others deck their pride with scars,
And of their wounds make brave lame shows;
First let them die, then pass the stars,
10 When rotten Fame will tell their blows.
      But eye from blade, and ear from cry:
      Who hath saved all? It is e'en I.

II.xiii [Basilius, Gynecia, Pamela and Philoclea]

Apollo great, whose beams the greater world do light,
And in our little world dost clear our inward sight,
Which ever shines, though hid from earth by earthly shade,
Whose lights do ever live, but in our darkness fade;
Thou god, whose youth was decked with spoil of *Python*'s
5   skin
(So humble knowledge can throw down the snakish sin),
Latona's son, whose birth in pain and travail long
Doth teach to learn the good what travails do belong;
In travail of our life (a short but tedious space)
10 While brickle hour-glass runs) guide thou our panting race:
Give us foresightful minds; give us minds to obey
What foresight tells; our thoughts upon thy knowledge
      stay.
Let so our fruits grow up that Nature be maintained;
But so our hearts keep down, with vice they be not stained.
15 Let this assured hold our judgements ever take,
That nothing wins the heav'n but what doth earth forsake.

The Second Eclogues

II.1 [Dicus and Dorus]

Dicus.   *Dorus*, tell me, where is thy wonted motion
   To make these woods resound thy lamentation?
   Thy saint is dead, or dead is thy devotion.
  For who doth hold his love in estimation,
5   To witness that he thinks his thoughts delicious,
   Seeks to make each thing badge of his sweet passion.

Dorus.   But what doth make thee, *Dicus*, so suspicious
   Of my due faith, which needs must be immutable?
   Who others' virtue doubt, themselves are vicious.
10 Not so; although my metal were most mutable,
   Her beams have wrought therein most sure
    impression:
   To such a force soon change were nothing suitable.

Dicus.   The heart well set doth never shun confession;
   If noble be thy bands, make them notorious;
15   Silence doth seem the mask of base oppression.
  Who glories in his love doth make love glorious;
   But who doth fear, or bideth muett wilfully,
   Shows guilty heart doth deem his state opprobrious.
  Thou, then, that fram'st both words and voice most
    skilfully,
20   Yield to our ears a sweet and sound relation,
   If Love took thee by force, or caught thee guilefully.

Dorus.   If sunny beams shame heav'nly habitation;
   If three-leaved grass seem to the sheep unsavoury,
   Then base and sour is Love's most high vocation.
25 Or if sheep's cries can help the sun's own bravery,
   Then may I hope my pipe may have ability
   To help her praise, who decks me in her slavery.

No, no: no words ennoble self–nobility.
 As for your doubts, her voice was it deceived me,
30 Her eyes the force beyond my possibility.

Dicus. Thy words well voiced, well graced, had almost
   heaved me
 Quite from myself to love Love's contemplation;
 Till of these thoughts thy sudden end bereaved me.
Go on, therefore, and tell us by what fashion
35 In thy own proof he gets so strange possession,
 And, how possessed, he strengthens his invasion?

Dorus. Sight is his root, in thought is his progression,
 His childhood wonder, 'prenticeship attention,
 His youth delight, his age the soul's oppression;
40 Doubt is his sleep, he waketh in invention;
 Fancy his food, his clothing is of carefulness;
 Beauty his book, his play lovers' dissension;
His eyes are curious search, but veiled with warefulness;
 His wings desire oft clipped with desperation;
45 Largess his hands could never skill of sparefulness.
But how he doth by might or by persuasion
 To conquer, and his conquest how to ratify,
 Experience doubts, and schools hold disputation.

Dicus. But so thy sheep may thy good wishes satisfy
50 With large increase, and wool of fine perfection,
 So she thy love, her eyes thy eyes may gratify,
As thou wilt give our souls a dear refection,
 By telling how she was, how now she framed is
 To help or hurt in thee her own infection.

Dorus. Blest be the name wherewith my mistress named
55   is,
 Whose wounds are salves, whose yokes please more
  than pleasure doth;
 Her stains are beams, virtue the fault she blamed is.
The heart, eye, ear here only find his treasure doth;
 All numb'ring arts her endless graces number not;
 Time, place, life, wit scarcely her rare gifts measure
60   doth.

Is she in rage? So is the sun in summer hot,
   Yet harvest brings. Doth she, alas, absent herself?
   The sun is hid; his kindly shadows cumber not.
But when to give some grace she doth content herself,
65   O then it shines; then are the heav'ns distributed,
   And *Venus* seems, to make up her, she spent herself.
Thus then (I say) my mischiefs have contributed
   A greater good by her divine reflection;
   My harms to me, my bliss to her attributed.
70   Thus she is framed: her eyes are my direction;
   Her love my life; her anger my instruction;
   Lastly, what so she be, that's my protection.

Dicus.   Thy safety sure is wrapped in destruction;
   For that construction thy own words do bear.
75   A man to fear a woman's moody eye,
Or reason lie a slave to servile sense,
   There seek defence where weakness is the force,
   Is late remorse in folly dearly bought.

Dorus.   If I had thought to hear blasphemous words,
80   My breast to swords, my soul to hell have sold
I sooner would than thus my ears defile
With words so vile, which viler breath doth breed.
O herds, take heed! for I a wolf have found
Who, hunting round the strongest for to kill,
85   His breast doth fill with earth of others' woe,
And loaden so, pulls down; pulled down, destroys.
O shepherd boys, eschew these tongues of venom
Which do envenom both the soul and senses!
Our best defences are to fly these adders.
90   O tongues, right ladders made to climb dishonour,
Who judge that honour which hath scope to slander!

Dicus.   *Dorus*, you wander far in great reproaches,
   So love encroaches on your charmed reason;
   But it is season for to end our singing,
95   Such anger bringing; as for me, my fancy
In sick man's franzy rather takes compassion
   Than rage for rage: rather my wish I send to thee,

       Thou soon may have some help or change of passion.
    She oft her looks, the stars her favour, bend to thee;
100   Fortune store, Nature health, Love grant persuasion.
    A quiet mind none but thyself can lend to thee,
       Thus I commend to thee all our former love.

Dorus.   Well do I prove error lies oft in zeal;
       Yet is it seal (though error) of true heart.
105   Naught could impart such heats to friendly mind,
    But for to find thy words did her disgrace,
       Whose only face the little heaven is,
    Which who doth miss his eyes are but delusions,
       Barred from their chiefest object of delightfulness,
110   Thrown on this earth the chaos of confusions.
    As for thy wish to my enraged spitefulness,
       The lovely blow with rare reward, my prayer is
       Thou mayst love her that I may see thy sightfulness.
    The quiet mind (whereof myself impairer is,
115   As thou dost think) should most of all disquiet me
       Without her love, than any mind who fairer is.
    Her only cure from surfeit woes can diet me:
       She holds the balance of my contentation;
       Her cleared looks (naught else) in storms can quiet
         me.
120   Nay, rather than my ease discontentation
       Should breed to her, let me for ay dejected be
       From any joy which might her grief occasion.
    With so sweet plagues my happy harms infected be:
       Pain wills me die, yet will of death I mortify,
125   For though life irks, in life my loves protected be.
    Thus for each change my changeless heart I fortify.

II.2 [Philisides]   *[Echo]*

Fair rocks, goodly rivers, sweet woods, when shall I see
        peace?   Peace.
Peace? What bars me my tongue? Who is it that comes me
        so nigh?   I.

O! I do know what guest I have met: it is *Echo*.   'Tis *Echo*.
Well met, *Echo*, approach; then tell me thy will
      too.   I will too.
5   *Echo*, what do I get yielding my sprite to my griefs?   Griefs.
What medicine may I find for a pain that draws me
      to death?   Death.
O poisonous medicine! What worse to me can be than
      it?   It.
In what state was I then, when I took this deadly
      disease?   Ease.
And what manner a mind which had to that humour a
      vein?   Vain.
Hath not reason enough vehemence the desire to
10   reprove?   Prove.
Oft prove I; but what salve when reason seeks to be
      gone?   One.
O! what is it? What is it that may be a salve to my
      love?   Love.
What do lovers seek for, long seeking for to enjoy?   Joy.
What be the joys for which to enjoy they went to the
      pains?   Pains.
15   Then to an earnest love what doth best victory lend?   End.
End? But I can never end; Love will not give me the
      leave.   Leave.
How be the minds disposed that cannot taste thy
      physic?   Sick.
Yet say again thy advice for th'ills that I told
      thee.   I told thee.
Doth th'infected wretch of his ill th'extremity know?   No.
But if he know not his harms what guides hath he whilst
20   he be blind?   Blind.
What blind guides can he have that leans to a
      fancy?   A fancy.
Can fancies want eyes, or he fall that steppeth aloft?   Oft.
What causes first made these torments on me to
      light?   Light.
Can then a cause be so light that forceth a man to go
      die?   Aye.
Yet tell what light thing I had in me to draw me to
25   die?   Eye.

Eyesight made me to yield, but what first pierced to mine
      eyes?   Eyes.
Eyes' hurters, eyes' hurt; but what from them to me
      falls?   Falls.
But when I first did fall, what brought most fall to my
      heart?   Art.
Art? What can be that art which thou dost mean by thy
      speech?   Speech.
What be the fruits of speaking art? What grows by the
30   words?   Words.
O much more than words: those words served more to me
      bless.   Less.
O when shall I be known where most to be known I do
      long?   Long.
Long be thy woes for such news; but how recks she my
      thoughts?   Oughts.
Then, then what do I gain, since unto her will I do
      wind?   Wind.
Wind, tempests, and storms; yet in end what gives she
35   desire?   Ire.
Silly reward! Yet among women hath she of virtue the
      most.   Most.
What great name may I give to·so heav'nly a woman?
                                          A woe-man.
Woe? But seems to me joy that agrees to my
      thought so.   I thought so.
Think so, for of my desired bliss it is only the
      course.   Curse.
Cursed be thyself for cursing that which leads me to
40   joys.   Toys.
What be the sweet creatures where lowly demands be not
      heard?   Hard.
Hard to be got, but got, constant, to be held like
      steels.   Eels.
How can they be unkind? Speak, for th'hast narrowly
      pried.   Pride.
Whence can pride come there, since springs of beauty be
      thence?   Thence.
Horrible is this blasphemy unto the most holy.   O lie.

Thou liest, false *Echo*, their minds as virtue be just.　　Just.
Mock'st thou those diamonds which only be matched
　　　　by the gods?　　　　　　　　　　　　　　　Odds.
Odds? What an odds is there since them to the heav'ns I
　　　　prefer?　　　　　　　　　　　　　　　　　Err.
Tell yet again me the names of these fair formed to do
　　　　ev'ls.　　　　　　　　　　　　　　　　　Dev'ls.
Dev'ls? If in hell such dev'ls do abide, to the hells I do
50　　　go.　　　　　　　　　　　　　　　　　　Go.

II.3 [Cleophila]

My Muse what ails this ardour
To blaze my only secrets?
Alas, it is no glory
To sing my own decayed state.
5　Alas, it is no comfort
To speak without an answer.
Alas, it is no wisdom
To show the wound without cure.

My Muse what ails this ardour?
10　My eyes be dim, my limbs shake,
My voice is hoarse, my throat scorched,
My tongue to this my roof cleaves,
My fancy amazed, my thoughts dulled,
My heart doth ache, my life faints,
15　My soul begins to take leave.
So great a passion all feel,
To think a sore so deadly
I should so rashly rip up.

My Muse what ails this ardour?
20　If that to sing thou art bent,
Go sing the fall of old *Thebes*,
The wars of ugly centaurs,
The life, the death of *Hector*,

So may thy song be famous;
25   Or if to love thou art bent,
Recount the rape of *Europe*,
Adonis' end, *Venus'* net,
The sleepy kiss the Moon stale;
So may thy song be pleasant.

30   My Muse what ails this ardour
To blaze my only secrets?
Wherein do only flourish
The sorry fruits of anguish,
The song thereof a last will,
35   The tunes be cries, the words plaints,
The singer is the song's theme
Wherein no ear can have joy,
Nor eye receives due object,
Ne pleasure here, ne fame got.

40   My Muse what ails this ardour?
'Alas,' she saith, 'I am thine,
So are thy pains my pains too.
Thy heated heart my seat is,
Wherein I burn, thy breath is
45   My voice, too hot to keep in.
Besides, lo here the author
Of all thy harms; lo here she
That only can redress thee,
Of her I will demand help.'

50   My Muse, I yield, my Muse sing,
But all thy song herein knit:
The life we lead is all love,
The love we hold is all death,
Nor aught I crave to feed life,
55   Nor aught I seek to shun death,
But only that my goddess
My life, my death, do count hers.

II. 4 [Cleophila]

Reason, tell me thy mind, if here be reason
In this strange violence, to make resistance;
Where sweet graces erect the stately banner
Of virtue's regiment, shining in harness
5   Of fortune's diadems, by beauty mustered.
Say then, Reason, I say what is thy counsel?

Her loose hair be the shot, the breasts the pikes be,
Scouts each motion is, the hands the horsemen,
Her lips are the riches the wars to maintain,
10   Where well couched abides a coffer of pearl,
Her legs carriage is of all the sweet camp.
Say then, Reason, I say what is thy counsel?

Her cannons be her eyes, mine eyes the walls be,
Which at first volley gave too open entry,
15   Nor rampire did abide; my brain was up-blown,
Undermined with a speech, the piercer of thoughts.
Thus weakened by myself, no help remaineth.
Say then, Reason, I say what is thy counsel?

And now Fame, the herald of her true honour,
20   Doth proclaim (with a sound made all by men's mouths)
That Nature, sovereign of earthly dwellers,
Commands all creatures to yield obeisance
Under this, this her own, her only darling.
Say then, Reason, I say what is thy counsel?

25   Reason sighs, but in end he thus doth answer:
'Naught can Reason avail in heav'nly matters.'
Thus Nature's diamond, receive thy conquest;
Thus pure pearl, I do yield my senses and soul;
Thus sweet pain, I do yield whate'er I can yield.
30   Reason, look to thyself, I serve a goddess.

II.5 *[Dorus]*

O sweet woods, the delight of solitariness!
O how much I do like your solitariness!
Where man's mind hath a freed consideration
Of goodness to receive lovely direction;
5   Where senses do behold th'order of heav'nly host,
And wise thoughts do behold what the creator is.
Contemplation here holdeth his only seat,
Bounded with no limits, borne with a wing of hope,
Climbs e'en unto the stars; Nature is under it.
10   Naught disturbs thy quiet, all to thy service yield,
Each sight draws on a thought (thought mother of science),
Sweet birds kindly do grant harmony unto thee,
Fair trees' shade is enough fortification,
Nor danger to thyself, if be not in thyself.

15   O sweet woods, the delight of solitariness!
O how much I do like your solitariness!
Here no treason is hid, veiled in innocence,
Nor envy's snaky eye finds any harbour here,
Nor flatterers' venomous insinuations,
20   Nor cunning humorists' puddled opinions,
Nor courteous ruin of proffered usury,
Nor time prattled away, cradle of ignorance,
Nor causeless duty, nor cumber of arrogance,
Nor trifling title of vanity dazzleth us,
25   Nor golden manacles stand for a paradise;
Here wrong's name is unheard; slander a monster is.
Keep thy sprite from abuse, here no abuse doth haunt.
What man grafts in a tree dissimulation?

O sweet woods, the delight of solitariness!
30   O how well I do like your solitariness!
Yet dear soil, if a soul closed in a mansion
As sweet as violets, fair as a lily is,
Straight as cedar, a voice stains the canary birds,
Whose shade safety doth hold, danger avoideth her:
35   Such wisdom that in her lives speculation;

Such goodness that in her simplicity triumphs;
Where envy's snaky eye winketh or else dieth,
Slander wants a pretext, flattery gone beyond:
O! if such a one have bent to a lonely life,
40   Her steps glad we receive, glad we receive her eyes;
        And think not she doth hurt our solitariness,
        For such company decks such solitariness.

The Third Book or Act

III.i [Dorus]

Sweet glove, the witness of my secret bliss
(Which hiding didst preserve that beauty's light
That, opened forth, my seal of comfort is),
Be thou my star in this my darkest night,
5   Now that mine eyes their cheerful sun do miss
Which dazzling still, doth still maintain my sight;
     Be thou, sweet glove, the anchor of my mind,
     Till my frail bark his hav'n again do find.

Sweet glove, the sweet despoils of sweetest hand,
10 Fair hand, the fairest pledge of fairer heart,
True heart, whose truth doth yield to truest band,
Chief band, I say, which ties my chiefest part,
My chiefest part, wherein do chiefly stand
Those secret joys, which heav'n to me impart,
15   Unite in one, my state thus still to save;
     You have my thanks, let me your comfort have.

III.ii [Dorus]

The merchant man, whom gain doth teach the sea
Where rocks do wait for them the winds do chase,
Beaten with waves, no sooner kens the bay
Where he was bound to make his marting place,
5   But fear forgot, and pains all overpast,
     Make present ease receive the better taste.

The labourer, which cursed earth up tears,
With sweaty brows, sometimes with wat'ry eyes,
Oft scorching sun, oft cloudy darkness fears,
10 While upon chance his fruit of labour lies;

> But harvest come, and corn in fertile store,
> More in his own he toiled, he glads the more.

Thus in my pilgrimage of mated mind,
Seeking the saint in whom all graces dwell,
15 What storms found me, what torments I did find,
Who seeks to know acquaints himself with hell;
> But now success hath got above annoys,
> That sorrow's weight doth balance up these joys.

III.iii [Cleophila]

The merchant man, whom many seas have taught
What horrors breed where wind dominion bears,
Yet never rock, nor race, such terror brought
As near his home when storm or shelf he fears;
5 > For Nature hath that never failing scope,
> Most loath to lose, the most approaching hope.

The labourer, whom tired body makes
Hold dear his work, with sighs each change attends,
But at no change so pinching care he takes
10 As happy shows of corn when harvest sends;
> For reason will, great sight of hoped bliss,
> Make great the loss, so great the fear to miss.

Thus tossed in my ship of huge desire,
Thus toiled in my work of raging love,
15 Now that I spy the hav'n my thoughts require,
Now that some flow'r of fruit my pains do prove,
> My dreads augment the more in passion's might,
> Since love with care, and hope with fear do fight.

III.iv [Basilius]

Phoebus farewell, a sweeter saint I serve.
The high conceits thy heav'nly wisdoms breed
My thoughts forget: my thoughts which never swerve
From her in whom is sown their freedom's seed,
5   And in whose eyes my daily doom I read.

Phoebus farewell, a sweeter saint I serve.
Thou art far off, thy kingdom is above;
She heav'n on earth with beauties doth preserve.
Thy beams I like, but her clear rays I love;
10   Thy force I fear, her force I still do prove.

Phoebus yield up thy title in my mind.
She doth possess; thy image is defaste.
But if thy rage some brave revenge will find
On her, who hath in me thy temple raste,
15   Employ thy might, that she my fires may taste;
        And how much more her worth surmounteth thee,
        Make her as much more base by loving me.

III.v [Cleophila]

Since that the stormy rage of passions dark
(Of passions dark, made dark by beauty's light)
With rebel force hath closed in dungeon dark
My mind ere now led forth by reason's light;

5   Since all the things which give mine eyes their light
Do foster still the fruit of fancies dark,
So that the windows of my inward light
Do serve to make my inward powers dark;

Since, as I say, both mind and senses dark
10   Are hurt, not helped, with piercing of the light;
While that the light may show the horrors dark,
But cannot make resolved darkness light;
  I like this place where, at the least, the dark
  May keep my thoughts from thought of wonted light.

III. vi [Gynecia]

Hark, plaintful ghosts! Infernal furies, hark
Unto my woes the hateful heav'ns do send:
The heav'ns conspired to make my vital spark
A wretched wrack, a glass of ruin's end.

5   Seeing, alas, so mighty powers bend
Their ireful shot against so weak a mark,
Come cave, become my grave; come death, and lend
Receipt to me within thy bosom dark.

For what is life to daily dying mind
10   Where, drawing breath, I suck the air of woe;
Where too much sight makes all the body blind,
And highest thoughts downward most headlong throw?
  Thus then my form, and thus my state I find:
  Death wrapped in flesh, to living grave assigned.

    *   *   *

15   Like those sick folks, in whom strange humours flow,
Can taste no sweets, the sour only please;
So to my mind, while passions daily grow,
Whose fiery chains upon his freedom seize,
  Joys strangers seem; I cannot bide their show,
20   Nor brook aught else but well-acquainted woe.
  Bitter grief tastes me best, pain is my ease,
  Sick to the death, still loving my disease.

III.vii [Gynecia]

How is my sun, whose beams are shining bright,
Become the cause of my dark ugly night?
Or how do I, captived in this dark plight,
Bewail the case, and in the cause delight?

5   My mangled mind huge horrors still do fright,
With sense possessed, and claimed by reason's right:
Betwixt which two in me I have this fight,
Where whoso wins, I put myself to flight.

Come, cloudy fears, close up my dazzled sight;
10 Sorrow, suck up the marrow of my might;
Due sighs, blow out all sparks of joyful light;
Tire on, despair, upon my tired sprite.
An end, an end, my dulled pen cannot write,
Nor mazed head think, nor falt'ring tongue recite.

* * *

15 This cave is dark, but it had never light.
This wax doth waste itself, yet painless dies.
These words are full of woes, yet feel they
none.

I darkened am, who once had clearest sight.
I waste my heart, which still new torment tries.
20 I plain with cause, my woes are all mine own.

No cave, no wasting wax, no words of grief,
Can hold, show, tell, my pains without relief.

III.viii [Charita]

My true love hath my heart, and I have his,
By just exchange, one for the other giv'n.
I hold his dear, and mine he cannot miss:
There never was a better bargain driv'n.

5 His heart in me, keeps me and him in one,
   My heart in him, his thoughts and senses guides.
   He loves my heart, for once it was his own:
   I cherish his, because in me it bides.

   His heart his wound received from my sight;
10 My heart was wounded, with his wounded heart,
   For as from me on him his hurt did light,
   So still methought in me his hurt did smart;
        Both equal hurt, in this change sought our bliss:
        My true love hath my heart, and I have his.

III.ix [Dametas]

   O words which fall like summer dew on me,
   O breath more sweet than is the growing bean,
   O tongue in which all honeyed liquors be,
   O voice that doth the thrush in shrillness stain:
5   Do you say still, this is her promise due,
        That she is mine, as I to her am true.

   Gay hair, more gay than straw when harvest lies,
   Lips red and plum, as cherry's ruddy side,
   Eyes fair and great, like fair great ox's eyes,
10 O breast in which two white sheep swell in pride:
        Join you with me, to seal this promise due,
        That she be mine, as I to her am true.

   But thou, white skin, as white as cruds well pressed,
   So smooth as sleekstone-like it smooths each part,
15 And thou, dear flesh, as soft as wool new dressed,
   And yet as hard as brawn made hard by art;
        First four but say, next four their saying seal,
        But you must pay the gage of promised weal.

III. x [Pamela]

Do not disdain, O straight upraised pine,
That, wounding thee, my thoughts in thee I grave;
Since that my thoughts, as straight as straightness thine,
No smaller wound, alas, far deeper have:

5   Deeper engraved, which salve nor time can save,
Giv'n to my heart by my fore-wounded ey'n;
Thus cruel to myself, how canst thou crave
My inward hurt should spare thy outward rine?

Yet still, fair tree, lift up thy stately line,
10   Live long, and long witness my chosen smart,
Which barred desires (barred by myself) impart;

And in this growing bark grow verses mine.
My heart my word, my word hath giv'n my heart.
The giver giv'n from gift shall never part.

*   *   *

15   Sweet root, say thou, the root of my desire
Was virtue clad in constant love's attire.

III. xi [Musidorus]

You goodly pines, which still with brave ascent
In Nature's pride your heads to heav'nward heave,
Though you besides such graces earth hath lent,
Of some late grace a greater grace receive,

5   By her who was (O blessed you) content
With her fair hand your tender barks to cleave,
And so by you (O blessed you) hath sent
Such piercing words as no thoughts else conceive:

Yet yield your grant, a baser hand may leave
10   His thoughts in you, where so sweet thoughts were spent,
For how would you the mistress' thoughts bereave
Of waiting thoughts all to her service meant?

Nay, higher thoughts (though thralled thoughts) I call
My thoughts than hers, who first your rine did rent,
15   Than hers, to whom my thoughts alonely thrall
Rising from low, are to the highest bent;
Where hers, whom worth makes highest over all,
Coming from her, cannot but downward fall.

III.xii [Pamela]

Like diverse flowers, whose diverse beauties serve
To deck the earth with his well-coloured weed,
Though each of them his private form preserve,
Yet joining forms one sight of beauty breed:
5   Right so my thoughts whereon my heart I feed;

Right so my inward parts and outward glass,
Though each possess a diverse working kind,
Yet all well knit to one fair end do pass:
That he to whom these sundry gifts I bind,
10   All what I am, still one, his own, do find.

III.xiii [Musidorus]

All what you are still one, his own to find,
You that are born to be the world's eye,
What were it else, but to make each thing blind,
And to the sun with waxen wings to fly?

5   No, no, such force with my small force to try
     Is not my skill, nor reach of mortal mind.
     Call me but yours, my title is most high;
     Hold me most yours, then my long suit is signed.

     You none can claim but you yourself by right,
10   For you do pass yourself, in virtue's might.
     So both are yours: I, bound with gaged heart;
     You only yours, too far beyond desert.

III.xiv [Musidorus]

     Lock up, fair lids, the treasures of my heart:
     Preserve those beams, this age's only light;
     To her sweet sense, sweet sleep, some ease impart,
     Her sense too weak to bear her spirit's might.

5   And while, O sleep, thou closest up her sight
     (Her sight where Love did forge his fairest dart),
     O harbour all her parts in easeful plight:
     Let no strange dream make her fair body start.

     But yet, O dream, if thou wilt not depart
10   In this rare subject from thy common right,
     But wilt thyself in such a seat delight,

     Then take my shape, and play a lover's part:
     Kiss her from me, and say unto her sprite,
     Till her eyes shine, I live in darkest night.

III.xv [Basilius]

     Why dost thou haste away,
     O *Titan* fair, the giver of the day?
     Is it to carry news
     To western wights, what stars in east appear?
5   Or dost thou think that here

Is left a sun whose beams thy place may use?
Yet stay, and well peruse
What be her gifts that make her equal thee.
Bend all thy light to see
10 In earthly clothes enclosed a heav'nly spark.
Thy running course cannot such beauties mark.
No, no, thy motions be
Hastened from us with bar of shadow dark,
Because that thou, the author of our sight,
15 Disdain'st we see thee stained with other's light.

III. xvi [Philoclea]

O stealing time, the subject of delay
(Delay, the rack of unrefrained desire),
What strange design hast thou my hopes to stay,
My hopes which do but to mine own aspire?

5   Mine own? O word on whose sweet sound doth prey
My greedy soul, with gripe of inward fire.
Thy title great, I justly challenge may,
Since in such phrase his faith he did attire.

O time, become the chariot of my joys;
10 As thou draw'st on, so let my bliss draw near.
Each moment lost, part of my hap destroys.

Thou art the father of occasion dear:
Join with thy son to ease my long annoys.
In speedy help thank-worthy friends appear.

III. xvii [Gynecia]

My lute, within thyself thy tunes enclose;
Thy mistress' song is now a sorrow's cry;
Her hand benumbed with fortune's daily blows,
Her mind amazed, can neither's help apply.
5   Wear these my words as mourning weeds of woes,
Black ink becomes the state wherein I die.
       And though my moans be not in music bound,
       Of written griefs yet be the silent ground.

The world doth yield such ill-consorted shows
10 (With circled course, which no wise stay can try)
That childish stuff which knows not friends from foes
(Better despised) bewonder gazing eye.
Thus noble gold down to the bottom goes,
When worthless cork aloft doth floating lie.
15   Thus in thyself least strings are loudest found,
       And lowest stops do yield the highest sound.

III. xviii [Basilius]

When two suns do appear
Some say it doth betoken wonders near,
As prince's loss or change.
Two gleaming suns of splendour like I see,
5 And seeing feel in me
Of prince's heart quite lost the ruin strange.

But now eachwhere doth range
With ugly cloak the dark envious night;
Who, full of guilty spite
10 Such living beams should her black seat assail,
Too weak for them our weaker sight doth veil.

'No,' says fair moon, 'my light
Shall bar that wrong, and though it not prevail
Like to my brother's rays, yet those I send
15   Hurt not the face, which nothing can amend.'

III.xix [Cleophila]

Aurora, now thou show'st thy blushing light
(Which oft to hope lays out a guileful bait,
That trusts in time to find the way aright
To ease those pains which on desire do wait),

5   Blush on for shame that still with thee do light
On pensive souls (instead of restful bait)
Care upon care (instead of doing right)
To overpressed breasts, more grievous weight.

As O! myself, whose woes are never light,
10   Tied to the stake of doubt, strange passions bait;
While thy known course, observing Nature's right,
Stirs me to think what dangers lie in wait.
        For mischiefs great, day after day doth show;
        Make me still fear thy fair appearing show.

III.xx [Cleophila]

Beauty hath force to catch the human sight;
Sight doth bewitch the fancy ill awaked;
Fancy, we feel, includes all passion's might;
Passion rebelled, oft reason's strength hath shaked.

5   No wonder, then, though sight my sight did taint,
And though thereby my fancy was infected,
Though (yoked so) my mind with sickness faint,
Had reason's weight for passion's ease rejected.

But now the fit is passed; and time hath giv'n
10   Leisure to weigh what due desert requireth.
All thoughts so sprung are from their dwelling driv'n,
And wisdom to his wonted seat aspireth,
          Crying in me: 'Eye-hopes deceitful prove;
          Things rightly prized, love is the band of love.'

III. xxi [Basilius]

Get hence foul grief, the canker of the mind;
Farewell complaint, the miser's only pleasure;
Away vain cares, by which few men do find
          Their sought-for treasure.

5   Ye helpless sighs, blow out your breath to naught;
Tears, drown yourselves, for woe (your cause) is wasted;
Thought, think to end, too long the fruit of thought
          My mind hath tasted.

But thou, sure hope, tickle my leaping heart;
10   Comfort, step thou in place of wonted sadness;
Fore-felt desire, begin to savour part
          Of coming gladness.

Let voice of sighs into clear music run;
Eyes, let your tears with gazing now be mended;
15   Instead of thought, true pleasure be begun
          And never ended.

III. xxii [Philoclea]

    1   2   3   1   2   3
Virtue, beauty, and speech, did strike, wound, charm,
          1   2   3   1   2   3
My heart, eyes, ears, with wonder, love, delight:

    1   2   3   1   2   3
First, second, last, did bind, enforce, and arm,
     1   2   3   1   2   3
His works, shows, suits, with wit, grace, and vow's might.

         1   2   3   1 2   3
5 Thus honour, liking, trust, much, far, and deep,
    1   2   3   1   2   3
Held, pierced, possessed, my judgement, sense, and will,
      1   2   3   1   2   3
Till wrong, contempt, deceit, did grow, steal, creep,
    1   2   3   1   2   3
Bands, favour, faith, to break, defile, and kill.

        1   2   3   1   2   3
Then grief, unkindness, proof, took, kindled, taught,
       1   2   3   1   2   3
10 Well-grounded, noble, due, spite, rage, disdain,
   1 2 3   1   2   3
But ah, alas! (in vain) my mind, sight, thought,
     1   2   3   1   2   3
Doth him, his face, his words, leave, shun, refrain,
        1   2   3   1   2   3
For no thing, time, nor place, can loose, quench, ease,
       1   2   3   1   2   3
Mine own, embraced, sought, knot, fire, disease.

III.xxiii [Philoclea]

The love which is imprinted in my soul
With beauty's seal, and virtue fair disguised,
With inward cries puts up a bitter roll
Of huge complaints that now it is despised.

5   Thus, thus, the more I love, the wrong the more
     Monstrous appears, long truth received late;
     Wrong stirs remorsed grief, grief's deadly sore
     Unkindness breeds, unkindness fost'reth hate.

     But ah! the more I hate, the more I think
10   Whom I do hate; the more I think on him,
     The more his matchless gifts do deeply sink
     Into my breast, and loves renewed swim.
          What medicine, then, can such disease remove
          Where love draws hate, and hate engend'reth love?

III. xxiv [Pyrocles repeating Philisides]

     What tongue can her perfections tell
     In whose each part all pens may dwell?
     Her hair fine threads of finest gold
     In curled knots man's thought to hold,
5   But that her forehead says, 'In me
     A whiter beauty you may see.'
     Whiter indeed; more white than snow
     Which on cold winter's face doth grow;
     That doth present those even brows
10   Whose equal lines their angles bows,
     Like to the moon when after change
     Her horned head abroad doth range,
     And arches be to heav'nly lids,
     Whose wink each bold attempt forbids.
15   For the black stars those spheres contain,
     The matchless pair e'en praise doth stain.
     No lamp whose light by art is got,
     No sun which shines and seeth not,
     Can liken them without all peer,
20   Save one as much as other clear,
     Which only thus unhappy be
     Because themselves they cannot see.

Her cheeks with kindly claret spread,
Aurora-like new out of bed;
25   Or like the fresh queen-apple's side,
Blushing at sight of *Phoebus'* pride.
Her nose, her chin, pure ivory wears,
No purer than the pretty ears,
Save that therein appears some blood,
30   Like wine and milk that mingled stood;
In whose incirclets if you gaze
Your eyes may tread a lover's maze,
But with such turns the voice to stray
No talk untaught can find the way.
35   The tip no jewel needs to wear:
The tip is jewel of the ear.
      But who those ruddy lips can miss,
Which blessed still themselves do kiss?
Rubies, cherries, and roses new,
40   In worth, in taste, in perfect hue,
Which never part but that they show
Of precious pearl the double row,
The second sweetly-fenced ward
Her heav'nly-dewed tongue to guard,
45   Whence never word in vain did flow.
      Fair under these doth stately grow
The handle of this pleasant work,
The neck, in which strange graces lurk:
Such be, I think, the sumptuous towers
50   Which skill doth make in princes' bowers.
      So good a say invites the eye
A little downward to espy
The lovely clusters of her breasts,
Of *Venus'* babe the wanton nests,
55   Like pommels round of marble clear,
Where azured veins well mixed appear,
With dearest tops of porphyry.
      Betwixt these two a way doth lie,
A way more worthy beauty's fame
60   Than that which bears the milken name.

This leads unto the joyous field
Which only still doth lilies yield,
But lilies such whose native smell
The Indian odours doth excel.
65   Waist it is called, for it doth waste
Men's lives until it be embraced.
       There may one see, and yet not see,
Her ribs in white well armed be,
More white than *Neptune*'s foamy face
70   When struggling rocks he would embrace.
       In these delights the wand'ring thought
Might of each side astray be brought,
But that her navel doth unite
In curious circle busy sight,
75   A dainty seal of virgin wax
Where nothing but impression lacks.
       Her belly there glad sight doth fill,
Justly entitled *Cupid*'s hill;
A hill most fit for such a master,
80   A spotless mine of alabaster,
Like alabaster fair and sleek,
But soft and supple, satin-like:
In that sweet seat the boy doth sport.
Loath, I must leave his chief resort;
85   For such an use the world hath gotten,
The best things still must be forgotten.
       Yet never shall my song omit
Those thighs (for *Ovid*'s song more fit)
Which, flanked with two sugared flanks,
90   Lift up their stately swelling banks,
That *Albion* cliffs in whiteness pass,
With haunches smooth as looking-glass.
       But bow all knees, now of her knees
My tongue doth tell what fancy sees:
95   The knots of joy, the gems of love,
Whose motion makes all graces move;
Whose bought incaved doth yield such sight,
Like cunning painter shadowing white.

The gart'ring place with childlike sign
100   Shows easy print in metal fine.
      But there again the flesh doth rise
In her brave calves like crystal skies,
Whose *Atlas* is a smallest small,
More white than whitest bone of whale.
105   There oft steals out that round clean foot,
This noble cedar's precious root;
In show and scent pale violets,
Whose step on earth all beauty sets.
      But back unto her back, my Muse,
110   Where *Leda*'s swan his feathers mews,
Along whose ridge such bones are met,
Like comfits round in marchpane set.
      Her shoulders be like two white doves,
Perching within square royal rooves,
115   Which leaded are with silver skin,
Passing the hate-spot ermelin.
      And thence those arms derived are;
The phoenix' wings be not so rare
For faultless length and stainless hue.
120   Ah, woe is me, my woes renew;
Now course doth lead me to her hand,
Of my first love the fatal band,
Where whiteness doth for ever sit;
Nature herself enamelled it.
125   For there with strange compact doth lie
Warm snow, moist pearl, soft ivory.
There fall those sapphire-coloured brooks,
Which conduit-like, with curious crooks,
Sweet islands make in that sweet land.
130   As for the fingers of the hand,
The bloody shafts of *Cupid*'s war,
With amethysts they headed are.
      Thus hath each part his beauty's part:
But how the Graces do impart
135   To all her limbs a special grace,
Becoming every time and place,

Which doth e'en beauty beautify,
And most bewitch the wretched eye;
How all this is but a fair inn
140 Of fairer guest which dwells within,
Of whose high praise, and praiseful bliss,
Goodness the pen, heav'n paper is,
The ink immortal fame doth lend.
As I began, so must I end:
145   No tongue can her perfections tell,
          In whose each part all pens may dwell.

The Third Eclogues

III.1 [Dicus]

Let mother earth now deck herself in flowers,
To see her offspring seek a good increase,
Where justest love doth vanquish *Cupid*'s powers
And war of thoughts is swallowed up in peace
5   Which never may decrease,
       But like the turtles fair
       Live one in two, a well-united pair,
       Which, that no chance may stain,
       O *Hymen* long their coupled joys maintain.

10   O heav'n awake, show forth thy stately face;
Let not these slumb'ring clouds thy beauties hide,
But with thy cheerful presence help to grace
The honest bridegroom and the bashful bride,
       Whose loves may ever bide,
15   Like to the elm and vine,
       With mutual embracements them to twine;
       In which delightful pain,
       O *Hymen* long their coupled joys maintain.

Ye Muses all which chaste affects allow,
20   And have to *Lalus* showed your secret skill,
To this chaste love your sacred favours bow,
And so to him and her your gifts distil,
       That they all vice may kill;
       And like to lilies pure
25   Do please all eyes, and spotless do endure;
       Where, that all bliss may reign,
       O *Hymen* long their coupled joys maintain.

Ye nymphs which in the waters empire have,
Since *Lalus*' music oft doth yield you praise,
30   Grant to the thing which we for *Lalus* crave:

Let one time (but long first) close up their days,
  One grave their bodies seize,
  And like two rivers sweet
  When they, though diverse, do together meet,
35   One stream both streams contain;
  O *Hymen* long their coupled joys maintain.

Pan, father *Pan*, the god of silly sheep,
Whose care is cause that they in number grow,
Have much more care of them that them do keep,
40 Since from these good the others' good doth flow,
  And make their issue show
  In number like the herd
  Of younglings which thyself with love hast reared,
  Or like the drops of rain;
45   O *Hymen* long their coupled joys maintain.

Virtue, if not a god, yet God's chief part,
Be thou the knot of this their open vow:
That still he be her head, she be his heart,
He lean to her, she unto him do bow;
50   Each other still allow,
  Like oak and mistletoe,
  Her strength from him, his praise from her do grow;
  In which most lovely train,
  O *Hymen* long their coupled joys maintain.

55 But thou, foul *Cupid*, sire to lawless lust,
Be thou far hence with thy empoisoned dart
Which, though of glitt'ring gold, shall here take rust
Where simple love, which chasteness doth impart,
  Avoids thy hurtful art,
60   Not needing charming skill
  Such minds with sweet affections for to fill,
  Which being pure and plain,
  O *Hymen* long their coupled joys maintain.

All churlish words, shrewd answers, crabbed looks,
65 All privateness, self-seeking, inward spite,
All waywardness which nothing kindly brooks,
All strife for toys, and claiming master's right,

Be hence ay put to flight;
All stirring husband's hate
70   'Gainst neighbours good for womanish debate
Be fled as things most vain;
O *Hymen* long their coupled joys maintain.

All peacock pride, and fruits of peacock's pride,
Longing to be with loss of substance gay
75 With recklessness what may thy house betide,
So that you may on higher slippers stay,
    For ever hence away.
    Yet let not sluttery,
    The sink of filth, be counted housewifery;
80   But keeping wholesome mean,
    O *Hymen* long their coupled joys maintain.

But above all, away vile jealousy,
The ill of ills, just cause to be unjust
(How can he love, suspecting treachery?
85 How can she love where love cannot win trust?),
    Go snake, hide thee in dust,
    Ne dare once show thy face
    Where open hearts do hold so constant place
    That they thy sting restrain;
90   O *Hymen* long their coupled joys maintain.

The earth is decked with flow'rs, the heav'ns displayed,
Muses grant gifts, nymphs long and joined life,
Pan store of babes, virtue their thoughts well stayed;
Cupid's lust gone, and gone is bitter strife,
95   Happy man, happy wife.
    No pride shall them oppress,
    Nor yet shall yield to loathsome sluttishness,
    And jealousy is slain:
    For *Hymen* will their coupled joys maintain.

III. 2 *[Philisides]*

As I my little flock on *Ister* bank
(A little flock, but well my pipe they couthe)
Did piping lead, the sun already sank
Beyond our world, and, ere I gat my booth,
5   Each thing with mantle black the night did soothe,
  Saving the glow-worm, which would courteous be
  Of that small light oft watching shepherds see.

The welkin had full niggardly enclosed
In coffer of dim clouds his silver groats,
10   Ycleped stars; each thing to rest disposed:
The caves were full, the mountains void of goats;
The birds' eyes closed, closed their chirping notes.
  As for the nightingale, wood-music's king,
  It August was, he deigned not then to sing.

15   Amid my sheep, though I saw naught to fear,
Yet (for I nothing saw) I feared sore;
Then found I which thing is a charge to bear,
For for my sheep I dreaded mickle more
Than ever for myself since I was bore.
20   I sat me down, for see to go ne could,
  And sang unto my sheep lest stray they should.

The song I sang old *Languet* had me taught,
Languet, the shepherd best swift *Ister* knew,
For clerkly rede, and hating what is naught,
25   For faithful heart, clean hands, and mouth as true.
With his sweet skill my skill-less youth he drew
  To have a feeling taste of Him that sits
  Beyond the heav'n, far more beyond our wits.

He said the music best thilke powers pleased
30   Was jump concord between our wit and will,
Where highest notes to godliness are raised,

And lowest sink not down to jot of ill.
With old true tales he wont mine ears to fill,
    How shepherds did of yore, how now they thrive,
35   Spoiling their flock, or while 'twixt them they strive.

He liked me, but pitied lustful youth;
His good strong staff my slipp'ry years upbore;
He still hoped well, because I loved truth;
Till forced to part, with heart and eyes e'en sore,
40   To worthy *Coredens* he gave me o'er.
       But thus in oak's true shade recounted he
       Which now in night's deep shade sheep heard of me.

Such manner time there was (what time I n'ot)
When all this earth, this dam or mould of ours,
45   Was only woned with such as beasts begot;
Unknown as then were they that builden towers.
The cattle, wild or tame, in Nature's bowers
       Might freely roam or rest, as seemed them;
       Man was not man, their dwellings in to hem.

50   The beasts had sure some beastly policy,
For nothing can endure where order nis:
For once the lion by the lamb did lie;
The fearful hind the leopard did kiss;
Hurtless was tiger's paw and serpent's hiss.
55   This think I well, the beasts with courage clad
       Like senators a harmless empire had.

At which, whether the others did repine
(For envy harb'reth most in feeble hearts),
Or that they all to changing did incline
60   (As e'en in beasts their dams leave changing parts),
The multitude to *Jove* a suit imparts,
       With neighing, bleaing, braying, and barking,
       Roaring, and howling for to have a king.

A king in language theirs they said they would
65   (For then their language was a perfect speech).
The birds likewise with chirps and pewing could,

Cackling and chatt'ring, that of *Jove* beseech.
Only the owl still warned them not to seech
    So hastily that which they would repent;
70   But saw they would, and he to deserts went.

Jove wisely said (for wisdom wisely says):
'O beasts, take heed what you of me desire.
Rulers will think all things made them to please,
And soon forget the swink due to their hire.
75 But since you will, part of my hcav'nly fire
    I will you lend; the rest yourselves must give,
    That it both seen and felt may with you live.'

Full glad they were, and took the naked sprite,
Which straight the earth yclothed in his clay.
80 The lion, heart; the ounce gave active might;
The horse, good shape; the sparrow, lust to play;
Nightingale, voice, enticing songs to say.
    Elephant gave a perfect memory;
    And parrot, ready tongue, that to apply.

85 The fox gave craft; the dog gave flattery;
Ass, patience; the mole, a working thought;
Eagle, high look; wolf, secret cruelty;
Monkey, sweet breath; the cow, her fair eyes brought;
The ermine, whitest skin spotted with naught;
90   The sheep, mild-seeming face; climbing, the bear;
    The stag did give the harm-eschewing fear;

The hare, her sleights; the cat, his melancholy;
Ant, industry; and cony, skill to build;
Cranes, order; storks to be appearing holy;
95 Chameleon, ease to change; duck, ease to yield;
Crocodile, tears which might be falsely spilled;
    Ape great thing gave, though he did mowing stand:
    The instrument of instruments, the hand.

Each other beast likewise his present brings;
100 And (but they drad their prince they oft should want)
They all consented were to give him wings;

And ay more awe towards him for to plant,
To their own work this privilege they grant:
    That from thenceforth to all eternity
105   No beast should freely speak, but only he.

Thus man was made; thus man their lord became;
Who at the first, wanting or hiding pride,
He did to beasts' best use his cunning frame,
With water drink, herbs meat, and naked hide;
110 And fellow-like let his dominion slide,
    Not in his sayings saying 'I', but 'we',
    As if he meant his lordship common be.

But when his seat so rooted he had found
That they now skilled not how from him to wend,
115 Then gan in guiltless earth full many a wound,
Iron to seek, which 'gainst itself should bend,
To tear the bowels that good corn should send.
    But yet the common dam none did bemoan,
    Because (though hurt) they never heard her groan.

120 Then gan he factions in the beasts to breed:
Where helping weaker sort, the nobler beasts
(As tigers, leopards, bears, and lions' seed)
Disdained with this, in deserts sought their rests;
Where famine ravin taught their hungry chests,
125   That craftily he forced them to do ill;
    Which being done, he afterwards would kill

For murder done, which never erst was seen
By those great beasts. As for the weaker's good,
He chose themselves his guarders for to been,
130 'Gainst those of might of whom in fear they stood,
As horse and dog; not great, but gentle blood.
    Blithe were the commons, cattle of the field,
    Tho when they saw their foen of greatness killed.

But they, or spent or made of slender might,
135 Then quickly did the meaner cattle find;
The great beams gone, the house on shoulders light:

For by and by the horse fair bits did bind;
The dog was in a collar taught his kind;
    As for the gentle birds, like case might rue
140   When falcon they, and goshawk, saw in mew.

Worst fell to smallest birds, and meanest herd,
Who now his own, full like his own he used.
Yet first but wool, or feathers, off he teared;
And when they were well used to be abused,
145 For hungry throat their flesh with teeth he bruised;
    At length for glutton taste he did them kill;
    At last for sport their silly lives did spill.

But yet, O man, rage not beyond thy need:
Deem it no gloire to swell in tyranny.
150 Thou art of blood; joy not to make things bleed.
Thou fearest death; think they are loath to die.
A plaint of guiltless hurt doth pierce the sky.
    And you, poor beasts, in patience bide your hell,
    Or know your strengths, and then you shall do well.

155 Thus did I sing and pipe eight sullen hours
To sheep whom love, not knowledge, made to hear
Now fancy's fits, now fortune's baleful stours.
But then I homeward called my lambkins dear;
For to my dimmed eyes began t'appear
160   The night grown old, her black head waxen grey,
    Sure shepherd's sign that morn would soon fetch
        day.

The Fourth Book or Act

IV.i [Basilius]

O night, the ease of care, the pledge of pleasure,
Desire's best mean, harvest of hearts affected,
The seat of peace, the throne which is erected
Of human life to be the quiet measure,

5 Be victor still of *Phoebus*' golden treasure,
Who hath our sight with too much sight infected,
Whose light is cause we have our lives neglected,
Turning all Nature's course to self-displeasure.

These stately stars in their now shining faces,
10 With sinless sleep, and silence, wisdom's mother,
Witness his wrong which by thy help is eased.

Thou art therefore of these our desert places
The sure refuge; by thee and by no other
My soul is blest, sense joyed, and fortune raised.

IV.ii [Agelastus]

Since wailing is a bud of causeful sorrow,
    Since sorrow is the follower of ill fortune,
    Since no ill fortune equals public damage,
    Now prince's loss hath made our damage public,
5   Sorrow pay we unto the rights of Nature,
    And inward grief seal up with outward wailing.

Why should we spare our voice from endless wailing,
    Who justly make our hearts the seats of sorrow,
    In such a case where it appears that Nature
10   Doth add her force unto the sting of fortune,
    Choosing, alas, this our theatre public,
    Where they would leave trophies of cruel damage?

Then since such pow'rs conspire unto our damage
    (Which may be known, but never helped with
        wailing)
15   Yet let us leave a monument in public,
    Of willing tears, torn hair, and cries of sorrow.
    For lost, lost is by blow of cruel fortune
    Arcadia's gem, the noblest child of Nature.

O Nature doting old, O blinded Nature,
    How hast thou torn thyself, sought thine own
20   damage,
    In granting such a scope to filthy fortune,
    By thy imp's loss to fill the world with wailing!
    Cast thy stepmother eyes upon our sorrow,
    Public our loss: so, see, thy shame is public.

25 O that we had, to make our woes more public,
    Seas in our eyes, and brazen tongues by nature,
    A yelling voice, and hearts composed of sorrow,
    Breath made of flames, wits knowing naught but
        damage,
    Our sports murd'ring ourselves, our musics wailing,
30   Our studies fixed upon the falls of fortune.

No, no, our mischief grows in this vile fortune,
    That private pangs cannot breathe out in public
    The furious inward griefs with hellish wailing;
    But forced are to burden feeble Nature
35   With secret sense of our eternal damage,
    And sorrow feed, feeding our souls with sorrow.

Since sorrow then concludeth all our fortune,
    With all our deaths show we this damage public.
    His nature fears to die who lives still wailing.

The Fourth Eclogues

IV.1 [Strephon and Klaius]

Strephon.   Ye goat-herd gods, that love the grassy
            mountains,
    Ye nymphs, which haunt the springs in pleasant valleys,
    Ye satyrs, joyed with free and quiet forests,
    Vouchsafe your silent ears to plaining music
5   Which to my woes gives still an early morning,
    And draws the dolour on till weary evening.

Klaius.   O *Mercury*, foregoer to the evening,
    O heav'nly huntress of the savage mountains,
    O lovely star, entitled of the morning,
10   While that my voice doth fill these woeful valleys,
    Vouchsafe your silent ears to plaining music,
    Which oft hath *Echo* tired in secret forests.

Strephon.   I that was once free burgess of the forests,
    Where shade from sun, and sport I sought in evening,
15   I that was once esteemed for pleasant music,
    Am banished now among the monstrous mountains
    Of huge despair, and foul affliction's valleys,
    Am grown a screech-owl to myself each morning.

Klaius.   I that was once delighted every morning,
20   Hunting the wild inhabiters of forests,
    I that was once the music of these valleys,
    So darkened am that all my day is evening,
    Heart-broken so, that molehills seem high mountains,
    And fill the vales with cries instead of music.

25 *Strephon.*   Long since, alas, my deadly swannish music
    Hath made itself a crier of the morning,
    And hath with wailing strength climbed highest
            mountains;

Long since my thoughts more desert be than forests;
Long since I see my joys come to their evening,
30   And state thrown down to over-trodden valleys.

Klaius.   Long since the happy dwellers of these valleys
Have prayed me leave my strange exclaiming music,
Which troubles their day's work, and joys of evening;
Long since I hate the night, more hate the morning;
35   Long since my thoughts chase me like beasts in forests,
And make me wish myself laid under mountains.

Strephon.   Meseems I see the high and stately mountains
Transform themselves to low dejected valleys;
Meseems I hear in these ill-changed forests
40   The nightingales do learn of owls their music;
Meseems I feel the comfort of the morning
Turned to the mortal serene of an evening.

Klaius.   Meseems I see a filthy cloudy evening
As soon as sun begins to climb the mountains;
45   Meseems I feel a noisome scent the morning
When I do smell the flowers of these valleys;
Meseems I hear (when I do hear sweet music)
The dreadful cries of murdered men in forests.

Strephon.   I wish to fire the trees of all these forests;
50   I give the sun a last farewell each evening;
I curse the fiddling finders-out of music;
With envy I do hate the lofty mountains,
And with despite despise the humble valleys;
I do detest night, evening, day, and morning.

55   *Klaius.*   Curse to myself my prayer is, the morning;
My fire is more than can be made with forests;
My state more base than are the basest valleys;
I wish no evenings more to see, each evening;
Shamed, I hate myself in sight of mountains,
60   And stop mine ears lest I grow mad with music.

Strephon.   For she, whose parts maintained a perfect
            music,
Whose beauties shined more than the blushing morning,

Who much did pass in state the stately mountains,
In straightness passed the cedars of the forests,
65   Hath cast me, wretch, into eternal evening,
By taking her two suns from these dark valleys.

Klaius.   For she, with whom compared the Alps are
valleys,
She, whose least word brings from the spheres their
music,
At whose approach the sun rase in the evening,
70   Who, where she went, bare in her forehead morning,
Is gone, is gone from these our spoiled forests,
Turning to deserts our best pastured mountains.

Strephon.   These mountains witness shall, so shall these
valleys,
Klaius.   These forests eke, made wretched by our music,
75   Our morning hymn this is, and song at evening.

IV.2 [Strephon and Klaius]

Strephon.   I joy in grief, and do detest all joys;
Despise delight, am tired with thought of ease.
I turn my mind to all forms of annoys,
And with the change of them my fancy please.
5   I study that which most may me displease,
And in despite of that displeasure's might
Embrace that most that most my soul destroys;
Blinded with beams, fell darkness is my sight;
Dwell in my ruins, feed with sucking smart,
10   I think from me, not from my woes, to part.

Klaius.   I think from me, not from my woes, to part,
And loathe this time called life, nay think that life
Nature to me for torment did impart;
Think my hard haps have blunted death's sharp knife,
15   Not sparing me in whom his works be rife;
And thinking this, think Nature, life, and death

Place sorrow's triumph on my conquered heart;
Whereto I yield, and seek no other breath
But from the scent of some infectious grave;
20 Nor of my fortune aught but mischief crave.

Strephon. Nor of my fortune aught but mischief crave,
And seek to nourish that which now contains
All what I am. If I myself will save,
Then must I save what in me chiefly reigns,
25 Which is the hateful web of sorrow's pains.
Sorrow then cherish me, for I am sorrow;
No being now but sorrow I can have;
Then deck me as thine own; thy help I borrow,
Since thou my riches art, and that thou hast
30 Enough to make a fertile mind lie waste.

Klaius. Enough to make a fertile mind lie waste
Is that huge storm which pours itself on me:
Hailstones of tears, of sighs a monstrous blast,
Thunders of cries; lightnings my wild looks be,
35 The darkened heav'n my soul which naught can see;
The flying sprites which trees by roots up tear
Be those despairs which have my hopes quite waste.
The difference is: all folks those storms forbear,
But I cannot; who then myself should fly,
40 So close unto myself my wracks do lie.

Strephon. So close unto myself my wracks do lie;
Both cause, effect, beginning, and the end
Are all in me: what help then can I try?
My ship, myself, whose course to love doth bend,
45 Sore beaten doth her mast of comfort spend;
Her cable, reason, breaks from anchor, hope;
Fancy, her tackling, torn away doth fly;
Ruin, the wind, hath blown her from her scope;
Bruised with waves of care, but broken is
50 On rock, despair, the burial of my bliss.

Klaius. On rock, despair, the burial of my bliss,
I long do plough with plough of deep desire;
The seed fast-meaning is, no truth to miss;

I harrow it with thoughts, which all conspire
55   Favour to make my chief and only hire.
But, woe is me, the year is gone about,
And now I fain would reap, I reap but this,
Hate fully grown, absence new sprongen out;
So that I see, although my sight impair,
60   Vain is their pain who labour in despair.

Strephon.   Vain is their pain who labour in despair,
For so did I when with my angle, will,
I sought to catch the fish torpedo fair.
E'en then despair did hope already kill;
65   Yet fancy would perforce employ his skill,
And this hath got: the catcher now is caught,
Lamed with the angle which itself did bear,
And unto death, quite drowned in dolours, brought
To death, as then disguised in her fair face.
70   Thus, thus alas, I had my loss in chase.

Klaius.   Thus, thus alas, I had my loss in chase
When first that crowned basilisk I knew,
Whose footsteps I with kisses oft did trace,
Till by such hap as I must ever rue
75   Mine eyes did light upon her shining hue,
And hers on me, astonished with that sight.
Since then my heart did lose his wonted place,
Infected so with her sweet poison's might
That, leaving me for dead, to her it went.
80   But ah, her flight hath my dead relics spent.

Strephon.   But ah, her flight hath my dead relics spent,
Her flight from me, from me, though dead to me,
Yet living still in her, while her beams lent
Such vital spark that her mine eyes might see.
85   But now those living lights absented be,
Full dead before, I now to dust should fall,
But that eternal pains my soul have hent,
And keep it still within this body thrall;
That thus I must, while in this death I dwell,
90   In earthly fetters feel a lasting hell.

Klaius.   In earthly fetters feel a lasting hell
　　　Alas I do; from which to find release
　　　I would the earth, I would the heavens sell.
　　　But vain it is to think those pains should cease,
95　　Where life is death, and death cannot breed peace.
　　　O fair, O only fair, from thee, alas,
　　　These foul, most foul, disasters to me fell;
　　　Since thou from me (O me) O sun didst pass.
　　　Therefore esteeming all good blessings toys,
100　　I joy in grief, and do detest all joys.

Strephon.   I joy in grief, and do detest all joys.
　　　But now an end, O *Klaius*, now an end,
　　　For e'en the herbs our hateful music 'stroys,
　　　And from our burning breath the trees do bend.

IV.3 [Philisides]

Now was our heav'nly vault deprived of the light,
With sun's depart; and now the darkness of the night
Did light those beamy stars which greater light did dark;
Now each thing which enjoyed that fiery quick'ning spark
5　(Which life is called) were moved their spirits to repose,
And wanting use of eyes, their eyes began to close.
A silence sweet each where with one concent embraced
(A music sweet to one in careful musing placed);
And mother earth, now clad in mourning weeds, did
　　　　breathe
10　A dull desire to kiss the image of our death;
When I, disgraced wretch, not wretched then, did give
My senses such release as they which quiet live,
Whose brains boil not in woes, nor breasts with beatings
　　　　ache,
With Nature's praise are wont in safest home to take.
Far from my thoughts was aught whereto their minds
15　　　　aspire
Who under courtly pomps do hatch a base desire.

Free all my powers were from those captiving snares
Which heav'nly purest gifts defile in muddy cares.
Ne could my soul itself accuse of such a fault
20   As tender conscience might with furious pangs assault.
But like the feeble flow'r (whose stalk cannot sustain
His weighty top) his top doth downward drooping lean;
Or as the silly bird in well-acquainted nest
Doth hide his head with cares but only how to rest;
25   So I in simple course, and unentangled mind,
Did suffer drowsy lids mine eyes, then clear, to blind;
And laying down my head, did Nature's rule observe,
Which senses up doth shut the senses to preserve.
They first their use forgot; then fancies lost their force,
30   Till deadly sleep at length possessed my living corse.
A living corse I lay; but ah, my wakeful mind
(Which, made of heav'nly stuff, no mortal change doth
            bind)
Flew up with freer wings, of fleshly bondage free;
And having placed my thoughts, my thoughts thus placed
            me:
35   Methought, nay sure I was, I was in fairest wood
Of *Samothea* land; a land which whilom stood
An honour to the world, while honour was their end,
And while their line of years they did in virtue spend.
But there I was, and there my calmy thoughts I fed
40   On Nature's sweet repast, as healthful senses led.
Her gifts my study was; her beauties were my sport;
My work her works to know; her dwelling my resort.
Those lamps of heav'nly fire to fixed motion bound,
The ever-turning spheres, the never-moving ground;
45   What essence dest'ny hath; if fortune be or no;
Whence our immortal souls to mortal earth do flow;
What life it is, and how that all these lives do gather
With outward maker's force, or like an inward father:
Such thoughts, methought, I thought, and strained my
            single mind,
50   Then void of nearer cares, the depth of things to find.
When lo, with hugest noise (such noise a tower makes
When it blown up with mine a fall of ruin takes;

Or such a noise it was as highest thunders send,
Or cannons, thunder-like, all shot together lend),
55   The moon asunder rent (O gods, O pardon me,
That forced with grief reveals what grieved eyes did see),
The moon asunder rent; whereat with sudden fall
(More swift than falcon's stoop to feeding falconer's call)
There came a chariot fair by doves and sparrows guided,
60   Whose storm-like course stayed not till hard by me it
         bided.
I, wretch, astonished was, and thought the deathful doom
Of heav'n, of earth, of hell, of time and place was come.
But straight there issued forth two ladies (ladies sure
They seemed to me) on whom did wait a virgin pure.
Strange were the ladies' weeds, yet more unfit than
65   strange:
The first with clothes tucked up, as nymphs in woods do
         range,
Tucked up e'en with the knees, with bow and arrows prest;
Her right arm naked was, discovered was her breast;
But heavy was her pace, and such a meagre cheer
70   As little hunting mind (God knows) did there appear.
The other had with art (more than our women know,
As stuff meant for the sale set out to glaring show)
A wanton woman's face, and with curled knots had twined
Her hair which, by the help of painter's cunning, shined.
75   When I such guests did see come out of such a house,
The mountains great with child I thought brought forth a
         mouse.
But walking forth, the first thus to the second said,
'*Venus*, come on.' Said she, '*Diane*, you are obeyed.'
Those names abashed me much, when those great names I
         heard;
Although their fame (meseemed) from truth had greatly
80   jarred.
As I thus musing stood, *Diana* called to her
Her waiting nymph, a nymph that did excel as far
All things that erst I saw, as orient pearls exceed
That which their mother hight, or else their silly seed;

85 Indeed a perfect hue, indeed a sweet concent
Of all those graces' gifts the heav'ns have ever lent.
And so she was attired, as one that did not prize
Too much her peerless parts, nor yet could them despise.
But called, she came apace; a pace wherein did move
90 The band of beauties all, the little world of love;
And bending humbled eyes (O eyes, the sun of sight)
She waited mistress' will, who thus disclosed her sprite:
'Sweet *Mira* mine,' quoth she, 'the pleasure of my mind,
In whom of all my rules the perfect proof I find,
95 To only thee thou seest we grant this special grace
Us to attend, in this most private time and place.
Be silent therefore now, and so be silent still
Of what thou seest; close up in secret knot thy will.'
She answered was with look, and well-performed behest;
100 And *Mira* I admired; her shape sank in my breast.
But thus with ireful eyes, and face that shook with spite,
Diana did begin: 'What moved me to invite
Your presence, sister dear, first to my moony sphere,
And hither now, vouchsafe to take with willing ear.
105 I know full well you know what discord long hath reigned
Betwixt us two; how much that discord foul hath stained
Both our estates, while each the other did deprave;
Proof speaks too much to us, that feeling trial have.
Our names are quite forgot, our temples are defaced,
Our off'rings spoiled, our priests from priesthood are
110   displaced.
Is this thy fruit, O strife? Those thousand churches high,
Those thousand altars fair, now in the dust to lie?
In mortal minds our minds but planets' names preserve;
No knee once bowed, forsooth, for them they say we serve.
115 Are we their servants grown? No doubt a noble stay:
Celestial pow'rs to worms, *Jove*'s children serve to clay.
But such they say we be: this praise our discord bred,
While we for mutual spite a striving passion fed.
But let us wiser be; and what foul discord brake,
120 So much more strong again let fastest concord make.
Our years do it require; you see we both do feel
The weak'ning work of time's for ever whirling wheel.

Although we be divine, our grandsire *Saturn* is
With age's force decayed, yet once the heav'n was his.
125 And now, before we seek by wise *Apollo*'s skill
Our young years to renew (for so he saith he will),
Let us a perfect peace betwixt us two resolve;
Which, lest the ruinous want of government dissolve,
Let one the princess be, to her the other yield;
130 For vain equality is but contention's field.
And let her have the gifts that should in both remain:
In her let beauty both and chasteness fully reign;
So as, if I prevail, you give your gifts to me;
If you, on you I lay what in my office be.
135 Now resteth only this: which of us two is she
To whom precedence shall of both accorded be?
For that (so that you like) hereby doth lie a youth,'
(She beckoned unto me), 'as yet of spotless truth,
Who may this doubt discern; for better wit than lot
140 Becometh us; in us fortune determines not.
This crown of amber fair,' (an amber crown she held),
'To worthiest let him give when both he hath beheld,
And be it as he saith.' *Venus* was glad to hear
Such proffer made, which she well showed with smiling
cheer,
145 As though she were the same as when, by *Paris*' doom,
She had chief goddesses in beauty overcome,
And smirkly thus gan say: 'I never sought debate,
Diana dear; my mind to love and not to hate
Was ever apt; but you my pastimes did despise.
150 I never spited you, but thought you over-wise.
Now kindness proffered is, none kinder is than I;
And so most ready am this mean of peace to try.
And let him be our judge: the lad doth please me well.'
Thus both did come to me, and both began to tell
155 (For both together spake, each loath to be behind)
That they by solemn oath their deities would bind
To stand unto my will; their will they made me know.
I, that was first aghast when first I saw their show,

Now bolder waxed, waxed proud that I such sway might
      bear;
160 For near acquaintance doth diminish reverent fear.
And having bound them fast by *Styx* they should obey
To all what I decreed, did thus my verdict say:
'How ill both you can rule, well hath your discord taught;
Ne yet, for what I see, your beauties merit aught.
165 To yonder nymph, therefore,' (to *Mira* I did point),
'The crown above you both for ever I appoint.'
I would have spoken out, but out they both did cry:
'Fie, fie, what have we done? Ungodly rebel, fie!
But now we must needs yield to what our oaths require.'
170 'Yet thou shalt not go free,' quoth *Venus*; 'such a fire
Her beauty kindle shall within thy foolish mind
That thou full oft shalt wish thy judging eyes were blind.'
'Nay then,' *Diana* said, 'the chasteness I will give
In ashes of despair, though burnt, shall make thee live.'
'Nay thou,' said both, 'shalt see such beams shine in her
175   face
That thou shalt never dare seek help of wretched case.'
And with that cursed curse away to heav'n they fled,
First having all their gifts upon fair *Mira* spread.
The rest I cannot tell, for therewithal I waked
180 And found with deadly fear that all my sinews shaked.
Was it a dream? O dream, how hast thou wrought in me
That I things erst unseen should first in dreaming see?
And thou, O traitor sleep, made for to be our rest,
How hast thou framed the pain wherewith I am oppressed?
185 O coward *Cupid*, thus dost thou thy honour keep,
Unarmed, alas unwarned, to take a man asleep?

IV. 4 [Philisides]

Unto the caitiff wretch whom long affliction holdeth,
    and now fully believes help to be quite perished,
Grant yet, grant yet a look, to the last monument of his
    anguish,

O you (alas so I find) cause of his only ruin.
5   Dread not a whit (O goodly cruel) that pity may enter
      into thy heart by the sight of this epistle I send;
And so refuse to behold of these strange wounds the recital,
      lest it might thee allure home to thyself to return
(Unto thyself I do mean, those graces dwell so within thee,
10   gratefulness, sweetness, holy love, hearty regard).
Such thing cannot I seek (despair hath giv'n me my
      answer,
      despair most tragical clause to a deadly request);
Such thing cannot he hope that knows thy determinate
      hardness;
      hard like a rich marble; hard, but a fair diamond.
Can those eyes, that of eyes drowned in most hearty flowing
15   tears
      (tears, and tears of a man) had no return to remorse;
Can those eyes now yield to the kind conceit of a sorrow,
      which ink only relates, but ne laments ne replies?
Ah, that, that do I not conceive, though that to me lief
      were
20   more than *Nestor*'s years, more than a king's diadem.
Ah, that, that do I not conceive; to the heaven when a
      mouse climbs
      then may I hope t'achieve grace of a heavenly tiger.
But, but alas, like a man condemned doth crave to be heard
      speak,
      not that he hopes for amends of the disaster he feels,
25   But finding th'approach of death with an inly relenting,
      gives an adieu to the world, as to his only delight;
Right so my boiling heart, inflamed with fire of a fair eye,
      bubbling out doth breathe signs of his hugy dolours,
Now that he finds to what end his life and love be
      reserved,
      and that he thence must part where to live only I
30   lived.
O fair, O fairest, are such the triumphs to thy fairness?
      Can death beauty become? Must I be such a
      monument?

Must I be only the mark shall prove that virtue is angry?
    Shall prove that fierceness can with a white dove
      abide?
35 Shall to the world appear that faith and love be rewarded
    with mortal disdain, bent to unendly revenge?
Unto revenge? O sweet, on a wretch wilt thou be revenged?
    Shall such high planets tend to the loss of a worm?
And to revenge who do bend would in that kind be
    revenged
40   as th'offence was done, and go beyond if he can.
All my offence was love; with love then must I be
    chastened,
    and with more, by the laws that to revenge do
      belong.
If that love be a fault, more fault in you to be lovely;
    love never had me oppressed, but that I saw to be
      loved.
You be the cause that I love; what reason blameth a
45   shadow
    that with a body't goes, since by a body it is?
If the love hate you did, you should your beauty have
    hidden;
    you should those fair eyes have with a veil covered.
But fool, fool that I am, those eyes would shine from a
    dark cave;
50   what veils then do prevail, but to a more miracle?
Or those golden locks (those locks which lock me to
    bondage)
    torn you should disperse unto the blasts of a wind.
But fool, fool that I am, though I had but a hair of her
    head found,
    e'en as I am, so I should unto that hair be a thrall.
Or with a fair hand's nails (O hand which nails me to this
55   death)
    you should have your face (since love is ill)
      blemished.
O wretch, what do I say? Should that fair face be defaced?
    Should my too much sight cause so true a sun to be
      lost?

First let Cimmerian darkness be my onl'habitation,
　　　first be mine eyes pulled out, first be my brain
60　　　　　perished,
Ere that I should consent to do such excessive a damage
　　　unto the earth by the hurt of this her heavenly jewel.
O not but such love you say you could have afforded,
　　　as might learn temp'rance void of a rage's events.
65　O sweet simplicity, from whence should love be so learned?
　　　　Unto *Cupid*, that boy, shall a pedant be found?
Well, but faulty I was; reason to my passion yielded,
　　　passion unto my rage, rage to a hasty revenge.
But what's this for a fault, for which such faith be
　　　　abolished,
70　　　　such faith, so stainless, inviolate, violent?
Shall I not? O may I not thus yet refresh the remembrance
　　　what sweet joys I had once, and what a place I did hold?
Shall I not once object that you, you granted a favour
　　　unto the man whom now such miseries you award?
Bend your thoughts to the dear sweet words which then to
75　　　　me giv'n were;
　　　　think what a world is now, think who hath altered
　　　　her heart.
What? Was I then worthy such good, now worthy so much
　　　　ill?
　　　　Now fled, then cherished? Then so nigh, now so
　　　　remote?
Did not a rosed breath, from lips more rosy proceeding,
80　　　say that I well should find in what a care I was had?
With much more: now what do I find but care to abhor
　　　　me,
　　　care that I sink in grief, care that I live banished?
And banished do I live, nor now will seek a recov'ry,
　　　since so she will, whose will is to me more than a
　　　　law.
85　If then a man in most ill case may give you a farewell:
　　　farewell, long farewell, all my woe, all my delight.

The Fifth Book or Act

V.i [Musidorus]

Since Nature's works be good, and death doth serve
As Nature's work, why should we fear to die?
Since fear is vain but when it may preserve,
Why should we fear that which we cannot fly?

5   Fear is more pain than is the pain it fears,
Disarming human minds of native might;
While each conceit an ugly figure bears,
Which were not ill, well viewed in reason's light.

Our owly eyes, which dimmed with passions be,
10   And scarce discern the dawn of coming day,
Let them be cleared, and now begin to see
Our life is but a step in dusty way.
        Then let us hold the bliss of peaceful mind,
        Since this we feel, great loss we cannot find.

Poems from *Certain Sonnets*

i

Since, shunning pain, I ease can never find;
Since bashful dread seeks where he knows me harmed;
Since will is won, and stopped ears are charmed;
Since force doth faint, and sight doth make me blind;
5 Since loosing long, the faster still I bind;
Since naked sense can conquer reason armed;
Since heart in chilling fear with ice is warmed;
In fine, since strife of thought but mars the mind,
I yield, O Love, unto thy loathed yoke,
10 Yet craving law of arms, whose rule doth teach
That hardly used, whoever prison broke,
In justice quit, of honour made no breach:
     Whereas, if I a grateful guardian have,
     Thou art my lord, and I thy vowed slave.

ii

When Love, puffed up with rage of high disdain,
Resolved to make me pattern of his might,
Like foe, whose wits inclined to deadly spite,
Would often kill, to breed more feeling pain;
5 He would not, armed with beauty, only reign
On those affects which eas'ly yield to sight,
But virtue sets so high, that reason's light,
For all his strife can only bondage gain:
So that I live to pay a mortal fee,
10 Dead-palsy sick of all my chiefest parts;
Like those whom dreams make ugly monsters see,
And can cry 'Help!' with naught but groans and starts.
     Longing to have, having no wit to wish:
     To starving minds such is god *Cupid*'s dish.

iii

The scourge of life, and death's extreme disgrace,
    The smoke of hell, the monster called Pain,
Long shamed to be accursed in every place
    By them who of his rude resort complain,
5 Like crafty wretch, by time and travel taught
    His ugly ill in others' good to hide,
Late harbours in her face, whom Nature wrought
    As treasure-house where her best gifts abide.
And so, by privilege of sacred seat,
10   A seat where beauty shines and virtue reigns,
He hopes for some small praise, since she hath great,
    Within her beams wrapping his cruel stains.
      Ah, saucy Pain, let not thy error last;
      More loving eyes she draws, more hate thou hast.

iv

Thou Pain, the only guest of loathed constraint,
    The child of curse, man's weakness' foster-child,
Brother to woe, and father of complaint;
    Thou Pain, thou hated Pain, from heav'n exiled,
5 How hold'st thou her, whose eyes constraint doth fear,
    Whom cursed do bless, whose weakness virtues arm,
Who others' woes and plaints can chastely bear,
    In whose sweet heav'n angels of high thoughts swarm?
What courage strange hath caught thy caitiff heart?
10   Fear'st not a face that oft whole hearts devours,
Or art thou from above bid play this part,
    And so no help 'gainst envy of those powers?
      If thus, alas; yet while those parts have woe,
      So stay her tongue that she no more say no.

v

You better sure shall live, not evermore
 Trying high seas, nor, while sea's rage you flee,
 Pressing too much upon ill-harboured shore.

The golden mean who loves, lives safely free
5 From filth of forworn house, and quiet lives,
 Released from court, where envy needs must be.

The wind most oft the hugest pine-tree grieves;
 The stately towers come down with greater fall;
 The highest hills the bolt of thunder cleaves;

10 Ill haps do fill with hope, good haps appal
 With fear of change the courage well prepared;
 Foul winters, as they come, away they shall.

Though present times and past with ills be snared,
 They shall not last; with cithern silent Muse
15 *Apollo* wakes, and bow hath sometime spared.

In hard estate with stout show valour use;
 The same man still in whom wisdom prevails,
 In too full wind draw in thy swelling sails.

vi

Like as the dove which seeled–up doth fly,
 Is neither freed, nor yet to service bound,
But hopes to gain some help by mounting high
 Till want of force doth force her fall to ground;
5 Right so my mind, caught by his guiding eye
 And thence cast off, where his sweet hurt he found,
Hath neither leave to live, nor doom to die,
 Nor held in ill, nor suffered to be sound,

But with his wings of fancies up he goes
10   To high conceits whose fruits are oft but small,
Till wounded, blind, and wearied spirits lose
    Both force to fly and knowledge where to fall.
        O happy dove, if she no bondage tried;
        More happy I, might I in bondage bide.

vii

Oft have I mused, but now at length I find
    Why those that die, men say they do depart;
'Depart', a word so gentle to my mind,
    Weakly did seem to paint death's ugly dart.
5 But now the stars with their strange course do bind
    Me one to leave, with whom I leave my heart.
I hear a cry of spirits faint and blind,
    That, parting thus, my chiefest part I part.
Part of my life, the loathed part to me,
10   Lives to impart my weary clay some breath;
But that good part, wherein all comforts be,
    Now dead, doth show departure is a death;
        Yea, worse than death: death parts both woe and joy;
        From joy I part, still living in annoy.

viii

Thou blind man's mark, thou fool's self-chosen snare,
Fond fancy's scum, and dregs of scattered thought,
Band of all ills, cradle of causeless care,
Thou web of will, whose end is never wrought;
5 Desire, desire, I have too dearly bought,
With price of mangled mind, thy worthless ware;
Too long, too long, asleep thou hast me brought,
Who shouldst my mind to higher things prepare.

But yet in vain thou hast my ruin sought;
10   In vain thou mad'st me to vain things aspire;
In vain thou kindlest all thy smoky fire;
For virtue hath this better lesson taught,
Within myself to seek my only hire,
Desiring naught but how to kill desire.

ix

Leave me, O Love, which reachest but to dust,
And thou, my mind, aspire to higher things;
Grow rich in that which never taketh rust;
Whatever fades, but fading pleasure brings.
5   Draw in thy beams, and humble all thy might
To that sweet yoke where lasting freedoms be,
Which breaks the clouds, and opens forth the light
That doth both shine and give us sight to see.
O take fast hold, let that light be thy guide
10   In this small course which birth draws out to death,
And think how ill becometh him to slide
Who seeketh heav'n, and comes of heav'nly breath.
    Then farewell, world; thy uttermost I see;
    Eternal love, maintain thy life in me.

    Splendidis longum valedico nugis

Astrophil and Stella

I

Loving in truth, and fain in verse my love to show,
That the dear she might take some pleasure of my pain,
Pleasure might cause her read, reading might make her
     know,
Knowledge might pity win, and pity grace obtain:
5   I sought fit words to paint the blackest face of woe,
Studying inventions fine, her wits to entertain;
Oft turning others' leaves, to see if thence would flow
Some fresh and fruitful showers upon my sunburnt brain.
     But words came halting forth, wanting invention's
          stay;
10 Invention, Nature's child, fled step-dame study's blows,
And others' feet still seemed but strangers in my way.
Thus great with child to speak, and helpless in my throes,
     Biting my truant pen, beating myself for spite,
     'Fool,' said my Muse to me, 'look in thy heart and
          write.'

2

Not at first sight, nor with a dribbed shot
     Love gave the wound which while I breathe will
          bleed;
     But known worth did in mine of time proceed,
Till by degrees it had full conquest got.
5 I saw and liked, I liked but loved not,
     I loved, but straight did not what Love decreed;
     At length to Love's decrees I, forced, agreed,
Yet with repining at so partial lot.

Now e'en that footstep of lost liberty
10 Is gone, and now, like slave-born Muscovite,
I call it praise to suffer tyranny;
And now employ the remnant of my wit
To make myself believe that all is well,
While with a feeling skill I paint my hell.

3

Let dainty wits cry on the sisters nine,
That, bravely masked, their fancies may be told;
Or, *Pindar*'s apes, flaunt they in phrases fine,
Enam'lling with pied flowers their thoughts of gold;
5   Or else let them in statelier glory shine,
Ennobling new-found tropes with problems old;
Or with strange similes enrich each line
Of herbs or beasts which *Ind* or *Afric* hold.
For me, in sooth, no Muse but one I know:
10   Phrases and problems from my reach do grow,
And strange things cost too dear for my poor sprites.
How then? E'en thus: in *Stella*'s face I read
What love and beauty be; then all my deed
But copying is, what in her Nature writes.

4

Virtue, alas, now let me take some rest.
Thou sett'st a 'bate between my will and wit:
If vain love have my simple soul oppressed,
Leave what thou lik'st not, deal not thou with it.
5   Thy sceptre use in some old *Cato*'s breast;
Churches or schools are for thy seat more fit.
I do confess, pardon a fault confessed,
My mouth too tender is for thy hard bit.

But if that needs thou wilt usurping be
10   The little reason that is left in me,
And still th'effect of thy persuasions prove:
          I swear my heart such one shall show to thee,
          That shrines in flesh so true a deity,
That, Virtue, thou thyself shalt be in love.

5

It is most true, that eyes are formed to serve
The inward light; and that the heav'nly part
Ought to be king, from whose rules who do swerve,
Rebels to Nature, strive for their own smart.
5   It is most true, what we call *Cupid*'s dart
An image is, which for ourselves we carve,
And, fools, adore in temple of our heart,
Till that good god make Church and churchman starve.
          True, that true beauty virtue is indeed,
10 Whereof this beauty can be but a shade,
Which elements with mortal mixture breed;
True, that on earth we are but pilgrims made,
          And should in soul up to our country move:
          True, and yet true that I must *Stella* love.

6

Some lovers speak, when they their Muses entertain,
Of hopes begot by fear, of wot not what desires,
Of force of heav'nly beams, infusing hellish pain,
Of living deaths, dear wounds, fair storms and freezing
          fires;
          Some one his song in *Jove* and *Jove*'s strange tales
5   attires,
Broidered with bulls and swans, powdered with golden
          rain;

Another humbler wit to shepherd's pipe retires,
Yet hiding royal blood full oft in rural vein;
    To some, a sweetest plaint a sweetest style affords,
    While tears pour out his ink, and sighs breathe out
10   his words,
His paper, pale despair, and pain his pen doth move.
    I can speak what I feel, and feel as much as they,
    But think that all the map of my state I display
When trembling voice brings forth that I do *Stella* love.

7

When Nature made her chief work, *Stella*'s eyes,
In colour black, why wrapped she beams so bright?
Would she in beamy black, like painter wise,
Frame daintiest lustre, mixed of shades and light?
5   Or did she else that sober hue devise
In object best to knit and strength our sight,
 Lest, if no veil those brave gleams did disguise,
 They, sun-like, should more dazzle than delight?
    Or would she her miraculous power show,
10   That, whereas black seems beauty's contrary,
She e'en in black doth make all beauties flow?
But so, and thus: she minding Love should be
    Placed ever there, gave him this mourning weed,
    To honour all their deaths, who for her bleed.

8

Love, born in *Greece*, of late fled from his native place,
    Forced by a tedious proof, that Turkish hardened
      heart
    Is no fit mark to pierce with his fine-pointed dart;
And, pleased with our soft peace, stayed here his flying
      race.

5 But finding these north climes do coldly him embrace,
> Not used to frozen clips, he strave to find some part
> Where with most ease and warmth he might employ
> his art.
At length he perched himself in *Stella*'s joyful face,
> Whose fair skin, beamy eyes, like morning sun on
> snow,
10 Deceived the quaking boy, who thought from so pure light
Effects of lively heat must needs in nature grow.
But she, most fair, most cold, made him thence take his
> flight
> To my close heart, where, while some firebrands he
> did lay,
> He burnt unwares his wings, and cannot fly away.

9

Queen Virtue's court, which some call *Stella*'s face,
> Prepared by Nature's chiefest furniture,
> Hath his front built of alabaster pure;
Gold is the covering of that stately place;
5 The door, by which sometimes comes forth her grace,
> Red porphyr is, which lock of pearl makes sure,
> Whose porches rich (which name of cheeks endure)
Marble mixed red and white do interlace;
> The windows now through which this heav'nly guest
10 Looks o'er the world, and can find nothing such
Which dare claim from those lights the name of best,
Of touch they are, that without touch doth touch,
> Which *Cupid*'s self from beauty's mine did draw:
> Of touch they are, and poor I am their straw.

10

Reason, in faith thou art well served, that still
Wouldst brabbling be with sense and love in me.
I rather wished thee climb the Muses' hill,
Or reach the fruit of Nature's choicest tree,
5   Or seek heav'n's course, or heav'n's inside to see.
Why shouldst thou toil our thorny soil to till?
Leave sense, and those which sense's objects be;
Deal thou with powers of thoughts, leave love to will.
          But thou wouldst needs fight both with love and
          sense,
10   With sword of wit giving wounds of dispraise,
Till downright blows did foil thy cunning fence:
For soon as they strake thee with *Stella*'s rays,
          Reason thou kneeled'st, and offered'st straight to
          prove
          By reason good, good reason her to love.

11

In truth, O Love, with what a boyish kind
          Thou dost proceed in thy most serious ways,
          That when the heav'n to thee his best displays,
Yet of that best thou leav'st the best behind.
5   For like a child that some fair book doth find,
          With gilded leaves or coloured vellum plays,
          Or at the most on some fine picture stays,
But never heeds the fruit of writer's mind;
          So when thou saw'st in Nature's cabinet
10   *Stella*, thou straight look'st babies in her eyes,
In her cheek's pit thou didst thy pit-fold set,
And in her breast bo-peep or couching lies,
          Playing and shining in each outward part:
          But, fool, seek'st not to get into her heart.

12

Cupid, because thou shin'st in *Stella*'s eyes,
    That from her locks, thy day-nets, none 'scapes free,
    That those lips swell, so full of thee they be,
That her sweet breath makes oft thy flames to rise,
5 That in her breast thy pap well sugared lies,
    That her grace gracious makes thy wrongs, that she,
    What words so e'er she speaks, persuades for thee,
That her clear voice lifts thy fame to the skies:
    Thou countest *Stella* thine, like those whose powers,
10 Having got up a breach by fighting well,
Cry, 'Victory, this fair day all is ours.'
O no, her heart is such a citadel,
    So fortified with wit, stored with disdain,
    That to win it is all the skill and pain.

13

Phoebus was judge between *Jove*, *Mars*, and Love,
    Of those three gods, whose arms the fairest were:
    Jove's golden shield did eagle sables bear,
Whose talons held young *Ganymede* above;
5 But in vert field *Mars* bare a golden spear
    Which through a bleeding heart his point did shove;
    Each had his crest: *Mars* carried *Venus*' glove,
Jove on his helm the thunderbolt did rear.
Cupid then smiles, for on his crest there lies
10   *Stella*'s fair hair, her face he makes his shield,
    Where roses gules are borne in silver field.
Phoebus drew wide the curtains of the skies
    To blaze these last, and sware devoutly then,
    The first, thus matched, were scarcely gentlemen.

14

Alas, have I not pain enough, my friend,
    Upon whose breast a fiercer gripe doth tire
    Than did on him who first stale down the fire,
While Love on me doth all his quiver spend,
5   But with your rhubarb words you must contend
    To grieve me worse, in saying that desire
    Doth plunge my well-formed soul e'en in the mire
Of sinful thoughts, which do in ruin end?
    If that be sin which doth the manners frame,
10 Well swayed with truth in word and faith of deed,
Ready of wit and fearing naught but shame;
If that be sin which in fixed hearts doth breed
    A loathing of all loose unchastity:
    Then love is sin, and let me sinful be.

15

You that do search for every purling spring
    Which from the ribs of old *Parnassus* flows,
    And every flower, not sweet perhaps, which grows
Near thereabout, into your poesy wring;
5   You that do dictionary's method bring
    Into your rhymes, running in rattling rows;
    You that poor *Petrarch*'s long-deceased woes
With new-born sighs and denizened wit do sing;
    You take wrong ways, those far-fet helps be such
10   As do bewray a want of inward touch:
And sure at length stol'n goods do come to light.
    But if (both for your love and skill) your name
    You seek to nurse at fullest breasts of Fame,
Stella behold, and then begin t'indite.

16

In nature apt to like when I did see
    Beauties which were of many carats fine,
    My boiling sprites did thither soon incline,
And, Love, I thought that I was full of thee;
5 But finding not those restless flames in me
    Which others said did make their souls to pine,
    I thought those babes of some pin's hurt did whine,
By my love judging what Love's pain might be.
    But while I thus with this young lion played,
10 Mine eyes (shall I say cursed or blest?) beheld
Stella: now she is named, need more be said?
In her sight I a lesson new have spelled;
    I now have learned love right, and learned e'en so,
    As who by being poisoned doth poison know.

17

His mother dear *Cupid* offended late,
    Because that *Mars*, grown slacker in her love,
    With pricking shot he did not throughly move
To keep the pace of their first loving state.
5 The boy refused for fear of *Mars*'s hate,
    Who threatened stripes if he his wrath did prove;
    But she in chafe him from her lap did shove,
Brake bow, brake shafts, while *Cupid* weeping sate,
    Till that his grandame Nature pitying it,
10 Of *Stella*'s brows made him two better bows,
And in her eyes of arrows infinite.
O how for joy he leaps, O how he crows,
    And straight therewith, like wags new got to play,
    Falls to shrewd turns, and I was in his way.

18

With what sharp checks I in myself am shent
    When into Reason's audit I do go,
    And by just counts myself a bankrupt know
Of all those goods, which heav'n to me hath lent,
5   Unable quite to pay e'en Nature's rent,
    Which unto it by birthright I do owe;
    And, which is worse, no good excuse can show
But that my wealth I have most idly spent.
    My youth doth waste, my knowledge brings forth
        toys,
10   My wit doth strive those passions to defend,
Which for reward spoil it with vain annoys.
I see my course to lose myself doth bend:
    I see and yet no greater sorrow take,
    Than that I lose no more for *Stella*'s sake.

19

On *Cupid*'s bow how are my heart-strings bent,
    That see my wrack, and yet embrace the same!
    When most I glory, then I feel most shame;
I willing run, yet while I run, repent;
5   My best wits still their own disgrace invent;
    My very ink turns straight to *Stella*'s name,
    And yet my words, as them my pen doth frame,
Avise themselves that they are vainly spent;
    For though she pass all things, yet what is all
10   That unto me, who fare like him that both
Looks to the skies, and in a ditch doth fall?
O let me prop my mind, yet in his growth,
    And not in nature, for best fruits unfit:
    'Scholar,' saith Love, 'bend hitherward your wit.'

20

Fly, fly, my friends, I have my death-wound, fly;
See there that boy, that murd'ring boy, I say,
Who like a thief, hid in dark bush doth lie,
Till bloody bullet get him wrongful prey;
5   So tyrant he no fitter place could spy,
Nor so fair level in so secret stay,
As that sweet black which veils the heav'nly eye:
There himself with his shot he close doth lay.
      Poor passenger, pass now thereby I did,
10 And stayed, pleased with the prospect of the place,
While that black hue from me the bad guest hid;
But straight I saw motions of lightning grace,
      And then descried the glist'ring of his dart:
      But ere I could fly thence, it pierced my heart.

21

Your words my friend (right healthful caustics) blame
      My young mind marred, whom Love doth windlass
         so,
      That mine own writings like bad servants show
My wits, quick in vain thoughts, in virtue lame;
5 That *Plato* I read for naught, but if he tame
      Such coltish geres; that to my birth I owe
      Nobler desires, lest else that friendly foe,
Great expectation, wear a train of shame.
      For since mad March great promise made of me,
10 If now the May of my years much decline,
What can be hoped my harvest time will be?
Sure you say well, your wisdom's golden mine
      Dig deep with learning's spade; now tell me this,
      Hath this world aught so fair as *Stella* is?

22

In highest way of heav'n the sun did ride,
　　Progressing then from fair twins' golden place:
　　Having no scarf of clouds before his face,
But shining forth of heat in his chief pride;
5　When some fair ladies, by hard promise tied,
　　On horseback met him in his furious race,
　　Yet each prepared, with fan's well-shading grace,
From that foe's wounds their tender skins to hide.
Stella alone with face unarmed marched,
10　Either to do like him, which open shone,
　　Or careless of the wealth because her own:
Yet were the hid and meaner beauties parched,
　　Her daintiest bare went free; the cause was this,
　　The sun which others burned, did her but kiss.

23

The curious wits, seeing dull pensiveness
　　Bewray itself in my long settled eyes,
　　Whence those same fumes of melancholy rise,
With idle pains, and missing aim, do guess.
5　Some, that know how my spring I did address,
　　Deem that my Muse some fruit of knowledge plies;
　　Others, because the prince my service tries,
Think that I think state errors to redress;
　　But harder judges judge ambition's rage,
10　Scourge of itself, still climbing slipp'ry place,
Holds my young brain captived in golden cage.
O fools, or over-wise, alas, the race
　　Of all my thoughts hath neither stop nor start,
　　But only *Stella*'s eyes and *Stella*'s heart.

24

Rich fools there be, whose base and filthy heart
Lies hatching still the goods wherein they flow:
And damning their own selves to *Tantal*'s smart,
Wealth breeding want, more blest, more wretched grow.
5   Yet to those fools heav'n such wit doth impart,
As what their hands do hold, their heads do know,
And knowing, love, and loving, lay apart,
As sacred things, far from all danger's show.
      But that rich fool, who by blind fortune's lot
10 The richest gem of love and life enjoys,
And can with foul abuse such beauties blot;
Let him, deprived of sweet but unfelt joys,
      (Exiled for ay from those high treasures, which
      He knows not) grow in only folly rich.

25

The wisest scholar of the wight most wise,
By *Phoebus*' doom, with sugared sentence says
That virtue, if it once met with our eyes,
Strange flames of love it in our souls would raise.
5   But for that man with pain this truth descries,
While he each thing in sense's balance weighs,
And so nor will nor can behold those skies
Which inward sun to heroic mind displays,
      Virtue of late, with virtuous care to stir
10 Love of herself, takes *Stella*'s shape, that she
To mortal eyes might sweetly shine in her.
It is most true, for since I her did see,
      Virtue's great beauty in that face I prove,
      And find th'effect, for I do burn in love.

26

Though dusty wits dare scorn astrology,
And fools can think those lamps of purest light,
Whose numbers, ways, greatness, eternity,
Promising wonders, wonder to invite,
5   To have for no cause birthright in the sky,
But for to spangle the black weeds of night;
Or for some brawl, which in that chamber high,
They should still dance to please a gazer's sight:
   For me, I do Nature unidle know,
10 And know great causes, great effects procure,
And know these bodies high reign on the low.
And if these rules did fail, proof makes me sure,
   Who oft fore-judge my after-following race,
   By only those two stars in *Stella*'s face.

27

Because I oft, in dark abstracted guise,
   Seem most alone in greatest company,
   With dearth of words, or answers quite awry,
To them that would make speech of speech arise,
5 They deem, and of their doom the rumour flies,
   That poison foul of bubbling pride doth lie
   So in my swelling breast that only I
Fawn on myself, and others do despise:
   Yet pride I think doth not my soul possess,
10 Which looks too oft in his unflatt'ring glass;
But one worse fault, ambition, I confess,
That makes me oft my best friends overpass,
   Unseen, unheard, while thought to highest place
   Bends all his powers, e'en unto *Stella*'s grace.

28

You that with allegory's curious frame
    Of others' children changelings use to make,
    With me those pains for God's sake do not take:
I list not dig so deep for brazen fame.
5   When I say '*Stella*', I do mean the same
    Princess of beauty, for whose only sake
    The reins of Love I love, though never slake,
And joy therein, though nations count it shame.
    I beg no subject to use eloquence,
10 Nor in hid ways to guide philosophy;
Look at my hands for no such quintessence,
But know that I, in pure simplicity,
    Breathe out the flames which burn within my heart,
    Love only reading unto me this art.

29

Like some weak lords, neighboured by mighty kings,
    To keep themselves and their chief cities free,
    Do eas'ly yield, that all their coasts may be
Ready to store their camps of needful things:
5   So *Stella*'s heart, finding what power Love brings,
    To keep itself in life and liberty,
    Doth willing grant, that in the frontiers he
Use all to help his other conquerings;
And thus her heart escapes, but thus her eyes
10   Serve him with shot, her lips his heralds are,
    Her breasts his tents, legs his triumphal car,
Her flesh his food, her skin his armour brave;
And I, but for because my prospect lies
Upon that coast, am giv'n up for a slave.

30

Whether the Turkish new moon minded be
    To fill his horns this year on Christian coast;
    How Poles' right king means, without leave of host,
To warm with ill-made fire cold *Muscovy*;
5 If French can yet three parts in one agree;
    What now the Dutch in their full diets boast;
    How *Holland* hearts, now so good towns be lost,
Trust in the shade of pleasing *Orange* tree;
    How *Ulster* likes of that same golden bit
10 Wherewith my father once made it half tamè;
If in the Scottish court be welt'ring yet;
These questions busy wits to me do frame;
    I, cumbered with good manners, answer do,
    But know not how, for still I think of you.

31

With how sad steps, O Moon, thou climb'st the skies,
    How silently, and with how wan a face;
    What, may it be that e'en in heav'nly place
That busy archer his sharp arrows tries?
5 Sure, if that long-with-love-acquainted eyes
    Can judge of love, thou feel'st a lover's case;
    I read it in thy looks; thy languished grace,
To me that feel the like, thy state descries.
    Then e'en of fellowship, O Moon, tell me,
10 Is constant love deemed there but want of wit?
Are beauties there as proud as here they be?
Do they above love to be loved, and yet
    Those lovers scorn whom that love doth possess?
    Do they call virtue there ungratefulness?

32

Morpheus, the lively son of deadly sleep,
  Witness of life to them that living die,
  A prophet oft, and oft an history,
A poet eke, as humours fly or creep;
5 Since thou in me so sure a power dost keep,
  That never I with closed-up sense do lie
  But by thy work my *Stella* I descry,
Teaching blind eyes both how to smile and weep,
  Vouchsafe of all acquaintance this to tell:
10 Whence hast thou ivory, rubies, pearl and gold
To show her skin, lips, teeth and head so well?
'Fool,' answers he, 'no *Ind's* such treasures hold,
  But from thy heart, while my sire charmeth thee,
  Sweet *Stella's* image I do steal to me.'

33

I might, unhappy word, O me, I might,
And then would not, or could not see my bliss;
Till now, wrapped in a most infernal night,
I find how heav'nly day, wretch, I did miss.
5 Heart rend thyself, thou dost thyself but right;
No lovely *Paris* made thy *Helen* his,
No force, no fraud, robbed thee of thy delight,
Nor Fortune of thy fortune author is;
  But to myself myself did give the blow,
10 While too much wit (forsooth) so troubled me,
That I respects for both our sakes must show:
And yet could not by rising morn foresee
  How fair a day was near; O punished eyes,
  That I had been more foolish or more wise.

34

Come, let me write. 'And to what end?' To ease
         A burdened heart. 'How can words ease, which are
         The glasses of thy daily vexing care?'
Oft cruel fights well pictured forth do please.
5 'Art not ashamed to publish thy disease?'
         Nay, that may breed my fame, it is so rare.
         'But will not wise men think thy words fond ware?'
Then be they close, and so none shall displease.
         'What idler thing, than speak and not be heard?'
10 What harder thing, than smart and not to speak?
Peace, foolish wit, with wit my wit is marred.
Thus write I while I doubt to write, and wreak
         My harms on ink's poor loss; perhaps some find
         Stella's great powers, that so confuse my mind.

35

What may words say, or what may words not say,
Where truth itself must speak like flattery?
Within what bounds can one his liking stay,
Where Nature doth with infinite agree?
5   What Nestor's counsel can my flames allay,
Since reason's self doth blow the coal in me?
And ah, what hope that hope should once see day,
Where Cupid is sworn page to chastity?
Honour is honoured that thou dost possess
10   Him as thy slave, and now long needy fame
         Doth e'en grow rich, naming my Stella's name.
Wit learns in thee perfection to express,
         Not thou by praise, but praise in thee is raised:
         It is a praise to praise, when thou art praised.

36

Stella, whence doth this new assault arise,
A conquered, yelden, ransacked heart to win?
Whereto long since, through my long battered eyes,
Whole armies of thy beauties entered in;
5   And there long since, Love thy lieutenant lies,
My forces razed, thy banners raised within:
Of conquest, do not these effects suffice,
But wilt new war upon thine own begin?
      With so sweet voice, and by sweet nature so,
10   In sweetest strength, so sweetly skilled withal,
In all sweet stratagems sweet art can show,
That not my soul, which at thy foot did fall,
      Long since forced by thy beams, but stone nor tree
      By sense's privilege, can 'scape from thee.

37

My mouth doth water, and my breast doth swell,
      My tongue doth itch, my thoughts in labour be:
      Listen then, lordings, with good ear to me,
For of my life I must a riddle tell.
5   Towards *Aurora*'s court a nymph doth dwell,
      Rich in all beauties which man's eye can see;
      Beauties so far from reach of words, that we
Abase her praise, saying she doth excel;
      Rich in the treasure of deserved renown,
10   Rich in the riches of a royal heart,
Rich in those gifts which give th'eternal crown;
Who though most rich in these and every part,
      Which make the patents of true worldly bliss,
      Hath no misfortune, but that Rich she is.

38

This night, while sleep begins with heavy wings
   To hatch mine eyes, and that unbitted thought
   Doth fall to stray, and my chief powers are brought
To leave the sceptre of all subject things,
5 The first that straight my fancy's error brings
   Unto my mind is *Stella*'s image, wrought
   By Love's own self, but with so curious draught
That she, methinks, not only shines but sings.
   I start, look, heark, but what in closed-up sense
10 Was held, in opened sense it flies away,
Leaving me naught but wailing eloquence:
I, seeing better sights in sight's decay,
   Called it anew, and wooed sleep again:
   But him her host that unkind guest had slain.

39

Come sleep, O sleep, the certain knot of peace,
The baiting place of wit, the balm of woe,
The poor man's wealth, the prisoner's release,
Th'indifferent judge between the high and low;
5 With shield of proof shield me from out the prease
Of those fierce darts despair at me doth throw:
O make in me those civil wars to cease;
I will good tribute pay if thou do so.
  Take thou of me smooth pillows, sweetest bed,
10 A chamber deaf to noise, and blind to light,
A rosy garland, and a weary head:
And if these things, as being thine by right,
   Move not thy heavy grace, thou shalt in me,
   Livelier than elsewhere, *Stella*'s image see.

40

As good to write as for to lie and groan.
  O *Stella* dear, how much thy power hath wrought,
  That hast my mind, none of the basest, brought
My still kept course, while others sleep, to moan.
5 Alas, if from the height of virtue's throne
  Thou canst vouchsafe the influence of a thought
  Upon a wretch that long thy grace hath sought,
Weigh then how I by thee am overthrown:
  And then think thus: although thy beauty be
10 Made manifest by such a victory,
Yet noblest conquerors do wrecks avoid.
  Since then thou hast so far subdued me,
  That in my heart I offer still to thee,
O do not let thy temple be destroyed.

41

Having this day my horse, my hand, my lance
  Guided so well, that I obtained the prize,
  Both by the judgement of the English eyes,
And of some sent from that sweet enemy, *France*;
5 Horsemen my skill in horsemanship advance;
  Town-folks my strength; a daintier judge applies
  His praise to sleight, which from good use doth rise;
Some lucky wits impute it but to chance;
  Others, because of both sides I do take
10 My blood from them who did excel in this,
Think Nature me a man of arms did make.
How far they shoot awry! The true cause is,
  Stella looked on, and from her heav'nly face
  Sent forth the beams, which made so fair my race.

42

O eyes, which do the spheres of beauty move,
Whose beams be joys, whose joys all virtues be,
Who while they make love conquer, conquer love,
The schools where *Venus* hath learned chastity;
5   O eyes, where humble looks most glorious prove
Only loved tyrants, just in cruelty:
Do not, O do not from poor me remove;
Keep still my zenith, ever shine on me.
        For though I never see them, but straight ways
10   My life forgets to nourish languished sprites,
Yet still on me, O eyes, dart down your rays:
And if from majesty of sacred lights,
        Oppressing mortal sense, my death proceed,
        Wracks triumphs be, which love (high set) doth
            breed.

43

Fair eyes, sweet lips, dear heart, that foolish I
Could hope by *Cupid*'s help on you to prey;
Since to himself he doth your gifts apply,
As his main force, choice sport, and easeful stay.
5   For when he will see who dare him gainsay,
Then with those eyes he looks; lo, by and by
Each soul doth at Love's feet his weapons lay,
Glad if for her he give them leave to die.
        When he will play, then in her lips he is,
10   Where blushing red, that Love's self them doth love,
With either lip he doth the other kiss:
But when he will for quiet's sake remove
        From all the world, her heart is then his room,
        Where well he knows, no man to him can come.

44

My words I know do well set forth my mind;
　　My mind bemoans his sense of inward smart;
　　Such smart may pity claim of any heart;
Her heart, sweet heart, is of no tiger's kind:
5　And yet she hears, yet I no pity find;
　　But more I cry, less grace she doth impart.
　　Alas, what cause is there so overthwart
That nobleness itself makes thus unkind?
　　I much do guess, yet find no truth save this:
10　That when the breath of my complaints doth touch
Those dainty doors unto the court of bliss,
The heav'nly nature of that place is such
　　That, once come there, the sobs of mine annoys
　　Are metamorphosed straight to tunes of joys.

45

Stella oft sees the very face of woe
　　Painted in my beclouded stormy face:
　　But cannot skill to pity my disgrace,
Not though thereof the cause herself she know;
5　Yet hearing late a fable, which did show
　　Of lovers never known a grievous case,
　　Pity thereof gat in her breast such place
That, from that sea derived, tears' spring did flow.
　　Alas, if fancy, drawn by imaged things,
10　Though false, yet with free scope more grace doth breed
Than servant's wrack, where new doubts honour brings;
Then think, my dear, that you in me do read
　　Of lover's ruin some sad tragedy:
　　I am not I; pity the tale of me.

46

I cursed thee oft, I pity now thy case,
    Blind-hitting boy, since she that thee and me
    Rules with a beck, so tyrannizeth thee,
That thou must want or food, or dwelling-place.
5   For she protests to banish thee her face;
    Her face? O Love, a rogue thou then shouldst be,
    If Love learn not alone to love and see,
Without desire to feed of further grace.
    Alas, poor wag, that now a scholar art
10 To such a school-mistress, whose lessons new
Thou needs must miss, and so thou needs must smart.
Yet dear, let me this pardon get of you,
    So long (though he from book miche to desire)
    Till without fuel you can make hot fire.

47

What, have I thus betrayed my liberty?
    Can those black beams such burning marks engrave
    In my free side? Or am I born a slave,
Whose neck becomes such yoke of tyranny?
5   Or want I sense to feel my misery?
    Or sprite, disdain of such disdain to have?
    Who for long faith, though daily help I crave,
May get no alms but scorn of beggary.
    Virtue awake, beauty but beauty is,
10 I may, I must, I can, I will, I do
Leave following that which it is gain to miss.
Let her go. Soft, but here she comes. Go to,
    Unkind, I love you not: O me, that eye
    Doth make my heart give to my tongue the lie.

48

Soul's joy, bend not those morning stars from me,
    Where virtue is made strong by beauty's might,
    Where love is chasteness, pain doth learn delight,
And humbleness grows one with majesty.
5 Whatever may ensue, O let me be
    Co-partner of the riches of that sight;
    Let not mine eyes be hell-driv'n from that light;
O look, O shine, O let me die and see.
    For though I oft myself of them bemoan,
10   That through my heart their beamy darts be gone,
Whose cureless wounds e'en now most freshly bleed:
    Yet since my death-wound is already got,
    Dear killer, spare not thy sweet cruel shot:
A kind of grace it is to slay with speed.

49

I on my horse, and Love on me doth try
    Our horsemanships, while by strange work I prove
    A horseman to my horse, a horse to Love;
And now man's wrongs in me, poor beast, descry.
5 The reins wherewith my rider doth me tie
    Are humbled thoughts, which bit of reverence move,
    Curbed in with fear, but with gilt boss above
Of hope, which makes it seem fair to the eye.
    The wand is will, thou, fancy, saddle art,
10 Girt fast by memory; and while I spur
My horse, he spurs with sharp desire my heart;
He sits me fast, however I do stir;
    And now hath made me to his hand so right,
    That in the manage myself takes delight.

50

Stella, the fullness of my thoughts of thee
Cannot be stayed within my panting breast,
But they do swell and struggle forth of me,
Till that in words thy figure be expressed.
5   And yet as soon as they so formed be,
According to my lord Love's own behest,
With sad eyes I their weak proportion see,
To portrait that which in this world is best.
      So that I cannot choose but write my mind,
10 And cannot choose but put out what I write,
While those poor babes their death in birth do find:
And now my pen these lines had dashed quite,
      But that they stopped his fury from the same,
      Because their forefront bare sweet *Stella*'s name.

51

Pardon mine ears; both I and they do pray,
      So may your tongue still fluently proceed
      To them that do such entertainment need,
So may you still have somewhat new to say.
5 On silly me do not the burden lay
      Of all the grave conceits your brain doth breed,
      But find some *Hercules* to bear, in steed
Of *Atlas* tired, your wisdom's heav'nly sway.
      For me, while you discourse of courtly tides,
10 Of cunning'st fishers in most troubled streams,
Of straying ways, when valiant error guides,
Meanwhile my heart confers with *Stella*'s beams,
      And is e'en irked that so sweet comedy
      By such unsuited speech should hindered be.

52

A strife is grown between Virtue and Love,
　　While each pretends that *Stella* must be his:
　　Her eyes, her lips, her all, saith Love, do this,
Since they do wear his badge, most firmly prove.
5　But Virtue thus that title doth disprove,
　　That *Stella* (O dear name), that *Stella* is
　　That virtuous soul, sure heir of heav'nly bliss,
Not this fair outside, which our hearts doth move;
　　And therefore, though her beauty and her grace
10　Be Love's indeed, in *Stella*'s self he may
By no pretence claim any manner place.
Well, Love, since this demur our suit doth stay,
　　Let Virtue have that *Stella*'s self; yet thus,
　　That Virtue but that body grant to us.

53

In martial sports I had my cunning tried,
　　And yet to break more staves did me address,
　　While with the people's shouts, I must confess,
Youth, luck, and praise e'en filled my veins with pride;
5　When *Cupid*, having me his slave descried
　　In *Mars*'s liv'ry, prancing in the press:
　　'What now, sir fool,' said he, 'I would no less,
Look here, I say.' I looked, and *Stella* spied,
　　Who hard by made a window send forth light.
10　My heart then quaked, then dazzled were mine eyes,
One hand forgot to rule, th'other to fight;
Nor trumpets' sound I heard, nor friendly cries;
　　My foe came on, and beat the air for me,
　　Till that her blush taught me my shame to see.

54

Because I breathe not love to every one,
     Nor do not use set colours for to wear,
     Nor nourish special locks of vowed hair,
Nor give each speech a full point of a groan,
5   The courtly nymphs, acquainted with the moan
     Of them, who in their lips Love's standard bear:
     'What, he?' say they of me, 'now I dare swear,
He cannot love: no, no, let him alone.'
     And think so still, so *Stella* know my mind.
10 Profess indeed I do not *Cupid*'s art;
But you, fair maids, at length this true shall find,
That his right badge is but worn in the heart:
     Dumb swans, not chatt'ring pies, do lovers prove;
     They love indeed, who quake to say they love.

55

Muses, I oft invoked your holy aid,
     With choicest flowers my speech t'engarland so
     That it, despised in true but naked show,
Might win some grace in your sweet skill arrayed;
5   And oft whole troops of saddest words I stayed,
     Striving abroad a-foraging to go,
     Until by your inspiring I might know
How their black banner might be best displayed.
     But now I mean no more your help to try,
10 Nor other sugaring of my speech to prove,
But on her name incessantly to cry:
For let me but name her whom I do love,
     So sweet sounds straight mine ear and heart do hit,
     That I well find no eloquence like it.

56

Fie, school of Patience, fie; your lesson is
    Far, far too long to learn it without book:
    What, a whole week without one piece of look,
And think I should not your large precepts miss?
5 When I might read those letters fair of bliss,
    Which in her face teach virtue, I could brook
    Somewhat thy leaden counsels, which I took
As of a friend that meant not much amiss:
    But now that I, alas, do want her sight,
10 What, dost thou think that I can ever take
In thy cold stuff a phlegmatique delight?
No, Patience, if thou wilt my good, then make
    Her come, and hear with patience my desire,
    And then with patience bid me bear my fire.

57

Woe, having made with many fights his own
    Each sense of mine, each gift, each power of mind,
    Grown now his slaves, he forced them out to find
The thorough'st words, fit for woe's self to groan,
5 Hoping that when they might find *Stella* alone,
    Before she could prepare to be unkind,
    Her soul, armed but with such a dainty rind,
Should soon be pierced with sharpness of the moan.
    She heard my plaints, and did not only hear,
10 But them (so sweet is she) most sweetly sing,
With that fair breast making woe's darkness clear.
A pretty case! I hoped her to bring
    To feel my griefs, and she with face and voice
    So sweets my pains, that my pains me rejoice.

58

Doubt there hath been, when with his golden chain
    The orator so far men's hearts doth bind
    That no pace else their guided steps can find
But as he them more short or slack doth rein,
5 Whether with words this sovereignty he gain,
    Clothed with fine tropes, with strongest reasons lined,
    Or else pronouncing grace, wherewith his mind
Prints his own lively form in rudest brain.
    Now judge by this: in piercing phrases late
10 Th'anatomy of all my woes I wrate,
Stella's sweet breath the same to me did read.
    O voice, O face, maugre my speech's might,
    Which wooed woe, most ravishing delight
E'en those sad words e'en in sad me did breed.

59

Dear, why make you more of a dog than me?
    If he do love, I burn, I burn in love;
    If he wait well, I never thence would move;
If he be fair, yet but a dog can be.
5 Little he is, so little worth is he;
    He barks, my songs thine own voice oft doth prove;
    Bidden, perhaps he fetcheth thee a glove,
But I unbid fetch e'en my soul to thee.
    Yet while I languish, him that bosom clips,
10 That lap doth lap, nay lets, in spite of spite,
This sour-breathed mate taste of those sugared lips.
    Alas, if you grant only such delight
    To witless things, then love, I hope (since wit
Becomes a clog), will soon ease me of it.

60

When my good angel guides me to the place
    Where all my good I do in *Stella* see,
    That heav'n of joys throws only down on me
Thundered disdains and lightnings of disgrace:
5 But when the rugged'st step of fortune's race
    Makes me fall from her sight, then sweetly she
    With words, wherein the Muses' treasures be,
Shows love and pity to my absent case.
    Now I, wit-beaten long by hardest fate,
10 So dull am, that I cannot look into
The ground of this fierce love and lovely hate:
Then some good body tell me how I do,
    Whose presence, absence, absence presence is;
    Blest in my curse, and cursed in my bliss.

61

Oft with true sighs, oft with uncalled tears,
Now with slow words, now with dumb eloquence,
I *Stella*'s eyes assail, invade her ears;
But this at last is her sweet-breathed defence:
5   That who indeed infelt affection bears,
So captives to his saint both soul and sense,
That, wholly hers, all selfness he forbears,
Thence his desires he learns, his life's course thence.
    Now since her chaste mind hates this love in me,
10   With chastened mind, I straight must show that she
Shall quickly me from what she hates remove.
    O Doctor *Cupid*, thou for me reply,
    Driv'n else to grant by angel's sophistry,
That I love not, without I leave to love.

62

Late tired with woe, e'en ready for to pine
With rage of love, I called my love unkind;
She in whose eyes love, though unfelt, doth shine,
Sweet said that I true love in her should find.
5   I joyed, but straight thus watered was my wine,
That love she did, but loved a love not blind,
Which would not let me, whom she loved, decline
From nobler course, fit for my birth and mind:
      And therefore by her love's authority,
10   Willed me these tempests of vain love to fly,
And anchor fast myself on virtue's shore.
      Alas, if this the only metal be
      Of love, new-coined to help my beggary,
Dear, love me not, that you may love me more.

63

O grammar rules, O now your virtues show;
      So children still read you with awful eyes,
      As my young dove may in your precepts wise
Her grant to me, by her own virtue know.
5 For late with heart most high, with eyes most low,
      I craved the thing which ever she denies:
      She, lightning love, displaying *Venus*' skies,
Lest once should not be heard, twice said, 'No, no.'
      Sing then my Muse, now *Io Paean* sing,
10   Heav'ns envy not at my high triumphing,
But grammar's force with sweet success confirm:
      For grammar says (O this dear *Stella* weigh),
      For grammar says (to grammar who says nay?)
That in one speech two negatives affirm.

First Song

Doubt you to whom my Muse these notes intendeth,
Which now my breast o'ercharged to music lendeth?
To you, to you, all song of praise is due,
Only in you my song begins and endeth.

5 Who hath the eyes which marry state with pleasure,
Who keeps the key of Nature's chiefest treasure?
To you, to you, all song of praise is due,
Only for you the heav'n forgat all measure.

Who hath the lips, where wit in fairness reigneth,
10 Who womankind at once both decks and staineth?
To you, to you, all song of praise is due,
Only by you *Cupid* his crown maintaineth.

Who hath the feet, whose step all sweetness planteth,
Who else for whom Fame worthy trumpets wanteth?
15 To you, to you, all song of praise is due,
Only to you her sceptre *Venus* granteth.

Who hath the breast, whose milk doth passions nourish,
Whose grace is such, that when it chides doth cherish?
To you, to you, all song of praise is due,
20 Only through you the tree of life doth flourish.

Who hath the hand which without stroke subdueth,
Who long-dead beauty with increase reneweth?
To you, to you, all song of praise is due,
Only at you all envy hopeless rueth.

25 Who hath the hair which, loosest, fasteth tieth,
Who makes a man live then glad when he dieth?
To you, to you, all song of praise is due,
Only of you the flatterer never lieth.

Who hath the voice which soul from senses sunders,
30 Whose force but yours the bolts of beauty thunders?
To you, to you, all song of praise is due,
Only with you not miracles are wonders.

Doubt you to whom my Muse these notes intendeth,
Which now my breast o'ercharged to music lendeth?
35   To you, to you, all song of praise is due,
Only in you my song begins and endeth.

64

No more, my dear, no more these counsels try,
    O give my passions leave to run their race;
    Let Fortune lay on me her worst disgrace,
Let folk o'ercharged with brain against me cry,
5   Let clouds bedim my face, break in mine eye,
    Let me no steps but of lost labour trace,
    Let all the earth with scorn recount my case,
But do not will me from my love to fly.
    I do not envy *Aristotle*'s wit,
10   Nor do aspire to *Caesar*'s bleeding fame,
Nor aught do care, though some above me sit,
Nor hope, nor wish another course to frame,
    But that which once may win thy cruel heart:
    Thou art my wit, and thou my virtue art.

65

Love, by sure proof I may call thee unkind,
That giv'st no better ear to my just cries;
Thou whom to me such my good turns should bind,
As I may well recount, but none can prize;
5   For when, nak'd boy, thou couldst no harbour find
In this old world, grown now so too too wise,
I lodged thee in my heart, and being blind
By nature born, I gave to thee mine eyes.
    Mine eyes, my light, my heart, my life, alas,
10   If so great services may scorned be,
Yet let this thought thy tig'rish courage pass,

That I perhaps am somewhat kin to thee;
    Since in thine arms, if learn'd fame truth hath
      spread,
    Thou bear'st the arrow, I the arrow head.

66

  And do I see some cause a hope to feed,
  Or doth the tedious burden of long woe,
  In weakened minds, quick apprehending breed
  Of every image which may comfort show?
5   I cannot brag of word, much less of deed;
  Fortune wheels still with me in one sort slow;
  My wealth no more, and no whit less my need,
  Desire still on the stilts of fear doth go.
     And yet amid all fears a hope there is
10 Stol'n to my heart, since last fair night, nay day,
  Stella's eyes sent to me the beams of bliss,
  Looking on me, while I looked other way:
     But when mine eyes back to their heav'n did move,
     They fled with blush, which guilty seemed of love.

67

  Hope, art thou true, or dost thou flatter me?
     Doth *Stella* now begin with piteous eye
     The ruins of her conquest to espy:
  Will she take time, before all wracked be?
5 Her eyes' speech is translated thus by thee:
     But fail'st thou not in phrase so heav'nly high?
     Look on again, the fair text better try:
  What blushing notes dost thou in margin see?

What sighs stol'n out, or killed before full born?
10   Hast thou found such and such like arguments?
Or art thou else to comfort me forsworn?
Well, how so thou interpret the contents,
    I am resolved thy error to maintain,
    Rather than by more truth to get more pain.

68

Stella, the only planet of my light,
    Light of my life, and life of my desire,
    Chief good, whereto my hope doth only aspire,
World of my wealth, and heav'n of my delight;
5   Why dost thou spend the treasures of thy sprite
    With voice more fit to wed *Amphion*'s lyre,
    Seeking to quench in me the noble fire,
Fed by thy worth, and kindled by thy sight?
    And all in vain, for while thy breath most sweet,
10   With choicest words, thy words with reasons rare,
Thy reasons firmly set on virtue's feet,
Labour to kill in me this killing care:
    O think I then, what paradise of joy
    It is, so fair a virtue to enjoy.

69

O joy, too high for my low style to show:
    O bliss, fit for a nobler state than me:
    Envy, put out thine eyes, lest thou do see
What oceans of delight in me do flow.
5   My friend, that oft saw through all masks my woe,
    Come, come, and let me pour myself on thee;
    Gone is the winter of my misery,
My spring appears, O see what here doth grow:

For *Stella* hath, with words where faith doth shine,
10 Of her high heart giv'n me the monarchy:
I, I, O I may say that she is mine.
And though she give but thus condition'lly
  This realm of bliss, while virtuous course I take,
  No kings be crowned, but they some covenants
   make.

70

My Muse may well grudge at my heav'nly joy,
If still I force her in sad rhymes to creep:
She oft hath drunk my tears, now hopes t'enjoy
Nectar of mirth, since I *Jove*'s cup do keep.
5   Sonnets be not bound 'prentice to annoy;
Trebles sing high, as well as bases deep;
Grief but Love's winter liv'ry is; the boy
Hath cheeks to smile, as well as eyes to weep.
  Come then, my Muse, show thou height of delight
10 In well-raised notes; my pen the best it may
Shall paint out joy, though but in black and white.
Cease eager Muse, peace pen, for my sake stay,
  I give you here my hand for truth of this,
  Wise silence is best music unto bliss.

71

Who will in fairest book of Nature know
  How virtue may best lodged in beauty be,
  Let him but learn of Love to read in thee,
Stella, those fair lines which true goodness show.
5 There shall he find all vices' overthrow,
  Not by rude force, but sweetest sovereignty
  Of reason, from whose light those night-birds fly,
That inward sun in thine eyes shineth so.

And not content to be perfection's heir
10   Thyself, dost strive all minds that way to move,
Who mark in thee what is in thee most fair.
So while thy beauty draws the heart to love,
    As fast thy virtue bends that love to good:
    'But ah,' Desire still cries, 'give me some food.'

72

Desire, though thou my old companion art,
    And oft so clings to my pure love, that I
    One from the other scarcely can descry,
While each doth blow the fire of my heart,
5   Now from thy fellowship I needs must part;
    Venus is taught with *Dian*'s wings to fly;
    I must no more in thy sweet passions lie;
Virtue's gold now must head my *Cupid*'s dart.
    Service and honour, wonder with delight,
10   Fear to offend, will worthy to appear,
Care shining in mine eyes, faith in my sprite,
These things are left me by my only dear;
    But thou, Desire, because thou wouldst have all,
    Now banished art, but yet alas how shall?

Second Song

Have I caught my heav'nly jewel
Teaching sleep most fair to be?
Now will I teach her that she,
When she wakes, is too too cruel.

5   Since sweet sleep her eyes hath charmed,
The only two darts of Love:
Now will I with that boy prove
Some play, while he is disarmed.

Her tongue waking still refuseth,
10 Giving frankly niggard No:
    Now will I attempt to know
    What No her tongue sleeping useth.

    See the hand which waking guardeth,
    Sleeping, grants a free resort:
15 Now will I invade the fort;
    Cowards Love with loss rewardeth.

    But, O fool, think of the danger
    Of her just and high disdain:
    Now will I alas refrain;
20 Love fears nothing else but anger.

    Yet those lips so sweetly swelling
    Do invite a stealing kiss:
    Now will I but venture this;
    Who will read must first learn spelling.

25 O sweet kiss, but ah she's waking,
    Louring beauty chastens me:
    Now will I away hence flee;
    Fool, more fool, for no more taking.

(73)

    Love still a boy, and oft a wanton is,
    Schooled only by his mother's tender eye;
    What wonder then if he his lesson miss,
    When for so soft a rod dear play he try?
5   And yet my star, because a sugared kiss
    In sport I sucked, while she asleep did lie,
    Doth lour, nay chide; nay, threat for only this:
    Sweet, it was saucy Love, not humble I.
         But no 'scuse serves, she makes her wrath appear
10   In beauty's throne; see now who dares come near

Those scarlet judges, threat'ning bloody pain?
   O heav'nly fool, thy most kiss-worthy face
   Anger invests with such a lovely grace
That anger's self I needs must kiss again.

74

I never drank of *Aganippe* well,
Nor ever did in shade of *Tempe* sit;
And Muses scorn with vulgar brains to dwell;
Poor layman I, for sacred rites unfit.
5   Some do I hear of poets' fury tell,
But (God wot) wot not what they mean by it;
And this I swear by blackest brook of hell,
I am no pick-purse of another's wit.
     How falls it then, that with so smooth an ease
10 My thoughts I speak, and what I speak doth flow
In verse, and that my verse best wits doth please?
Guess we the cause: 'What, is it thus?' Fie, no:
   'Or so?' Much less: 'How then?' Sure thus it is:
   My lips are sweet, inspired with *Stella*'s kiss.

75

Of all the kings that ever here did reign,
Edward named fourth, as first in praise I name,
Not for his fair outside, nor well-lined brain,
Although less gifts imp feathers oft on Fame;
5   Nor that he could young-wise, wise-valiant frame
His sire's revenge, joined with a kingdom's gain,
And gained by *Mars*, could yet mad *Mars* so tame,
That balance weighed what sword did late obtain;
     Nor that he made the flower-de-luce so 'fraid,
10 Though strongly hedged of bloody lion's paws,
That witty *Lewis* to him a tribute paid;

Nor this, nor that, nor any such small cause,
>But only for this worthy knight durst prove
>To lose his crown, rather than fail his love.

76

She comes, and straight therewith her shining twins do
>move
>>Their rays to me, who in her tedious absence lay
>>Benighted in cold woe; but now appears my day,
The only light of joy, the only warmth of love.
5 She comes with light and warmth, which like *Aurora* prove
>>Of gentle force, so that mine eyes dare gladly play
>>With such a rosy morn, whose beams most freshly
>>gay
Scorch not, but only do dark chilling sprites remove.
>>But lo, while I do speak, it groweth noon with me,
10 Her flamy glist'ring lights increase with time and place;
My heart cries 'Ah', it burns, mine eyes now dazzled be:
No wind, no shade can cool; what help then in my case,
>>But with short breath, long looks, stayed feet and
>>walking head,
>>Pray that my sun go down with meeker beams to
>>bed.

77

Those looks, whose beams be joy, whose motion is delight;
That face, whose lecture shows what perfect beauty is;
That presence, which doth give dark hearts a living light;
That grace, which *Venus* weeps that she herself doth miss;
>>That hand, which without touch holds more than
5 >>*Atlas'* might;
Those lips, which make death's pay a mean price for a kiss;

That skin, whose past-praise hue scorns this poor term of
      white;
Those words, which do sublime the quintessence of bliss;
    That voice, which makes the soul plant himself in the
      ears;
10 That conversation sweet, where such high comforts be,
As, construed in true speech, the name of heav'n it bears,
Makes me in my best thoughts and quietest judgement see
    That in no more but these I might be fully blest:
    Yet ah, my maiden Muse doth blush to tell the best.

78

O how the pleasant airs of true love be
    Infected by those vapours, which arise
    From out that noisome gulf, which gaping lies
Between the jaws of hellish Jealousy:
5 A monster, others' harm, self-misery,
    Beauty's plague, virtue's scourge, succour of lies;
    Who his own joy to his own hurt applies,
And only cherish doth with injury;
    Who since he hath, by Nature's special grace,
10   So piercing paws, as spoil when they embrace,
So nimble feet as stir still, though on thorns,
    So many eyes ay seeking their own woe,
    So ample ears as never good news know:
Is it not ev'l that such a dev'l wants horns?

79

Sweet kiss, thy sweets I fain would sweetly indite,
     Which e'en of sweetness sweetest sweet'ner art:
     Pleasing'st consort, where each sense holds a part,
Which, coupling doves, guides *Venus'* chariot right;
5 Best charge, and bravest retreat in *Cupid*'s fight;
     A double key, which opens to the heart,
     Most rich, when most his riches it impart;
Nest of young joys, schoolmaster of delight,
     Teaching the mean, at once to take and give;
10 The friendly fray, where blows both wound and heal;
The pretty death, while each in other live;
Poor hope's first wealth, hostage of promised weal,
     Breakfast of love: but lo, lo, where she is,
     Cease we to praise, now pray we for a kiss.

80

Sweet swelling lip, well mayst thou swell in pride,
     Since best wits think it wit thee to admire;
     Nature's praise, virtue's stall, *Cupid*'s cold fire,
Whence words, not words, but heav'nly graces slide;
5 The new *Parnassus*, where the Muses bide;
     Sweet'ner of music, wisdom's beautifier;
     Breather of life, and fast'ner of desire,
Where beauty's blush in honour's grain is dyed.
     Thus much my heart compelled my mouth to say,
10   But now, spite of my heart, my mouth will stay,
Loathing all lies, doubting this flattery is;
     And no spur can his resty race renew,
     Without how far this praise is short of you,
Sweet lip, you teach my mouth with one sweet kiss.

81

O kiss, which dost those ruddy gems impart,
Or gems, or fruits of new-found paradise,
Breathing all bliss and sweet'ning to the heart,
Teaching dumb lips a nobler exercise;
5   O kiss, which souls, e'en souls together ties
By links of love, and only Nature's art:
How fain would I paint thee to all men's eyes,
Or of thy gifts at least shade out some part.
      But she forbids: with blushing words, she says
10   She builds her fame on higher-seated praise.
But my heart burns, I cannot silent be:
      Then since (dear life) you fain would have me peace,
      And I, mad with delight, want wit to cease,
Stop you my mouth with still still kissing me.

82

Nymph of the garden where all beauties be;
      Beauties which do in excellency pass
      His who till death looked in a wat'ry glass,
Or hers whom naked the Trojan boy did see:
5   Sweet garden nymph, which keeps the cherry tree,
      Whose fruit doth far th'Hesperian taste surpass;
      Most sweet-fair, most fair-sweet, do not, alas,
From coming near those cherries banish me:
      For though full of desire, empty of wit,
10   Admitted late by your best-graced grace,
I caught at one of them a hungry bit;
Pardon that fault, once more grant me the place,
      And I do swear e'en by the same delight,
      I will but kiss, I never more will bite.

83

Good brother *Philip*, I have borne you long;
    I was content you should in favour creep,
    While craftily you seemed your cut to keep,
As though that fair soft hand did you great wrong.
5 I bare (with envy) yet I bare your song,
    When in her neck you did love-ditties peep;
    Nay, more fool I, oft suffered you to sleep
In lilies' nest, where Love's self lies along.
    What, doth high place ambitious thoughts augment?
10 Is sauciness reward of courtesy?
Cannot such grace your silly self content,
But you must needs with those lips billing be,
    And through those lips drink nectar from that
        tongue?
    Leave that, sir *Phip*, lest off your head be wrung.

Third Song

If *Orpheus*' voice had force to breathe such music's love
Through pores of senseless trees, as it could make them
    move;
If stones good measure danced, the Theban walls to build,
To cadence of the tunes which *Amphion*'s lyre did yield;
5 More cause a like effect at leastwise bringeth:
O stones, O trees, learn hearing, *Stella* singeth.

If love might sweeten so a boy of shepherd brood,
To make a lizard dull to taste love's dainty food;
If eagle fierce could so in Grecian maid delight,
10 As his light was her eyes, her death his endless night;
Earth gave that love, heav'n I trow love refineth:
O birds, O beasts, look, love, lo, *Stella* shineth.

The birds, beasts, stones and trees feel this, and feeling,
        love:
And if the trees, nor stones stir not the same to prove,
15 Nor beasts, nor birds do come unto this blessed gaze,
Know, that small love is quick, and great love doth amaze:
They are amazed, but you with reason armed,
O eyes, O ears of men, how are you charmed!

84

Highway, since you my chief *Parnassus* be,
        And that my Muse, to some ears not unsweet,
        Tempers her words to trampling horses' feet
More oft than to a chamber melody;
5   Now blessed you, bear onward blessed me
        To her, where I my heart safeliest shall meet.
        My Muse and I must you of duty greet
With thanks and wishes, wishing thankfully.
        Be you still fair, honoured by public heed,
10 By no encroachment wronged, nor time forgot;
Nor blamed for blood, nor shamed for sinful deed.
And that you know, I envy you no lot
        Of highest wish, I wish you so much bliss,
        Hundreds of years you *Stella*'s feet may kiss.

85

I see the house; my heart thyself contain:
        Beware full sails drown not thy tott'ring barge
        Lest joy, by Nature apt sprites to enlarge,
Thee to thy wrack beyond thy limits strain;
5   Nor do like lords, whose weak confused brain,
        Not pointing to fit folks each undercharge,
        While every office themselves will discharge,
With doing all, leave nothing done but pain;

But give apt servants their due place: let eyes
10   See beauty's total sum summed in her face,
Let ears hear speech, which wit to wonder ties,
Let breath suck up those sweets, let arms embrace
The globe of weal, lips Love's indentures make:
Thou but of all the kingly tribute take.

Fourth Song

Only joy, now here you are,
Fit to hear and ease my care;
Let my whisp'ring voice obtain
Sweet reward for sharpest pain:
5   Take me to thee, and thee to me.
'No, no, no, no, my dear, let be.'

Night hath closed all in her cloak,
Twinkling stars love-thoughts provoke;
Danger hence good care doth keep,
10   Jealousy itself doth sleep:
Take me to thee, and thee to me.
'No, no, no, no, my dear, let be.'

Better place no wit can find
Cupid's yoke to loose or bind;
15   These sweet flow'rs on fine bed too
Us in their best language woo:
Take me to thee, and thee to me.
'No, no, no, no, my dear, let be.'

This small light the moon bestows,
20   Serves thy beams but to disclose,
So to raise my hap more high;
Fear not else, none can us spy:
Take me to thee, and thee to me.
'No, no, no, no, my dear, let be.'

25   That you heard was but a mouse;
      Dumb sleep holdeth all the house;
      Yet, asleep, methinks they say,
      Young folks, take time while you may:
      Take me to thee, and thee to me.
30   'No, no, no, no, my dear, let be.'

      Niggard Time threats, if we miss
      This large offer of our bliss,
      Long stay ere he grant the same;
      Sweet then, while each thing doth frame,
35   Take me to thee, and thee to me.
      'No, no, no, no, my dear, let be.'

      Your fair mother is abed,
      Candles out, and curtains spread;
      She thinks you do letters write:
40   Write, but let me first indite:
      Take me to thee, and thee to me.
      'No, no, no, no, my dear, let be.'

      Sweet, alas, why strive you thus?
      Concord better fitteth us.
45   Leave to *Mars* the force of hands,
      Your power in your beauty stands:
      Take me to thee, and thee to me.
      'No, no, no, no, my dear, let be.'

      Woe to me, and do you swear
50   Me to hate? But I forbear;
      Cursed be my dest'nies all,
      That brought me so high to fall:
      Soon with my death I will please thee.
      'No, no, no, no, my dear, let be.'

86

Alas, whence came this change of looks? If I
    Have changed desert, let mine own conscience be
    A still felt plague to self-condemning me:
Let woe gripe on my heart, shame load mine eye.
5 But if all faith, like spotless ermine, lie
    Safe in my soul, which only doth to thee
    (As his sole object of felicity)
With wings of love in air of wonder fly,
    O ease your hand, treat not so hard your slave:
10 In justice pains come not till faults do call;
Or if I needs (sweet judge) must torments have,
Use something else to chasten me withal
    Than those blest eyes, where all my hopes do dwell;
    No doom should make one's heav'n become his hell.

Fifth Song

While favour fed my hope, delight with hope was brought,
Thought waited on delight, and speech did follow thought;
Then grew my tongue and pen records unto thy glory:
I thought all words were lost, that were not spent of thee;
I thought each place was dark but where thy lights would
5   be,
And all ears worse than deaf, that heard not out thy story.

I said thou wert most fair, and so indeed thou art;
I said thou wert most sweet, sweet poison to my heart;
I said my soul was thine (O that I then had lied);
10 I said thine eyes were stars, thy breasts the milken way,
Thy fingers *Cupid*'s shafts, thy voice the angels' lay:
And all I said so well, as no man it denied.

But now that hope is lost, unkindness kills delight,
Yet thought and speech do live, though metamorphosed
      quite:

For rage now rules the reins, which guided were by
15   pleasure.
I think now of thy faults, who late thought of thy praise;
That speech falls now to blame, which did thy honour
   raise;
The same key open can, which can lock up a treasure.

Thou then, whom partial heav'ns conspired in one to frame
20 The proof of beauty's worth, th'inheritrix of fame,
The mansion seat of bliss, and just excuse of lovers;
See now those feathers plucked, wherewith thou flew'st
   most high;
See what clouds of reproach shall dark thy honour's sky;
Whose own fault casts him down, hardly high seat
   recovers.

25 And O my Muse, though oft you lulled her in your lap,
And then, a heav'nly child, gave her ambrosian pap,
And to that brain of hers your hidd'nest gifts infused;
Since she, disdaining me, doth you in me disdain,
Suffer not her to laugh, while both we suffer pain:
Princes in subjects wronged, must deem themselves
30   abused.

Your client, poor myself, shall *Stella* handle so?
Revenge, revenge, my Muse, defiance' trumpet blow:
Threaten what may be done, yet do more than you
   threaten.
Ah, my suit granted is, I feel my breast doth swell;
35 Now child, a lesson new you shall begin to spell:
Sweet babes must babies have, but shrewd girls must be
   beaten.

Think now no more to hear of warm fine-odoured snow,
Nor blushing lilies, nor pearls' ruby-hidden row,
Nor of that golden sea, whose waves in curls are broken:
40 But of thy soul, so fraught with such ungratefulness,
As where thou mightest help, most faith dost most oppress;
Ungrateful who is called, the worst of ills is spoken.

Yet worse than worst, I say thou art a thief. A thief?
Now God forbid. A thief, and of worst thieves the chief:
Thieves steal for need, and steal but goods, which pain
45   recovers;
But thou, rich in all joys, dost rob my joys from me,
Which cannot be restored by time nor industry:
Of foes the spoil is ill, far worse of constant lovers.

Yet gentle English thieves do rob, but will not slay;
Thou, English murd'ring thief, wilt have hearts for thy
50   prey;
The name of murd'rer now on thy fair forehead sitteth;
And e'en while I do speak, my death-wounds bleeding be,
Which (I protest) proceed from only cruel thee:
Who may and will not save, murder in truth committeth.

55   But murder, private fault, seems but a toy to thee.
I lay then to thy charge unjustest tyranny,
If rule by force without all claim a tyrant showeth.
For thou dost lord my heart, who am not born thy slave,
And, which is worse, makes me, most guiltless, torments
          have:
60   A rightful prince by unright deeds a tyrant groweth.

Lo, you grow proud with this, for tyrants make folk bow.
Of foul rebellion then I do appeach thee now;
Rebel by nature's law, rebel by law of reason.
Thou, sweetest subject, wert born in the realm of Love,
65   And yet against thy prince thy force dost daily prove:
No virtue merits praise, once touched with blot of treason.

But valiant rebels oft in fools' mouths purchase fame;
I now then stain thy white with vagabonding shame,
Both rebel to the son, and vagrant from the mother:
70   For wearing *Venus'* badge, in every part of thee,
Unto *Diana*'s train thou runaway didst flee:
Who faileth one, is false, though trusty to another.

What, is not this enough? Nay, far worse cometh here:
A witch I say thou art, though thou so fair appear;
75 For I protest, my sight never thy face enjoyeth,
But I in me am changed: I am alive and dead,
My feet are turned to roots, my heart becometh lead.
No witchcraft is so ill, as which man's mind destroyeth.

Yet witches may repent; thou art far worse than they;
80 Alas, that I am forced such ev'l of thee to say.
I say thou art a dev'l, though clothed in angel's shining,
For thy face tempts my soul to leave the heav'n for thee,
And thy words of refuse do pour e'en hell on me:
Who tempt, and tempted plague, are dev'ls in true
defining.

85 You then ungrateful thief, you murd'ring tyrant, you,
You rebel runaway, to lord and lady untrue,
You witch, you dev'l, (alas) you still of me beloved,
You see what I can say; mend yet your froward mind,
And such skill in my Muse you reconciled shall find,
90 That all these cruel words your praises shall be proved.

Sixth Song

O you that hear this voice,
O you that see this face,
Say whether of the choice
Deserves the former place:
5 Fear not to judge this 'bate,
For it is void of hate.

This side doth Beauty take,
For that doth Music speak;
Fit orators to make
10 The strongest judgements weak:
The bar to plead their right
Is only true delight.

Thus doth the voice and face,
These gentle lawyers, wage,
15 Like loving brothers' case
For father's heritage,
That each, while each contends,
Itself to other lends.

For Beauty beautifies
20 With heav'nly hue and grace
The heav'nly harmonies;
And in this faultless face
The perfect beauties be
A perfect harmony.

25 Music more loft'ly swells
In speeches nobly placed;
Beauty as far excels
In action aptly graced:
A friend each party draws,
30 To countenance his cause.

Love more affected seems
To Beauty's lovely light,
And Wonder more esteems
Of Music's wondrous might:
35 But both to both so bent,
As both in both are spent.

Music doth witness call
The ear, his truth to try;
Beauty brings to the hall
40 The judgement of the eye:
Both in their objects such,
As no exceptions touch.

The Common Sense, which might
Be arbiter of this,
45 To be forsooth upright,
To both sides partial is:
He lays on this chief praise,
Chief praise on that he lays.

Then Reason, princess high,
50 Whose throne is in the mind,
Which music can in sky
And hidden beauties find,
Say whether thou wilt crown
With limitless renown.

Seventh Song

Whose senses in so ill consort their step-dame Nature lays,
That ravishing delight in them most sweet tunes do not
        raise;
Or if they do delight therein, yet are so cloyed with wit,
As with sententious lips to set a title vain on it:
O let them hear these sacred tunes, and learn in wonder's
5   schools
To be, in things past bounds of wit, fools, if they be not
        fools.

Who have so leaden eyes, as not to see sweet beauty's
        show;
Or seeing, have so wooden wits, as not that worth to know;
Or knowing, have so muddy minds, as not to be in love;
10 Or loving, have so frothy thoughts, as eas'ly thence to move:
O let them see these heav'nly beams, and in fair letters
        read
A lesson fit, both sight and skill, love and firm love to
        breed.

Hear then, but then with wonder hear; see, but adoring
        see;
No mortal gifts, no earthly fruits, now here descended be.
15 See, do you see this face? A face? Nay, image of the skies,
Of which the two life-giving lights are figured in her eyes;
Hear you this soul-invading voice, and count it but a voice?
The very essence of their tunes, when angels do rejoice.

Eighth Song

In a grove most rich of shade,
Where birds wanton music made,
May, then young, his pied weeds showing,
New perfumed with flowers fresh growing,

5   *Astrophil* with *Stella* sweet
Did for mutual comfort meet,
Both within themselves oppressed,
But each in the other blest.

Him great harms had taught much care;
10 Her fair neck a foul yoke bare;
But her sight his cares did banish,
In his sight her yoke did vanish.

Wept they had, alas the while;
But now tears themselves did smile,
15 While their eyes, by love directed,
Interchangeably reflected.

Sigh they did, but now betwixt
Sighs of woes were glad sighs mixed,
With arms crossed, yet testifying
20 Restless rest, and living dying.

Their ears hungry of each word
Which the dear tongue would afford,
But their tongues restrained from walking
Till their hearts had ended talking.

25 But when their tongues could not speak,
Love itself did silence break;
Love did set his lips asunder,
Thus to speak in love and wonder:

'*Stella*, sovereign of my joy,
30 Fair triumpher of annoy,
Stella, star of heav'nly fire,
Stella, lodestar of desire;

'*Stella*, in whose shining eyes
Are the lights of *Cupid*'s skies,
35   Whose beams, where they once are darted,
Love therewith is straight imparted;

'*Stella*, whose voice when it speaks
Senses all asunder breaks;
Stella, whose voice when it singeth
40   Angels to acquaintance bringeth;

'*Stella*, in whose body is
Writ each character of bliss;
Whose face all, all beauty passeth,
Save thy mind, which yet surpasseth:

45   'Grant, O grant, but speech, alas,
Fails me, fearing on to pass;
Grant, O me, what am I saying?
But no fault there is in praying.

'Grant, O dear, on knees I pray,'
50   (Knees on ground he then did stay)
'That not I, but since I love you,
Time and place for me may move you.

'Never season was more fit,
Never room more apt for it;
55   Smiling air allows my reason,
These birds sing, "Now use the season."

'This small wind, which so sweet is,
See how it the leaves doth kiss,
Each tree in his best attiring,
60   Sense of love to love inspiring.

'Love makes earth the water drink,
Love to earth makes water sink;
And if dumb things be so witty,
Shall a heav'nly grace want pity?'

65   There his hands in their speech fain
Would have made tongue's language plain;
But her hands, his hands repelling,
Gave repulse, all grace excelling.

Then she spake; her speech was such
70 As not ears but heart did touch;
While such wise she love denied,
As yet love she signified.

'*Astrophil,*' said she, 'my love
Cease in these effects to prove:
75 Now be still, yet still believe me,
Thy grief more than death would grieve me.

'If that any thought in me
Can taste comfort but of thee,
Let me, fed with hellish anguish,
80 Joyless, hopeless, endless languish.

'If those eyes you praised be
Half so dear as you to me,
Let me home return, stark blinded
Of those eyes, and blinder minded.

85 'If to secret of my heart
I do any wish impart
Where thou art not foremost placed,
Be both wish and I defaced.

'If more may be said, I say,
90 All my bliss in thee I lay;
If thou love, my love content thee,
For all love, all faith is meant thee.

'Trust me while I thee deny,
In myself the smart I try;
95 Tyrant honour doth thus use thee,
Stella's self might not refuse thee.

'Therefore, dear, this no more move,
Lest, though I leave not thy love,
Which too deep in me is framed,
100 I should blush when thou art named.'

Therewithal away she went,
Leaving him so passion rent
With what she had done and spoken,
That therewith my song is broken.

Ninth Song

Go, my flock, go get you hence,
Seek a better place of feeding,
Where you may have some defence
From the storms in my breast breeding,
5   And showers from mine eyes proceeding.

Leave a wretch, in whom all woe
Can abide to keep no measure;
Merry flock, such one forgo,
Unto whom mirth is displeasure,
10   Only rich in mischief's treasure.

Yet, alas, before you go,
Hear your woeful master's story,
Which to stones I else would show:
Sorrow only then hath glory,
15   When 'tis excellently sorry.

Stella, fiercest shepherdess,
Fiercest but yet fairest ever;
Stella, whom O heav'ns do bless,
Though against me she persever,
20   Though I bliss inherit never;

Stella hath refused me,
Stella, who more love hath proved
In this caitiff heart to be
Than can in good ewes be moved
25   Toward lambkins best beloved.

Stella hath refused me,
Astrophil, that so well served;
In this pleasant spring must see,
While in pride flowers be preserved,
30   Himself only winter-starved.

Why, alas, doth she then swear
That she loveth me so dearly,
Seeing me so long to bear
Coals of love that burn so clearly,
35   And yet leave me helpless merely?

Is that love? Forsooth, I trow,
If I saw my good dog grieved,
And a help for him did know,
My love should not be believed
40   But he were by me relieved.

No, she hates me, wellaway,
Feigning love somewhat to please me:
For she knows, if she display
All her hate, death soon would seize me,
45   And of hideous torments ease me.

Then adieu, dear flock, adieu:
But, alas, if in your straying
Heav'nly *Stella* meet with you,
Tell her in your piteous blaying,
50   Her poor slave's unjust decaying.

87

When I was forced from *Stella* ever dear,
Stella, food of my thoughts, heart of my heart,
Stella, whose eyes make all my tempests clear,
By iron laws of duty to depart;
5   Alas, I found that she with me did smart,
I saw that tears did in her eyes appear;
I saw that sighs her sweetest lips did part,
And her sad words my sadded sense did hear.
      For me, I wept to see pearls scattered so,
10   I sighed her sighs, and wailed for her woe,

Yet swam in joy, such love in her was seen.
  Thus while th'effect most bitter was to me,
  And nothing than the cause more sweet could be,
I had been vexed, if vexed I had not been.

88

Out, traitor absence: dar'st thou counsel me
From my dear captainess to run away,
Because in brave array here marcheth she
That to win me, oft shows a present pay?
  Is faith so weak? Or is such force in thee?
When sun is hid, can stars such beams display?
Cannot heav'n's food, once felt, keep stomachs free
From base desire on earthly cates to prey?
  Tush, absence: while thy mists eclipse that light,
  My orphan sense flies to the inward sight,
Where memory sets forth the beams of love;
  That where before heart loved and eyes did see,
  In heart both sight and love now coupled be;
United powers make each the stronger prove.

89

Now that of absence the most irksome night
  With darkest shade doth overcome my day;
  Since *Stella*'s eyes, wont to give me my day,
Leaving my hemisphere, leave me in night;
Each day seems long, and longs for long-stayed night;
  The night, as tedious, woos th'approach of day;
  Tired with the dusty toils of busy day,
Languished with horrors of the silent night,
Suff'ring the ills both of the day and night,
  While no night is more dark than is my day,
Nor no day hath less quiet than my night:
  With such bad mixture of my night and day,

That living thus in blackest winter night,
    I feel the flames of hottest summer day.

90

Stella, think not that I by verse seek fame,
    Who seek, who hope, who love, who live but thee;
    Thine eyes my pride, thy lips my history;
If thou praise not, all other praise is shame.
5 Nor so ambitious am I, as to frame
    A nest for my young praise in laurel tree;
    In truth I swear, I wish not there should be
Gravcd in mine epitaph a poet's name:
    Ne if I would, could I just title make,
10 That any laud to me thereof should grow,
Without my plumes from others' wings I take.
For nothing from my wit or will doth flow,
    Since all my words thy beauty doth indite,
    And Love doth hold my hand, and makes me write.

91

Stella, while now by honour's cruel might
    I am from you, light of my life, misled,
    And that fair you, my sun, thus overspread
With absence' veil, I live in sorrow's night;
5 If this dark place yet show like candle-light
    Some beauty's piece, as amber-coloured head,
    Milk hands, rose cheeks, or lips more sweet, more red,
Or seeing jets, black, but in blackness bright:
    They please, I do confess, they please mine eyes.
10 But why? Because of you they models be,
Models such be wood-globes of glist'ring skies.
Dear, therefore be not jealous over me,
    If you hear that they seem my heart to move:
    Not them, O no, but you in them I love.

92

Be your words made (good sir) of Indian ware,
  That you allow me them by so small rate?
  Or do you cutted Spartans imitate?
Or do you mean my tender ears to spare,
5 That to my questions you so total are?
  When I demand of phoenix *Stella*'s state,
  You say, forsooth, you left her well of late.
O God, think you that satisfies my care?
  I would know whether she did sit or walk;
10 How clothed, how waited on; sighed she or smiled;
Whereof, with whom, how often did she talk;
With what pastime, time's journey she beguiled;
  If her lips deigned to sweeten my poor name.
  Say all, and all well said, still say the same.

Tenth Song

O dear life, when shall it be
  That mine eyes thine eyes may see?
  And in them thy mind discover,
  Whether absence have had force
5 Thy remembrance to divorce
  From the image of thy lover?

O if I myself find not
  After parting aught forgot,
  Nor debarred from beauty's treasure,
10 Let no tongue aspire to tell
  In what high joys I shall dwell;
  Only thought aims at the pleasure.

Thought, therefore, I will send thee
    To take up the place for me;
15   Long I will not after tarry.
    There unseen thou mayst be bold
    Those fair wonders to behold,
    Which in them my hopes do carry.

Thought, see thou no place forbear:
20   Enter bravely everywhere,
    Seize on all to her belonging;
    But if thou wouldst guarded be,
    Fearing her beams, take with thee
    Strength of liking, rage of longing.

25 Think of that most grateful time
    When my leaping heart will climb
    In my lips to have his biding,
    There those roses for to kiss
    Which do breathe a sugared bliss,
30   Op'ning rubies, pearls dividing.

Think of my most princely power
    When I, blessed, shall devour,
    With my greedy lickerous senses,
    Beauty, music, sweetness, love,
35   While she doth against me prove
    Her strong darts, but weak defences.

Think, think of those dallyings
    When with dove-like murmurings,
    With glad moaning passed anguish,
40   We change eyes, and heart for heart
    Each to other do impart,
    Joying till joy make us languish.

O my thought my thoughts surcease,
    Thy delights my woes increase,
45   My life melts with too much thinking;
    Think no more but die in me,
    Till thou shalt revived be
    At her lips my nectar drinking.

93

O fate, O fault, O curse, child of my bliss,
    What sobs can give words grace my grief to show?
    What ink is black enough to paint my woe?
Through me, wretch me, e'en *Stella* vexed is.
5   Yet truth (if caitiff's breath might call thee) this
    Witness with me, that my foul stumbling so,
    From carelessness did in no manner grow,
But wit confused with too much care did miss.
    And do I then myself this vain 'scuse give?
10 I have (live I and know this?) harmed thee,
Though worlds 'quit me, shall I myself forgive?
Only with pains my pains thus eased be,
    That all thy hurts in my heart's wrack I read;
    I cry thy sighs; my dear, thy tears I bleed.

94

Grief, find the words, for thou hast made my brain
    So dark with misty vapours, which arise
    From out thy heavy mould, that inbent eyes
Can scarce discern the shape of mine own pain.
5   Do thou then (for thou canst) do thou complain
    For my poor soul, which now that sickness tries,
    Which e'en to sense, sense of itself denies,
Though harbingers of death lodge there his train;
    Or if thy love of plaint yet mine forbears,
10 As of a caitiff worthy so to die,
Yet wail thyself, and wail with causeful tears,
That though in wretchedness thy life doth lie,
Yet growest more wretched than thy nature bears,
By being placed in such a wretch as I.

95

Yet sighs, dear sighs, indeed true friends you are,
    That do not leave your least friend at the worst,
    But, as you with my breast I oft have nursed,
So grateful now you wait upon my care.
5 Faint coward joy no longer tarry dare,
    Seeing hope yield when this woe strake him first:
    Delight protests he is not for th'accursed,
Though oft himself my mate-in-arms he sware.
    Nay, sorrow comes with such main rage, that he
10 Kills his own children, tears, finding that they
By love were made apt to consort with me.
Only true sighs, you do not go away:
    Thank may you have for such a thankful part,
    Thank-worthiest yet when you shall break my heart.

96

Thought, with good cause thou lik'st so well the night,
    Since kind or chance gives both one livery:
    Both sadly black, both blackly darkened be,
Night barred from sun, thou from thy own sun's light;
5 Silence in both displays his sullen might;
    Slow heaviness in both holds one degree;
    That full of doubts, thou of perplexity;
Thy tears express night's native moisture right;
    In both a mazeful solitariness;
10 In night of sprites the ghastly powers stir,
In thee or sprites or sprited ghastliness:
But, but (alas) night's side the odds hath, far,
    For that at length yet doth invite some rest,
    Thou, though still tired, yet still dost it detest.

97

Dian, that fain would cheer her friend the Night,
    Shows her oft at the full her fairest face,
    Bringing with her those starry nymphs, whose chase
From heav'nly standing hits each mortal wight.
5 But ah, poor Night, in love with *Phoebus'* light,
    And endlessly despairing of his grace,
    Herself (to show no other joy hath place)
Silent and sad in mourning weeds doth dight:
    E'en so (alas) a lady, *Dian*'s peer,
10 With choice delights and rarest company,
Would fain drive clouds from out my heavy cheer.
But woe is me, though joy itself were she,
    She could not show my blind brain ways of joy,
    While I despair my sun's sight to enjoy.

 98

Ah bed, the field where joy's peace some do see,
    The field where all my thoughts to war be trained,
    How is thy grace by my strange fortune stained!
How thy lee shores by my sighs stormed be!
5 With sweet soft shades thou oft invitest me
    To steal some rest, but wretch I am constrained
    (Spurred with love's spur, though galled and shortly reined
With care's hard hand) to turn and toss in thee,
    While the black horrors of the silent night
10   Paint woe's black face so lively to my sight
That tedious leisure marks each wrinkled line:
    But when *Aurora* leads out *Phoebus'* dance,
    Mine eyes then only wink, for spite perchance,
That worms should have their sun, and I want mine.

99

When far-spent night persuades each mortal eye,
　　To whom nor art nor nature granteth light,
　　To lay his then mark-wanting shafts of sight,
Closed with their quivers in sleep's armoury;
5　With windows ope then most my mind doth lie,
　　Viewing the shape of darkness and delight;
　　Takes in that sad hue, which with th'inward night
Of his mazed powers keeps perfect harmony:
　　But when birds charm, and that sweet air, which is
10　Morn's messenger, with rose-enamelled skies
Calls each wight to salute the flower of bliss;
In tomb of lids then buried are mine eyes,
　　Forced by their lord, who is ashamed to find
　　Such light in sense, with such a darkened mind.

100

O tears, no tears, but rain from beauty's skies,
　　Making those lilies and those roses grow
　　Which ay most fair, now more than most fair show,
While graceful pity beauty beautifies;
5　O honeyed sighs, which from that breast do rise,
　　Whose pants do make unspilling cream to flow,
　　Winged with whose breath so pleasing zephyrs blow
As can refresh the hell where my soul fries;
　　O plaints conserved in such a sugared phrase
10　　That eloquence itself envies your praise,
While sobbed-out words a perfect music give;
　　Such tears, sighs, plaints, no sorrow is, but joy:
　　Or if such heav'nly signs must prove annoy,
All mirth farewell, let me in sorrow live.

101

Stella is sick, and in that sick-bed lies
Sweetness, that breathes and pants as oft as she;
And grace, sick too, such fine conclusions tries
That sickness brags itself best graced to be.
5   Beauty is sick, but sick in so fair guise
That in that paleness beauty's white we see;
And joy, which is inseparate from those eyes,
Stella now learns (strange case) to weep in thee.
      Love moves thy pain, and like a faithful page,
10 As thy looks stir, runs up and down to make
All folks prest at thy will thy pain t'assuage;
Nature with care sweats for her darling's sake,
      Knowing worlds pass, ere she enough can find
      Of such heav'n stuff, to clothe so heav'nly mind.

102

Where be those roses gone, which sweetened so our eyes?
      Where those red cheeks, which oft with fair increase
         did frame
      The height of honour in the kindly badge of shame?
Who hath the crimson weeds stol'n from my morning
         skies?
5 How doth the colour vade of those vermilion dyes
      Which Nature's self did make, and self engrained the
         same?
      I would know by what right this paleness overcame
That hue, whose force my heart still unto thraldom ties?
      Galen's adoptive sons, who by a beaten way
      Their judgements hackney on, the fault on sickness
10   lay,
But feeling proof makes me say they mistake it far:
      It is but Love, which makes his paper perfect white
      To write therein more fresh the story of delight,
While beauty's reddest ink *Venus* for him doth stir.

103

O happy *Thames*, that didst my *Stella* bear,
I saw thyself, with many a smiling line
Upon thy cheerful face, joy's liv'ry wear,
While those fair planets on thy streams did shine.
5   The boat for joy could not to dance forbear,
While wanton winds, with beauties so divine
Ravished, stayed not, till in her golden hair
They did themselves (O sweetest prison) twine.
    And fain those *Aeol*'s youths there would their stay
10   Have made, but forced by Nature still to fly,
First did with puffing kiss those locks display:
She, so dishevelled, blushed; from window I
        With sight thereof cried out: O fair disgrace,
        Let honour's self to thee grant highest place.

104

Envious wits, what hath been mine offence,
        That with such poisonous care my looks you mark,
        That to each word, nay sigh of mine you hark,
As grudging me my sorrow's eloquence?
5   Ah, is it not enough, that I am thence,
        Thence, so far thence, that scarcely any spark
        Of comfort dare come to this dungeon dark,
Where rig'rous exile locks up all my sense?
        But if I by a happy window pass,
10   If I but stars upon mine armour bear,
Sick, thirsty, glad (though but of empty glass):
Your moral notes straight my hid meaning tear
        From out my ribs, and puffing prove that I
        Do *Stella* love. Fools, who doth it deny?

Eleventh Song

'Who is it that this dark night
Underneath my window plaineth?'
It is one who from thy sight
Being (ah) exiled, disdaineth
5   Every other vulgar light.

'Why alas, and are you he?
Be not yet those fancies changed?'
Dear, when you find change in me,
Though from me you be estranged,
10   Let my change to ruin be.

'Well, in absence this will die,
Leave to see, and leave to wonder.'
Absence sure will help, if I
Can learn how myself to sunder
15   From what in my heart doth lie.

'But time will these thoughts remove:
Time doth work what no man knoweth.'
Time doth as the subject prove;
With time still th'affection groweth
20   In the faithful turtle dove.

'What if you new beauties see,
Will not they stir new affection?'
I will think they pictures be,
(Image-like of saint's perfection)
25   Poorly counterfeiting thee.

'But your reason's purest light
Bids you leave such minds to nourish.'
Dear, do reason no such spite;
Never doth thy beauty flourish
30   More than in my reason's sight.

'But the wrongs love bears will make
Love at length leave undertaking.'
No, the more fools it do shake,
In a ground of so firm making,
35   Deeper still they drive the stake.

'Peace, I think that some give ear:
Come no more, lest I get anger.'
Bliss, I will my bliss forbear,
Fearing (sweet) you to endanger,
40   But my soul shall harbour there.

'Well, be gone, be gone, I say,
Lest that *Argus*' eyes perceive you.'
O unjustest fortune's sway,
Which can make me thus to leave you,
45   And from louts to run away.

105

Unhappy sight, and hath she vanished by,
        So near, in so good time, so free a place?
        Dead glass, dost thou thy object so embrace
As what my heart still sees thou canst not spy?
5   I swear by her I love and lack that I
        Was not in fault, who bent thy dazzling race
        Only unto the heav'n of *Stella*'s face,
Counting but dust what in the way did lie.
        But cease, mine eyes, your tears do witness well
10   That you, guiltless thereof, your nectar missed:
Cursed be the page from whom the bad torch fell,
Cursed be the night which did your strife resist,
        Cursed be the coachman which did drive so fast,
        With no worse curse than absence makes me taste.

106

O absent presence, *Stella* is not here;
  False flatt'ring hope, that with so fair a face
  Bare me in hand, that in this orphan place
Stella, I say my *Stella*, should appear.
5 What say'st thou now, where is that dainty cheer
  Thou told'st mine eyes should help their famished
   case?
  But thou art gone, now that self-felt disgrace
Doth make me most to wish thy comfort near.
  But here I do store of fair ladies meet,
10   Who may with charm of conversation sweet
Make in my heavy mould new thoughts to grow:
  Sure they prevail as much with me, as he
  That bade his friend, but then new-maimed, to be
Merry with him, and not think of his woe.

107

Stella, since thou so right a princess art
  Of all the powers which life bestows on me,
  That ere by them aught undertaken be,
They first resort unto that sovereign part;
5 Sweet, for a while give respite to my heart,
  Which pants as though it still should leap to thee;
  And on my thoughts give thy lieutenancy
To this great cause, which needs both use and art;
  And as a queen, who from her presence sends
10 Whom she employs, dismiss from thee my wit,
Till it have wrought what thy own will attends.
On servants' shame oft master's blame doth sit;
  O let not fools in me thy works reprove,
And scorning say, 'See what it is to love.'

108

When sorrow (using mine own fire's might)
    Melts down his lead into my boiling breast,
    Through that dark furnace to my heart oppressed,
There shines a joy from thee, my only light;
5 But soon as thought of thee breeds my delight,
    And my young soul flutters to thee, his nest,
    Most rude despair, my daily unbidden guest,
Clips straight my wings, straight wraps me in his night,
    And makes me then bow down my head, and say,
10 Ah, what doth *Phoebus'* gold that wretch avail
Whom iron doors do keep from use of day?
So strangely (alas) thy works in me prevail,
    That in my woes for thee thou art my joy,
    And in my joys for thee my only annoy.

Poems from *The Psalms of David*

Psalm XII

Lord, help, it is high time for me to call:
    No men are left that charity do love,
    Nay, e'en the race of good men are decayed.
Of things vain with vain mates they babble all;
5   Their abject lips no breath but flatt'ry move,
    Sent from false heart, on double meaning stayed.
But Thou (O Lord) give them a thorough fall;
    Those lying lips from cozening head remove,
    In falsehood wrapped, but in their pride displayed.

10 Our tongues, say they, beyond them all shall go;
    We both have pow'r and will our tales to tell,
    For what Lord rules our bold emboldened breast?
'Ah, now e'en for their sakes, that taste of woe,
    Whom troubles toss, whose natures need doth quell,
15   E'en for the sighs, true sighs of man distressed,
I will get up,' saith God, 'and my help show
    Against all them that against him do swell;
    Maugre their force, I will set him at rest.'

These are God's words, God's words are ever pure:
20   Pure, purer than the silver throughly tried
    When fire sev'n times hath spent his earthly parts.
Then Thou (O Lord) shalt keep the good still sure;
    By Thee preserved, in Thee they shall abide;
    Yea, in no age Thy bliss from them departs.
25 Thou seest each side the walking doth endure
    Of these bad folks, more lifted up with pride,
    Which, if it last, woe to all simple hearts.

Psalm XXII

Deus Deus meus

My God, my God, why hast Thou me forsaken?
    Woe me, from me why is Thy presence taken?
    So far from seeing mine unhealthful eyes,
    So far from hearing to my roaring cries.
5 O God, my God, I cry while day appeareth;
    But God, Thy ear my crying never heareth.
    O God, the night is privy to my plaint,
    Yet to my plaint Thou hast not audience lent.
But Thou art holy, and dost hold Thy dwelling
10 Where *Israel* Thy lauds is ever telling.
    Our fathers still in Thee their trust did bear;
    They trusted and by Thee delivered were.
They were set free when they upon Thee called;
    They hoped on Thee, and they were not appalled.
15 But I, a worm, not I of mankind am,
    Nay, shame of men, the people's scorning game;
The lookers now at me, poor wretch, be mocking,
    With mows and nods they stand about me flocking.
    'Let God help him,' say they, 'whom he did trust;
20 Let God save him, in whom was all his lust.'
And yet e'en from the womb Thyself didst take me;
    At mother's breasts, Thou didst good hope betake me.
    No sooner my child eyes could look abroad,
    Than I was giv'n to Thee, Thou wert my God.
25 O be not far, since pain so nearly presseth,
    And since there is not one who it redresseth.
    I am enclosed with young bulls' madded rout,
    Nay, *Bashan* mighty bulls close me about.
With gaping mouths, these folks on me have charged,
30 Like lions fierce, with roaring jaws enlarged.
    On me all this, who do like water slide,
    Whose loosed bones quite out of joint be wried,

Whose heart with these huge flames, like wax o'erheated,
Doth melt away, though it be inmost seated;
35 My moist'ning strength is like a potsherd dried,
My cleaving tongue close to my roof doth bide;
And now am brought, alas, brought by Thy power
Unto the dust of my death's running hour;
For bawling dogs have compassed me about,
40 Yea, worse than dogs, a naughty wicked rout.
My humble hands, my fainting feet they pierced;
They look, they gaze, my bones might be rehearsed;
Of my poor weeds they do partition make,
And do cast lots who should my vesture take.
45 But be not far, O Lord, my strength, my comfort;
Hasten to help me, in this deep discomfort.
Ah, from the sword yet save my vital sprite,
My desolated life from dogged might.
From lion's mouth O help, and show to hear me
50 By aiding when fierce unicorns come near me.
To brethren then I will declare Thy fame,
And with these words, when they meet, praise Thy
name:
'Who fear the Lord, all praise and glory bear Him;
You, *Israel*'s seed, you come of *Jacob*, fear Him.
55 For He hath not abhorred nor yet disdained
The silly wretch with foul affliction stained,
Nor hid from him His face's fair appearing;
But when he called this Lord did give him hearing.'
In congregation great I will praise Thee;
60 Who fear Thee shall my vows performed see.
Th'afflicted then shall eat, and be well pleased,
And God shall be by those His seekers praised.
Indeed, O you, you that be such of mind,
You shall the life that ever liveth find.
65 But what? I say from earth's remotest border
Unto due thoughts mankind his thoughts shall order
And turn to God; and all the nations be
Made worshippers before almighty Thee;
And reason, since the crown to God pertaineth,
70 And that by right upon all realms He reigneth,

They that be made e'en fat with earth's fat good,
Shall feed and laud the giver of their food.
To Him shall kneel who to the dust be stricken,
E'en he whose life no help of man can quicken.
75   As they so theirs, Him shall their offspring serve,
And God shall them in His own court reserve.
They shall to children's children make notorious
His righteousness, and this His doing glorious.

Psalm XXIII

Dominus regit me

The Lord, the Lord my shepherd is,
    And so can never I
        Taste misery.
He rests me in green pasture His;
5   By waters still and sweet
        He guides my feet.

He me revives; leads me the way
    Which righteousness doth take,
        For His name's sake.
10 Yea, though I should through valleys stray
    Of death's dark shade, I will
        No whit fear ill.

For Thou, dear Lord, Thou me besett'st;
    Thy rod and Thy staff be
15   To comfort me.
Before me Thou a table sett'st,
    E'en when foe's envious eye
        Doth it espy.

With oil Thou dost anoint my head,
20   And so my cup dost fill
        That it doth spill.
Thus, thus shall all my days be fed;
    This mercy is so sure
        It shall endure;
25 And long, yea long abide I shall,
    There where the Lord of all
        Doth hold His hall.

Psalm XXVIII

Ad te Domine clamabo

To Thee, Lord, my cry I send;
    O, my strength, stop not Thine ear
    Lest, if answer Thou forbear,
    I be like them that descend
5   To the pit where flesh doth end.
Therefore, while that I may cry,
    While I that way hold my hands
    Where Thy sanctuary stands,
    To Thyself those words apply
10   Which from 'suing voice do fly.
Link not me in selfsame chain
    With the wicked working folk
    Who, their spotted thoughts to cloak,
    Neighbours friendly entertain
15   When in hearts they malice mean.
Spare not them; give them reward
    As their deeds have purchased it,
    As deserves their wicked wit;
    Fare they as their hands have fared:
20   E'en so be their guerdon shared.
To Thy works they give no eye;
    Let them be thrown down by Thee;
    Let them not restored be;
    But let me give praises high
25   To the Lord that hears my cry.
That God is my strength, my shield;
    All my trust on Him was set,
    And so I did safety get;
    So shall I with joy be filled,
30   So my songs His lauds shall yield.

God on them His strength doth lay
Who His anointed helped have.
Lord then still Thy people save;
Bless Thine heritage, I say,
35   Feed and lift them up for ay.

Psalm XXXV

Speak Thou for me against wrong-speaking foes;
Thy force, O Lord, against their force oppose.
Take up Thy shield and for my succour stand;
Yea, take Thy lance and stop the way of those
5   That seek my bane; O make me understand
In sprite that I shall have Thy helping hand.

Confound those folks, thrust them in shameful hole
That hunt so poor a prey as is my soul.
Rebuke and wrack on those wrong-doers throw,
10 Who for my hurt each way their thoughts did roll;
And, as vile chaff away the wind doth blow,
Let angel Thine a-scatt'ring make them go.

Let angel Thine pursue them as they fly,
But let their flight be dark and slippery;
15 For causeless they both pit and net did set,
For causeless they did seek to make me die.
Let their sly wits unwares destruction get,
Fall in self pit, be caught in their own net.

Then shall I joy in Thee; then, saved by Thee,
20 I both in mind and bones shall gladded be.
E'en bones shall say, 'O God, who is Thy peer,
Who poor and weak from rich and strong dost free,
Who helpest those whose ruin was so near,
From him whose force did in their spoils appear?'

25 Who did me wrong, against me witness bare,
Laying such things as never in me were;
So my good deeds they pay with this ill share,
With cruel minds my very soul to tear.
And whose? E'en his who, when they sickness bare,
30 With inward woe an outward sackcloth ware.

I did pull down myself, fasting for such;
I prayed with prayers which my breast did touch;
   In sum, I showed that I to them was bent
As brothers, or as friends beloved much.
35   Still, still for them I humbly mourning went
Like one that should his mother's death lament.

But lo, soon as they did me stagg'ring see,
Who joy but they, when they assembled be?
   Then abjects, while I was unwitting quite,
40 Against me swarm, ceaseless to rail at me.
   With scoffers false, I was their feast's delight,
E'en gnashing teeth, to witness more their spite.

Lord, wilt Thou see, and wilt Thou suffer it?
O! on my soul let not these tumults hit.
45   Save me distressed from lion's cruel kind.
I will thank Thee where congregations sit,
   E'en where I do most store of people find;
Most to Thy lauds will I my speeches bind.

Then, then let not my foes unjustly joy;
50 Let them not fleer who me would causeless 'stroy,
   Who never word of peace yet utter would,
But hunt with craft the quiet man's annoy,
   And said to me, wide mowing as they could,
'Aha! Sir, now we see you where we should.'

55   This Thou hast seen, and wilt Thou silent be?
O Lord, do not absent Thyself from me,
   But rise, but wake that I may judgement get.
My Lord, my God, e'en to my equity,
   Judge, Lord, judge, God, e'en in Thy justice great,
60 Let not their joy upon my woes be set.

Let them not, Lord, within their hearts thus say:
'O soul, rejoice, we made this wretch our prey,'
   But throw them down, put them to endless blame,
Who make a cause to joy of my decay.
65   Let them be clothed in most confounding shame
That lift themselves my ruin for to frame.

But make such glad, and full of joyfulness,
That yet bear love unto my righteousness;
  Yet let them say, 'Laud be to God always,
70 Who loves with good His servants good to bless.'
  As for my tongue, while I have any days,
Thy justice witness shall and speak Thy praise.

Notes

Abbreviations

Ringler: W. A. Ringler, ed., *The Poems of Sir Philip Sidney* (Oxford, 1962).

Robertson: Jean Robertson, ed., *The Countess of Pembroke's Arcadia (The Old Arcadia)* (Oxford, 1973).

Skretkowicz: Victor Skretkowicz, ed., *The Countess of Pembroke's Arcadia (The New Arcadia)* (Oxford, 1987).

Miscellaneous Prose: Jan van Dorsten and Katherine Duncan-Jones, eds., *The Miscellaneous Prose of Sir Philip Sidney* (Oxford, 1973).

Apology for Poetry: Geoffrey Shepherd, ed., *An Apology for Poetry* (Manchester, 1973).

OED: *Oxford English Dictionary* (2nd edition).

Poems from *The Lady of May*

Sidney's pastoral entertainment (only later entitled *The Lady of May*) was written to be performed before Queen Elizabeth when she was visiting the Earl of Leicester at his house in Wanstead during May of 1578 or 1579. The action centres on the Lady of the May who finds herself unable to choose between two suitors, Therion (a forester) and Espilus (a shepherd). In the opening poem, the lady's mother invites Elizabeth to arbitrate the dispute, and, after a series of debates and competitions between the two rivals and their supporters, the *98* text records that 'it pleased her Majesty to judge that Espilus did the better deserve her' (*Miscellaneous Prose*, p. 30). The show was closely concerned with political issues preoccupying the English court in the 1570s, among them ongoing negotiations for Elizabeth's marriage to the Duke of Alençon which Sidney was to oppose in an open letter to the Queen in November or December 1579 (*Miscellaneous Prose*, pp. 33–57). Several critics have regarded Elizabeth's choice of Espilus as unplanned or unexpected on Sidney's part, but it is more likely that the entertainment follows the pattern of traditional courtly debates in being deliberately left open-ended. See Louis A. Montrose, 'Celebration and Insinuation: Sir Philip Sidney and the Motives of Elizabethan Courtship', *Renaissance Drama* 8 (1977), pp. 3–35; and Catherine Bates, *The Rhetoric of Courtship in Elizabethan Language and Literature* (Cambridge, 1992), pp. 61–9.

i The Suitor

The Suitor refers to the May Lady's mother, who here addresses the Queen directly, asking her to intervene in the debate that is to follow.

ii Therion and Espilus

Therion ('wild beast')   a forester, hunter.
Espilus ('hairy' or 'woolly one')   a shepherd.
31: Espilus here kneels before the Queen.

iii Espilus and Therion

The prose introducing this poem ascribes it to Espilus, but I follow the Oxford editors in giving lines 7–12 and 17–18 to Therion.
1: *Silvanus*   the god of forests.
4: *weal*   happiness, prosperity.
7: *Pan*   the god of shepherds, here identified with Faunus who mistook his mistress's bed for that of Hercules (Ovid, *Fasti*, ii. 303–58). That Espilus, a shepherd, invokes the god of forests, and Therion, a forester, the god of shepherds, suggests that 'Sidney must have been prepared for either choice' (Montrose, p. 20), and that 'the poem was ingeniously devised to be appropriate to whichever suitor was adjudged victor by the Queen' (Ringler, p. 363).
15: *bliss*   give joy or gladness to, bless.

Poems from the *Old Arcadia*

Sidney composed the *Old Arcadia* at some point between 1578 and 1580, before making some revisions and then wholly reorganizing it into the version now known as the *New Arcadia*. According to Sidney's dedication of the work to his sister, the *Old Arcadia* was never intended for publication – 'his chief safety shall be the not walking abroad' (quoted in Robertson, p. 3) – and it was perhaps for this reason that, after his death, his friend Fulke Greville advised against the publication of the *Old Arcadia* in favour of the *New Arcadia*, the 'correction of that old one don 4 or 5 years since', as he put it (ibid., p. xl). The latter, containing Sidney's most recent version of the *Arcadia* but incomplete and breaking off in mid-sentence, was accordingly published in 1590, and then reprinted in 1593 together with Books III–V of the earlier, 'old' version. This hybrid text was the version that came to be read for over three hundred years until the complete *Old Arcadia* was rediscovered by Bertram Dobell in 1907 and printed for the first time in 1926.

This complicated history has inevitably had some bearing on the interpretation and evaluation of the *Old Arcadia*, the very title by which it has come to be known suggesting a discarded, preliminary draft of the later version. Yet, quite apart from its relation to the *New Arcadia*, the narrative complexity of the *Old Arcadia* in itself makes for a tightly structured, rhetorically brilliant, morally and politically incisive text, one which combines the styles of classical and continental writers to produce its own peculiarly Renaissance blend of jest and earnest.

The *Old Arcadia* is divided into five 'Books or Acts' which are interspersed with four groups of pastoral interludes or 'Eclogues'. The story describes how Basilius, Duke of Arcadia, seeks to evade the terrible predictions of a prophecy by taking his family with him into pastoral retreat – the first step in the romantic comedy to which Sidney's five-act structure alludes. Two princes, Pyrocles and Musidorus, fall in love with the duke's daughters, Philoclea and Pamela, and, forced by Basilius' actions, go into disguise in order to woo and then to win them, Pyrocles as an Amazon ('Cleophila'), and Musidorus as a shepherd ('Dorus'). This sets up a conflict. On the one hand, Basilius takes the role of the prohibiting parent that is stock to the situation of romantic comedy and one that Sidney plays out to the full. On the other, Basilius' abortive efforts to evade the outcome of the oracle powerfully suggest his failure as a father and a king, whose chief ambition should be to secure the future succession of his kingdom through the dynastic alliances of his children. As a consequence of his folly, the otherwise wholly legitimate courtships of Pyrocles and Philoclea, Musidorus and Pamela, are compromised and driven to secrecy and deceit. The ambivalence of the ensuing situation allows Sidney to meditate on political issues of profound concern, including the specific question of royal marriage and succession, as well as the more general preoccupation with good rulership. The ambiguity comes to a head in the final Book when Pyrocles and Musidorus are arraigned for seducing and attempting to abduct the two princesses, actions which are, at one level, punishable by death; but, at another, simply the pursuit of the legitimate dynastic alliances which Basilius had blocked. A comic denouement resolves the narrative, but the moral conflict remains, returning the reader to the pronouncement of the opening pages that 'there is nothing so certain as our continual uncertainty' (Robertson, p. 5). For further reading, see A. C. Hamilton, 'Sidney's *Arcadia* as Prose Fiction: Its Relation to its Sources', *English Literary Renaissance* 2 (1972), pp. 29–60; Richard McCoy, *Sir Philip Sidney: Rebellion in Arcadia* (New Brunswick, NJ, 1979); and R. E. Stillman, *Sidney's Poetic Justice: The Old Arcadia, its Eclogues, and Renaissance Pastoral Traditions* (Lewisburg, PA, 1986).

In the present selection, all those poems embedded within the prose narrative of the *Old Arcadia* are designated by lower-case Roman numerals, the Eclogues by arabic numerals. The headings in square brackets refer to the speaker of each poem as it appears in the *Old Arcadia*.

The First Book or Act

I.i The Delphic Oracle

Desirous to know what the future holds, Basilius consults the Delphic oracle and receives, in riddling form, a plot summary of events as they are to unfold in the *Old Arcadia*.

Lines 5–7 were revised in the *New Arcadia* (90, 93) to read:

> Both they themselves unto such two shall wed,
> Who at thy bier, as at a bar, shall plead
> Why thee (a living man) they had made dead.
> In thy own seat a foreign state shall sit.
> And ere that all these blows thy head do hit,
> Thou with thy wife adult'ry shalt commit.

I.ii Cleophila

Cleophila having disguised himself as a woman in Amazon dress, Pyrocles assumes the anagrammatized name of his beloved, Philoclea.

Lines 9–10 were revised in the *New Arcadia* (90, 93) to read:

Thus are my eyes still captive to one sight:
Thus all my thoughts are slaves to one thought still:

I. iii Alethes

Alethes ('truthful')   'an honest man of that time' (Robertson, p. 30).
1: *Mopsa*   the ugly daughter of Basilius' herdsman, Dametas.
3: *shrewdly*   severely.
5–8:   Saturn is ugly, Venus wanton, Pan shaggy, Juno wrathful, Iris ephemeral, Cupid blind, Vulcan lame and Momus censorious.
6: *fast*   steadfast.
9: *jacinth*   a blue or yellow gem.
11: *crapal-stone*   crapaud-stone, a gem believed to have been produced in the heads of toads.
12: *silver ore untried*   unsmelted silver ore is black.

I. iv Dorus

Dorus   the pastoral name assumed by Musidorus when he adopts a shepherd's disguise in order to woo Pamela.
1 and 5: *weeds*   clothing, dress.
1: *become*   befit.
6: *Disuse*   cease to be accustomed to.
   Menalcas   the Arcadian shepherd with whom Musidorus exchanges clothes.

I. v Dametas

Dametas   Basilius' cowardly herdsman, guardian of Pamela.
   The poem is his response to Dorus' slaying of a bear that had threatened to attack Pamela.

The First Eclogues

The five Books of the *Old Arcadia* are divided by four sets of Eclogues: pastoral interludes which Sidney drew from a number of sources, including Jacopo Sannazaro's *Arcadia* (1504) and its imitation, the *Diana* (1559) by Jorge de Montemayor. In his *Apology for Poetry*, Sidney defends the pastoral as a form which 'under the pretty tales of wolves and sheep, can include the whole considerations of wrongdoing and patience' (*Apology for Poetry*, p. 116), articulating the Renaissance commonplace that this apparently escapist, rustic mode might also be a vehicle for social or political comment. Philisides' beast fable (*OA* III.2) is just such a 'pretty tale', while the other Eclogues frequently serve as an increasingly ironic commentary on the actions of Sidney's courtly characters. *OA* III.1, for example, celebrates a wedding (between Lalus and Kala) which is patently the outcome of a conventional courtship concluded 'with consent of both parents' (Robertson, p. 244). Meanwhile, the 'greater persons', Pyrocles and Philoclea, are, as the narrator wryly puts it, 'otherwise occupied', that is to say, in bed together (ibid., pp. 244–5). Much of this irony was lost with the rearrangement of the Eclogues in the revised *Arcadia*.

I. *1 Lalus and Dorus*

Lalus ('babbler') a shepherd. Lalus tests Dorus' technical virtuosity by challenging him to a singing contest in which Dorus has to answer each of the shepherd's stanzas in the same metre and using the same rhyme scheme. Dorus easily follows each challenge, and then reverses the roles at line 152 by beginning his reply with the last line of Lalus' stanza. Lalus has then to follow Dorus, which he does for one stanza before acknowledging defeat.

7: *pie*   magpie.

8: *throughly*   thoroughly.

23: *historify*   relate the history of (antedating *OED*, which gives as its first citation the Countess of Pembroke's translation of Psalm LXXVI, line 10).

26: *Kala* ('beautiful')   a shepherdess, beloved of Lalus. Their wedding is celebrated in *OA* III.1.

31: *cony*   rabbit.

35: *peised*   deliberated on, pondered.

40: *assumption*   reception into heaven.

55: *glasseth*   mirrors, reflects.

60: *shall I to keep inure myself?*   shall I accustom myself to taking care of sheep?

61: *harnished*   harnessed, armed.

88: *richesse*   richness, precious quality.

114: *thralls*   slaves.

126 and 140: *gins*   traps, snares.

130: *pelf*   wealth.

138: *waymenting*   lamenting.

149–50:   these lines were revised in the *New Arcadia* (90) to read:

> Let crows pick out mine eyes, which saw too much:
> If still her mind be such,

153: *resolve*   change their state, evaporate.

156–74:   these lines were revised in the *New Arcadia* (90) to read:

> So doth my life within itself dissolve.

Lalus.   So doth my life within itself dissolve
That I am like a flower
New plucked from the place where it did breed,
160   Life showing, dead indeed:
Such force hath love above poor Nature's power.

Dorus.   Such force hath love above poor Nature's power
That I grow like a shade
Which, being naught, seems somewhat to the eyen,
165   While that one body shine.
O he is marred that is for others made.

Lalus.   O he is marred that is for others made.
Which thought doth mar my piping declaration,
Thinking how it hath marred my shepherd's trade.
170   Now my hoarse voice doth fail this occupation,
And others long to tell their love's condition:
Of singing take to thee the reputation.

> *Dorus.* Of singing take to thee the reputation,
> New friend of mine: I yield to thy ability;

I.2 Dorus

9: *choler adusted*   choler (one of the four bodily humours) loses moisture when overheated, giving rise to melancholy.

12: *Heraclitus*   the weeping philosopher (*c*.540–*c*.480 BC), who bewailed 'the weakness of mankind and the wretchedness of the world' (*Apology for Poetry*, p. 116).

14: *a beauty divine*   Dorus' beloved, Pamela.

I.4 Dorus and Cleophila

2: *desert*   wild, uncultivated place.

13: *unfortunate Echo*   the wood-nymph who pined away to a mere voice for love of Narcissus (Ovid, *Metamorphoses*, iii.359–401).

15: *Idea*   the Platonic Idea, or ideal absolute; in this case, Pamela.

26: *Self-lost*   lost through one's own action (antedating *OED*, 1645).

38: *Which*   who.

40: *Silly*   harmless, innocent.

57: *grateful*   pleasing.

57 and 81: *richesse*   wealth, opulence.

75: *Olympus*   the highest mountain in Greece, home of the gods.

77: *emmet*   ant.

93: *silly*   weak, frail.

97: *carking*   burdening, fretting.
     to estates which still be adherent   which are still an attribute of high position.

116: *Laurel*   'victory' (this, and the following five glosses are Sidney's own).
     myrrh   'lamentation'.

117: *Olive*   'quietness'.

118: *Myrtle*   'love'.
     willow   'refusal'.

119: *Cypress*   'death'.

121: *boy*   Cupid.

138: *sensive*   having senses, capable of sensation.

153: *hostry*   hostelry, inn.

173: *moanful*   full of moaning or lamentation (first citation in *OED*).

The Second Book or Act

II. ii Basilius

Basilius ('king') falls in love with Cleophila, whom he mistakenly believes to be a woman.

5: *Ne*   nor.

II. iii Dorus

In this and the next poem, Dorus woos Pamela while appearing to address his words to her servant, Mopsa.

II. iv Dorus

5: *wanhope*   hopelessness, despair.

II. v Philoclea

Philoclea ('lover of glory')   younger daughter of Basilius, and beloved of Pyrocles/
Cleophila.
10: *after-livers*   survivors (first compounded by Sidney; first citation in *OED* is
Apology for Poetry, p. 116).
12: *Shame*   modesty.

II. vi Philoclea

1: *blaze*   proclaim, publish.
8: *store*   abundance.

II. vii Cleophila

In love with Philoclea, Cleophila also receives the unwanted attentions of Basilius
and his wife, Gynecia.
9: *god*   Cupid.
11: *silly*   innocent.

II. viii Cleophila

11: *refrain*   hold back, restrain.

II. ix Gynecia

Gynecia ('womanly')   the wife of Basilius, in love with Cleophila whom she
correctly perceives to be a man in disguise.

II. x Dorus

2: *sun's approach*   the favour of Pamela.
8: *murrain*   pestilence, plague.
10: *stricken*   lowered.

II. xi Philisides

Philisides ('star-lover')   a melancholy shepherd whose name anticipates that of
Astrophil as well as being a play on Sidney's own.
2: *My sun is gone*   Philisides' beloved, Mira, has withdrawn her favour.
10: *hoised*   hoist, raised.

II. xii Dametas

4: *bobbed*   struck, hit.
   bobs   blows.

8: *make brave lame shows*   give a resplendent yet paltry exhibition; show how their courage has lamed them.

II.xiii Basilius, Gynecia, Pamela and Philoclea

5: *Python*   Apollo's first feat was to win Delphi from its guardian deity, the dragon, Python.

7: *Latona*   Leto, the mother of Apollo by Jupiter, was denied a resting-place and aid in childbirth by the jealous Juno.

10: *brickle*   fragile, brittle.

11: *foresightful*   possessing foresight (first citation in *OED*).

The Second Eclogues

II.1 Dicus and Dorus

Dicus   a shepherd.

17: *muett*   mute.

35: *proof*   experience.

45: *sparefulness*   frugality (first citation in *OED*).

52: *refection*   refreshment, a meal.

63: *shadows cumber not*   all the *OA* manuscripts read 'shadow cumbers not', but I follow Robertson in adopting the reading of *90* here for the sake of the rhyme.

67: *mischiefs*   misfortunes.

96: *franzy*   frenzy.

104: *seal*   stamp, token.

113: *sightfulness*   power of seeing (first citation in *OED*).

117: *Her only cure from surfeit woes can diet me*   Only she can regulate my excessive suffering for her.

121: *for ay*   for ever.

124: *mortify*   kill, put to death.

126: *changeless*   unchanging, immutable (first citation in *OED*).

II.2 Philisides

3: *Echo*   see note to *OA* I.4, line 13. The echo device was common in Renaissance verse as an emblem both of self-love and of unrequited love.

33: *recks*   regards, cares for.

   Oughts   obligations, duties (antedating *OED*, 1678); also, possibly, *orts*: scraps, leftovers.

II.3 Cleophila

21: *fall of old Thebes*   the ancient city destroyed by the Epigonoi shortly before the Trojan war.

23: *Hector*   leader of the Trojans during the siege of Troy; his funeral concludes the *Iliad*.

26: *Europe*   Europa, the princess of Tyre whom Zeus seduced in the form of a bull (Ovid, *Metamorphoses*, ii.833–75).

27: *Adonis' end, Venus' net*   Adonis was the beautiful youth, beloved of Venus, who was killed by a boar while hunting; on discovering Venus' adulterous affair with Mars, Vulcan trapped them both in a net, thus exposing them to the ridicule of the gods (Ovid, *Metamorphoses*, x.708–39; iv.169–89).
28: *The sleepy kiss the Moon stale*   the kiss which the moon stole from her beloved, Endymion, while he slept.

II.4 Cleophila

15: *rampire*   rampart.
16: *Undermined*   mined or excavated as part of a military operation.

II.5 Dorus

14: *if be not*   if it be not.
20: *humorists*   persons of disturbed temperament or humour.
23: *cumber*   burden.

The Third Book or Act

III.i Dorus

8: *bark*   small ship.
9: *despoils*   plunder, booty.

III.ii Dorus

2: *them*   those whom.
3: *kens*   recognizes, catches sight of.
4: *marting*   trading.
13: *mated*   confounded, amazed.

III.iii Cleophila

3: *race*   strong current.
4: *shelf*   ledge, rock.

III.iv Basilius

12: *defaste*   defaced.
14: *raste*   razed.

III.v Cleophila

13: *this place*   the cave within which Cleophila sings this song.

III.vi Gynecia

4: *wrack*   ruin.
6: *ireful*   angry, wrathful.

8: *Receipt*   reception, admittance.
18: *his*   my mind's.

III. vii Gynecia

1: *sun*   Cleophila/Pyrocles.
12: *Tire on*   prey greedily upon (as a hawk).
14: *mazed*   stupefied, dazed.
20: *plain*   lament.

III. viii Charita

Charita ('love')   a fictional shepherdess, invented by Dorus, and supposedly beloved of Dametas.
9: *my sight*   from my eyes, from seeing me.

III. ix Dametas

Dorus claims that it was with this poem that Dametas answered Charita, thus persuading Miso of her husband's infidelity.
4: *stain*   out-do, eclipse.
8: *plum*   plump.
13: *cruds*   curds.
14: *sleekstone*   a polishing stone.
16: *brawn*   muscle.
18: *gage*   pledge.

III. x Pamela

Pamela ('all sweetness')   elder daughter of Basilius, beloved of Musidorus/Dorus.
2: *grave*   engrave.
6: *ey'n*   eyes.
8: *rine*   rind, bark.

III. xi Musidorus

Musidorus   no longer in disguise, Musidorus assumes his real name.
14: *rine*   see note to III.x, line 8 above.
15: *alonely*   solely, exclusively.

III. xii Pamela

9: *sundry gifts*   the posy of flowers Pamela makes while singing this song.

III. xiii Musidorus

4: *waxen wings*   alluding to Icarus, whose wings of wax and feathers melted when he flew too close to the sun, causing him to plummet to his death in the sea (Ovid, *Metamorphoses*, viii.183–235).

11: *gaged*   pledged

III.xv Basilius

4: *wights*   people

III.xvi Philoclea

1: *the subject of*   under the dominion of.
2: *unrefrained*   unrestrained, unchecked.
4: *mine own*   Pyrocles/Cleophila, who has since declared his love for Philoclea and been accepted as her suitor.
6: *gripe*   grip.
11: *hap*   fortune.

III.xvii Gynecia

6: *becomes*   befits.
9: *ill-consorted*   inharmonious, discordant.
16: *stops*   frets.

III.xviii Basilius

7: *eachwhere*   everywhere.

III.xix Cleophila

An elaborately punning poem in which the rhyme words (*light*, *bait*, *right*, *wait* and *show*) are repeated, but each time in a different sense.
1: *Aurora*   the goddess of the dawn.
2: *bait*   lure.
4: *wait*   attend.
5: *light*   alight.
6: *bait*   refreshment.
10: *bait*   worry, harass.
11: *right*   rite.

III.xx Cleophila

13: *Eye-hopes*   hopes arising from appearances (only citation in *OED*).

III.xxi Basilius

Basilius looks forward to an assignation with Cleophila, unaware that she has tricked him into sleeping with his own wife, Gynecia, thus fulfilling the oracle's prophecy that 'Thou with thy wife adult'ry shalt commit.' See also *OA* IV.i.
11: *Fore-felt*   previously felt (first citation in *OED*).

III. xxiii Philoclea

3: *roll*   scroll.
7: *remorsed*   affected with remorse (first citation in *OED*).

III. xxiv Pyrocles repeating Philisides

As Pyrocles and Philoclea consummate their love for the first time, Sidney's narrator occupies the reader's attention with this highly erotic blazon, composed by Philisides 'of his unkind mistress' (Robertson, p. 238) and here recalled by Pyrocles.

10: *bows*   so written for the rhyme; grammatically the line should read 'bow'.
23: *kindly*   natural.
24: *Aurora-like*   like the dawn.
25: *queen-apple*   an old variety of apple with red skin.
31: *incirclets*   spirals, convolutions (first citation in *OED*).
43: *ward*   a guarded place, as the court of a castle.
51: *say*   assay, trial.
55: *pommels*   round bosses.
57: *porphyry*   a hard red stone.
60: *milken name*   the Milky Way.
91: *Albion cliffs*   the white cliffs of Dover.
97: *bought*   curve, bend.
   incaved   hollowed (first citation in *OED*).
103: *Atlas*   the Titan who held up the sky.
110: *mews*   sheds, moults.
112: *comfits*   sweetmeats.
    marchpane   marzipan.
116: *ermelin*   the ermine, believed to give up its life rather than sully its skin, and thus an emblem of purity.
125: *compact*   combination, joining together (antedating *OED*, 1601).
132: *amethysts*   all the *OA* manuscripts use the old spelling 'amatists', punning on the Latin *amare*, 'to love'.

The Third Eclogues

III. 1 Dicus

One of the earliest epithalamia in English, this poem celebrates the wedding of Lalus and Kala.

9: *Hymen*   the deity who presided over weddings.
19: *affects*   affections, kind feelings.
37: *silly*   innocent, helpless.
68: *ay*   ever, always.
80: *mean*   moderation, balance.

III. 2 Philisides

This poem forms a tribute to Hubert Languet (1518–81), the Protestant statesman whom Sidney first met on his continental tour in 1572, and who subsequently became his friend and correspondent. They were together in Vienna in 1573 and 1574. The song here attributed to Languet takes the form of a beast fable, and could be interpreted either as an incitement to rebellion or as an expression of orthodox Tudor absolutism. For studies of the functional ambiguity of the poem see Annabel Patterson, *Censorship and Interpretation* (Madison, WN 1984) and Martin Ratière, *Faire Bitts: Sir Philip Sidney and Renaissance Political Theory* (Pittsburgh, PA 1984). Sidney's fable has affinities with the February eclogue of Spenser's *Shepheardes Calender* (1579) in that it adopts a deliberately archaic and rustic register.

1: *Ister*   the Danube.
2: *couthe*   knew, were familiar with.
4: *gat*   arrived at.
   booth   temporary shelter.
8: *welkin*   sky.
10: *Ycleped*   called.
18: *mickle*   much.
19: *bore*   born.
24: *clerkly rede*   learned counsel, advice.
29: *thilke*   those.
30: *jump*   coinciding, perfectly agreeing.
40: *Coredens*   a pastoral name, possibly alluding to one of Sidney's friends or mentors.
43: *n'ot*   do not know.
44, 60 and 118: *dam*   mother.
45: *woned*   inhabited.
51: *nis*   is not.
62: *bleaing*   bleating.
66: *pewing*   plaintive crying.
68: *seech*   seek.
74: *swink*   labour, toil.
80: *ounce*   lynx.
93: *cony*   rabbit.
97: *mowing*   making faces, grimacing.
124: *ravin*   seizing or devouring prey.
127: *erst*   before.
133: *Tho*   then.
   foen   foes, enemies.
140: *mew*   cage.
149: *gloire*   glory.
157: *stours*   times of turmoil and stress.

The Fourth Book or Act

IV.i Basilius

Basilius continues to labour under the delusion that the woman he has enjoyed is Cleophila (cf. *OA* III.xxi).
2: *affected*   fondly held, cherished (antedating *OED*, 1589).
12: *desert*   uncultivated, wild.

IV.ii Agelastus

Agelastus ('not laughing') once a high-born senator but now a shepherd, Agelastus sings this elegy over the supposedly dead body of Basilius.

1: *causeful*   well-grounded.
22: *imp*   offspring.

The Fourth Eclogues

IV.i Strephon and Klaius

Strephon ('writhe') *and Klaius* ('weep') two gentlemen who became shepherds for love of Urania, supposedly a shepherd's daughter though in fact of high birth.

7–9: *Mercury . . . heav'nly huntress . . . lovely star*   the planets Mercury, the moon (Diana) and Venus.
13: *burgess*   citizen.
23: *Heart-broken*   broken-hearted (antedating *OED*, which gives as its first citation the Countess of Pembroke's translation of Psalm LI, line 49).
25: *swannish*   pertaining to the swan, believed to sing only at the point of death (first citation in *OED*).
28: *desert*   uncultivated, desolate.
42: *serene*   evening dew, thought to be unwholesome or noxious.
61: *she*   Urania.
69: *rase*   rose.
74: *eke*   also.

IV.2 Strephon and Klaius

37: *waste*   wasted.
45: *spend*   destroy.
48: *scope*   intended goal; probably punning on the nautical sense, the length of cable at which a ship rides when at anchor (thus antedating *OED*, 1697).
53: *fast-meaning*   steadfast of purpose.
55: *hire*   reward, recompense, payment.
58: *sprongen*   sprung.
62: *angle*   fishing rod.
63: *torpedo*   the electric ray or cramp fish, which paralyses the fisherman when caught.
72: *basilisk*   the fabulous monster that killed by its look (Pliny, *Natural History*, viii.33).
74: *hap*   fortune.
87: *hent*   seized.

IV. 3 Philisides

2: *depart*   departure.
7 and 85: *concent*   concord, harmony (antedating *OED*, 1585).
16: *hatch*   plot, devise; also, perhaps, close, cover: see note to *AS* 38, line 2 (p. 206).
30 and 31: *corse*   corpse.

36: *Samothea*   a name for Ancient Britain.
   whilom   once, formerly.
39: *calmy*   tranquil, peaceful.
61 and 145: *doom*   judgement.
67: *prest*   ready, close to hand.
83 and 182: *erst*   before.
84: *mother*   mother-of-pearl.
   seed   tiny seed pearls.
93: *Mira* ('wonderful')   beloved of Philisides.
103: *moony*   belonging to the moon (first citation in *OED*).
115: *stay*   condition.
145: *Paris*   the Trojan prince who, when asked to settle a dispute between Juno, Venus and Diana as to which was the most beautiful, chose Venus.
147: *smirkly*   smirkingly (first citation in *OED*).
161: *Styx*   the river of the underworld; also, according to Herodotus, a small, reputedly poisonous river in Arcadia by which solemn oaths were sworn (vi.74).

IV. 4 Philisides

1: *caitiff*   miserable.
3: *monument*   written document.
19: *lief*   precious, dear.
20: *Nestor*   an old king, represented in the *Iliad* as having outlived two generations.
28: *hugy*   huge.
36: *unendly*   unending (first citation in *OED*).
59: *Cimmerian*   describing a legendary kingdom on the edge of the world, shrouded in perpetual darkness (antedates *OED*, 1598).
66: *pedant*   schoolmaster (antedates *OED*, 1588).

The Fifth Book or Act

V.i Musidorus

Musidorus sings this song as he and Pyrocles are in prison, awaiting execution for their attempts on the two princesses, Pamela and Philoclea.
9: *owly*   owlish (first citation in *OED*).

Poems from *Certain Sonnets*

Probably composed between 1577 and 1581, the *Certain Sonnets* form a group of thirty-two poems and verse translations on various subjects. The collection begins with a yielding to love (*CS* i, ii) and ends with the renunciation of desire in favour of 'higher things' (*CS* viii, ix), a traditional structure that has led some critics to look for a thematic coherence within the sequence. The miscellaneous nature of the anthology, however, is suggested by the way it was entitled in each of its sixteenth-century versions: 'divers and sundry sonnets' (Clifford manuscript), 'certain loose sonnets and songs' (Bodleian manuscript), and 'Certain Sonnets', the title in the 1598 folio and in all subsequent printed editions.

i

13: *grateful guardian*   pleasing gaoler.

ii

6: *affects*   affections, kindly feelings.
10: *Dead-palsy sick*   suffering complete paralysis (*dead-palsy* antedates *OED*, 1592).

iii

Some commentators suggest that the woman's pain here refers to the toothache, although a note in one of the manuscript versions of the poem suggests smallpox, a disease capable of inflicting the 'cruel stains' of line 12. Sidney's mother was severely scarred by smallpox in 1562, and the image of the beautiful woman's scarred face recurs in the story of Parthenia in the *New Arcadia* (Skretkowicz, p. 30). The identity of the lady in this and the following poem is unknown.

v

This poem is a close translation of Horace, *Odes*, ii.10.
5: *forworn*   decayed, ancient.
14: *cithern*   a stringed, guitar-like instrument.

vi

Two manuscripts entitle this poem: 'Upon the device of a seeled dove, with this word of Petrarch: *Non mi vuol e non mi trahe d'impaccio*' ('[Love] does not want me for his own, nor does he release me from my trouble', from *Canzoniere*, 134).
1: *seeled-up*   the eyelids of birds were 'seeled' or stitched together as part of the taming process.

vii

Two manuscripts and *98* entitle this poem 'A Farewell'.

ix

6: *yoke*   cf. Matthew xi.30, 'my yoke is easy, and my burden light.'
15: *Splendidis longum valedico nugis*   'I bid a long farewell to splendid trifles.' The Ottley manuscript reads: '*Virtus secura sequatur*': 'Let virtue follow in safety', a motto which Sidney used elsewhere; see Katherine Duncan-Jones, 'Sidney's Personal Imprese', *Journal of the Warburg and Courtauld Institutes* 33 (1970), p. 323.

Astrophil and Stella

Both external and internal evidence suggest that Sidney wrote *Astrophil and Stella* between 1581 and 1582. The sequence of 108 sonnets and eleven songs charts the frustrated desire of Astrophil ('star-lover') for Stella ('star'), and is modelled broadly on the pattern of Petrarch's *Canzoniere*. Astrophil's name, his identification with Stella's sparrow, Philip (*AS* 83), his constant references to horsemanship (philip: 'horse-lover', see *AS* 4, 28, 49, 98), and his allusions to the Sidney arms (*AS* 65, 72) were among the many signals that led Sidney's contemporaries to identify the poetic voice with that of the author. Similar hints, including the references to 'Rich' (*AS* 24, 35, 37) and to the Devereux arms (*AS* 13), prompted Sidney's earliest readers to identify Stella with Penelope Devereux, the eldest daughter of the first Earl of Essex, who came to court in 1581 (then aged 18), and who was married, apparently against her will, to Robert, Lord Rich, in November of that year. Stella appears throughout the sonnet sequence as virtuous and unyielding, a conflation of the traditional pose of the besought mistress with the authentic portrayal of an actual married woman.

Courtly texts lend themselves to personal identifications of this kind, and, with its references to contemporary political issues and events at court (e.g. *AS* 30, 41, 53), *Astrophil and Stella* clearly invites them. What was once read as the autobiographical account of an intense personal experience, or as a purely artistic 'prolonged lyrical meditation' (C. S. Lewis, *English Literature in the Sixteenth Century* (Oxford, 1954), p. 327) has, however, been seen more recently to raise incisive questions about the ways in which a text relates to its immediate social, political and historical context. See, for example, Arthur Marotti, '"Love is Not Love": Elizabethan Sonnet Sequences and the Social Order', *Journal of English Literary History* 49 (1982), pp. 396–428; Maureen Quilligan, 'Sidney and his Queen', in Heather Dubrow and Richard Strier, eds., *The Historical Renaissance* (Chicago, 1988); and Peter Stallybrass and Ann Rosalind Jones, 'The Politics of *Astrophil and Stella*', *Studies in English Literature* 24 (1984), pp. 53–68.

Ringler describes how the songs and sonnets in *Astrophil and Stella* mark a new departure in English poetry, for Sidney introduces and experiments with a whole series of technical and metrical forms, including Petrarchan rhyme schemes, sonnets in alexandrines (*AS* 1, 6, 8, 76, 77, 103), and the trochaic metre of songs ii, iv, viii and ix. In 1599, John Hoskins was moved to illustrate 'all the figures of rhetoric' from the *Arcadia*, and the same could equally be said of the sonnet sequence, with its pervasive use of rhetorical figures, among them *gradatio* (*AS* 1, 2, 24, 44, 68, 75), *antimetabole* (*AS* 10, 42, 60, 82, 84, 87), oxymoron (*AS* 21, 32, 41, 60, 106) and paronomasia (*AS* 15, 16, 36, 66, 79). The sonnets' highly disciplined form artfully creates the illusion of sincerity and spontaneity, and provides a structured literary framework for Astrophil's lack of emotional discipline. The initial image of Astrophil as a petulant schoolboy learning his lesson becomes a habitual pose (*AS* 1, 16, 18, 19, 21, 23, 46, 56, 63, 79), while the suggestion that Astrophil is 'somewhat kin' to Cupid (*AS* 65), and the references to his 'young mind', 'brain' and 'soul' (*AS* 21, 23, 108), all associate his passion with immature sexual desire, what Castiglione had called the 'bitterness and wretchedness that young men feel' (*The Book of the Courtier*, trans. Sir Thomas Hoby, ed. W. H. D. Rouse (1928), p. 317).

Astrophil and Stella ends unresolved, the failure to move his mistress typifying the Petrarchan scenario to which Astrophil, for all his protestations to the contrary (*AS* 15), largely conforms. Like so many traditional courtly debates in which questions of love were discussed but left undecided, *Astrophil and Stella* remains inconclusive, its very structure hinting at the lack of an ending: the 108 sonnets and the 108 stanzas that go to make up the songs allude to the number of suitors who unsuccessfully woo Penelope in the *Odyssey*. For additional further reading, see: Joseph Lowenstein, 'Sidney's Truant Pen', *Modern Language Quarterly* 46 (1985), pp. 128–42; and Thomas Roche, '*Astrophil and Stella*: A Radical Reading', *Spenser Studies* 3 (1982), pp. 139–91.

Although Sidney provided no title for the sequence himself, the first printed edition was entitled *Syr P. S. his Astrophel and Stella* (1591), from which arose the alternative if erroneous spelling of Astrophil's name. In order to retain the meaning ('star-lover') and the pun on Sidney's own name, Philip, Astrophil is the correct form.

2

1: *dribbed*   wide of the mark.
3: *mine*   tunnel dug during siege operations.
10: *Muscovite*   in the sixteenth century, popularly believed to prefer tyranny to freedom.

3

1: *sisters nine*   the Muses.
3: *Pindar's apes*   imitators of Pindar (518–after 446 BC), the Greek lyric poet.

4

5: *Cato*   Cato 'the Elder' or 'the Censor' (234–149 BC), a Roman disciplinarian proverbial for his severity.

5

2: *inward light*   reason.
13: *our country*   heaven.

6

5–6:   Jove raped Europa, Leda and Danaë by transforming himself into a bull, a swan, and a shower of gold (Ovid, *Metamorphoses*, vi.103–14).
6: *Broidered*   embroidered.
  powdered   sprinkled, spangled.

7

6: *strength*   strengthen.
8: *sun-like*   resembling the sun (antedating *OED*, 1596).

8

1: *Greece*   in the sixteenth century Greece was part of the Ottoman empire and lay under the power of the proverbially cruel Turks.

6: *clips*   embraces.

9

6: *porphyr*   a hard red stone.
12: *Of touch they are*   touchstone, a glossy black stone used to test the purity of gold and silver; also associated with jet, thought to attract light objects such as straws with static electricity induced by rubbing.

10

2: *brabbling*   cavilling, quibbling.
11: *fence*   the attitude of self-defence in sword-fighting.

11

9: *cabinet*   a case for valuables, treasures.
11: *pit-fold*   pit-fall, a trap for birds.

12

2: *day-nets*   nets used for catching larks and other small birds.
10: *got up*   made.

13

3–6:   Jove transformed himself into an eagle in order to carry off the beautiful Trojan youth, Ganymede; Mars had a love affair with Venus (Ovid, *Metamorphoses*, x.155–61; iv.167–89).
3: *sables*   sable, black.
5: *vert*   green.
11: *gules*   red.
13: *blaze*   blazon, describe the arms of; also, to shine, glow.
14: *gentlemen*   those entitled to coats of arms.

14

2: *gripe*   griffin, vulture, alluding to the vulture which tore out Prometheus' liver as an eternal punishment for his gift of fire to mankind.
   tire   tear, prey greedily upon.
5: *rhubarb*   a purgative.

15

1: *purling*   rippling, flowing (first citation in *OED*).
2: *Parnassus*   the sacred mountain of the Muses.
8: *denizened*   naturalized.
9: *far-fet*   far-fetched.
10: *bewray*   expose, reveal.

14: *indite*   express or describe in a literary composition.

17

3: *With pricking shot he did not throughly move*   Cupid failed to wound Mars thoroughly with his piercing arrows.
6: *stripes*   blows.
7: *chafe*   anger, vexation.
13: *wags*   mischievous fellows.

18

1: *checks*   rebukes, reproofs.
    shent   shamed, disgraced.

19

2: *wrack*   ruin.
10–11:   Plato recounts how the Greek scientist, Thales, fell into a well as he was contemplating the stars (*Theaetetus*, 174a), an anecdote which became a commonplace; see 'the astronomer looking to the stars might fall into a ditch', *Apology for Poetry*, p. 104.

20

5: *tyrant*   tyrannical.
6: *level*   aim.
9: *passenger*   passer-by.

21

1: *caustics*   burning, corroding substances.
2: *windlass*   decoy, ensnare (first citation in *OED*).
6: *geres*   sudden fits of passion, changes of mood (see Priscilla Bawcutt, 'A Crux in *Astrophil and Stella*, Sonnet 21', *Notes and Queries* 29 (1982), pp. 406–8).

22

2: *twins*   the zodiacal sign of Gemini, from which the sun emerges in late June.

23

2: *Bewray*   expose, reveal.

24

1: *Rich*   a punning reference to Robert, Lord Rich, the husband of Penelope Devereux (see also *AS* 35 and 37).
3: *Tantal's smart*   the punishment of Tantalus, condemned to perpetual thirst amid water. Tantalus was son of the Titaness, Pluto ('wealth').

25

1: *wisest scholar*   Plato, pupil of Socrates, judged by the Delphic oracle to be the wisest of men. See 'the saying of Plato and Tully ... that who could see virtue would be wonderfully ravished with the love of her beauty', *Apology for Poetry*, p. 119.

26

7: *brawl*   a kind of dance.
9: *unidle*   busy, industrious (first citation in *OED*).

27

5: *doom*   judgement.
12: *overpass*   pass by, ignore.

28

7: *slake*   slacken, loosen.

30

The seven questions with which the 'busy wits' ply Astrophil were political issues topical during the summer of 1582.
1–2:   long a threat to western Europe, the Turks (here represented by their standard, the crescent) were expected to attack Spain at this time.
3–4:   the elected king of Poland (Stephen Báthory) invaded Russia ('*Muscovy*') in 1580 and laid siege to Pskov until December 1581.
5:   three factions (the Catholics, Huguenots and Politiques) struggled for control of France until the accession of Henri IV in 1589.
6:   the Germans (Deutsch) held the Diet of the Holy Roman Empire at Augsburg from July to September 1582.
7–8:   having lost the towns of Breda, Tournai, Oudenarde, Lier and Ninove to the Spaniards between 1581 and 1582, the Dutch placed yet greater hope in their leader, William of Orange.
9–10:   as Lord Deputy Governor of Ireland, Sir Henry Sidney had sought to revive and impose the 'cess' or land tax on the great landowners of Ulster. It was in support of his father's controversial action that Sidney wrote his 'Discourse on Irish Affairs' (1577).
11:   the 'welt'ring' or political agitation of the Scottish court may refer to the intrigues preceding the Raid of Ruthven on 22 August 1582. *98* reads 'no weltring', presumably to avoid giving offence to James VI of Scotland, who, in 1598, was expected to be the future king of England.

32

1: *Morpheus*   son of Somnus (the god of sleep), and skilled in making human forms appear to dreamers (Ovid, *Metamorphoses*, xi. 633–8).
4: *eke*   also.

12: *Ind's*   Indies.

33

Possibly alluding to the abortive scheme to betroth Sidney to Penelope Devereux in 1576, when she would have been thirteen years old.

34

7: *fond ware*   foolish trifles.
8: *close*   private, secret.

35

5: *Nestor*   see note to *OA* IV. 4, line 20 (p. 199).

36

2: *yelden*   surrendered, yielded.

37

5: *Towards Aurora s court*   in the east, possibly alluding to the family seat of Lord Rich, Leighs, in Essex.
13: *make the patents*   constitute the grants, endowments.

38

2: *hatch*   close as with a hatch (first citation in *OED*).
   unbitted   unbridled, unrestrained (first citation in *OED*).
5: *error*   wandering, roaming (antedating *OED* in this sense, 1594).
7: *draught*   draughtsmanship, drawing.

39

2: *baiting place*   resting place.
5: *prease*   press, crowd, throng.
11: *rosy garland*   a garland of silence or secrecy, as in the expression *sub rosa*.

41

Astrophil is presented as taking part in a tournament at court, possibly the spectacular triumph, *The Four Foster Children of Desire*, put on before Queen Elizabeth and the French delegation (negotiating the match with the Duke of Alençon) in May 1581, and in which Sidney participated.
7: *sleight*   skill, dexterity.

44

7: *overthwart*   perverse, contrary.

45

2: *beclouded*   covered with clouds (first citation in *OED*).
7: *gat*   got, obtained.
9: *imaged*   represented by an image (antedating *OED*, 1718).

46

3: *beck*   a nod of the head.
4: *or . . . or*   either . . . or.
13: *miche*   play truant.

47

2: *burning marks*   brands indicating slavery.

49

4: *descry*   declare, disclose.
7: *boss*   metal knob on either side of a horse-bit.
14: *manage*   the training and handling of a horse in its paces (first citation in *OED*).

51

7: *in steed*   instead.
8: *Atlas*   see note to *OA* III.xxiv, line 103 (p. 196).

52

12: *demur*   demurrer, a tactic whereby one party (here Virtue) admits the facts of the other (Love), but denies any legal entitlement by shifting the ground of the argument (whether Stella's 'self' exists on the inside or the outside). This stops the action until the point can be determined by the court.

53

11: *rule*   control (the horse).

54

13: *pies*   magpies.

55

2: *engarland*   put a garland upon (*OED* gives as its first citation *Apology for Poetry*, p. 130).

56

11: *phlegmatique*   phlegmatic, cool.

57

4: *thorough'st*   most piercing.

58

This sonnet refers to the debate in classical rhetoric as to whether the matter of a speech or the manner of its delivery was most important (Cicero, *De Oratore*, iii.223; Quintilian, XI.iii.2–4). See also: 'For if *oratio* next to *ratio*, speech next to reason, be the greatest gift bestowed upon mortality, that cannot be praiseless which doth most polish that blessing of speech,' *Apology for Poetry*, pp. 121–2.
12: *maugre*   in spite of, notwithstanding.

59

6: *prove*   make trial of, test the genuineness of.

61

5: *infelt*   inwardly felt or experienced (first citation in *OED*).
7: *selfness*   self-centredness, egoism (first citation in *OED*).

63

14: *two negatives affirm*   a rule applying to Latin rather than to sixteenth-century English grammar.

First Song

2: *music*   etymologically related to the Muse of line 1.

64

10: *Caesar*   assassinated in 44 BC.

65

14: *arrow head*   probably alluding to Sidney's own arms, a blue arrow head on a gold background.

66

8: *stilts*   crutches.

68

6: *Amphion*   'Amphion was said to move stones with his poetry to build Thebes,' *Apology for Poetry*, p. 96; a Renaissance commonplace.

70

4: *Jove's cup*   Ganymede mixed nectar for Jove.

Second Song

10: *niggard*   miserly.

74

1: *Aganippe*   a spring sacred to the Muses.
2: *Tempe*   the wooded valley in Thessaly where Daphne, pursued by the amorous Apollo, was transformed into a laurel tree (Ovid, *Metamorphoses*, i. 567–9).

75

2: *Edward named fourth*   Edward IV (1442–82), who usurped the throne in 1461 after his father, the Duke of York, was killed fighting the Lancastrians. Edward was notorious among sixteenth-century chroniclers for his licentiousness, and Shakespeare presents him as enjoying 'his hateful luxury / And bestial appetite in change of lust . . . / Even where his raging eye or savage heart, / Without control, lusted to make a prey' (*Richard III*, III.v. 80–84). Astrophil's identification with this king invites a degree of irony at his own expense.
4: *imp*   a term in falconry for engrafting feathers on the wing of a bird in order to restore or improve its powers of flight.
9–11:   Edward IV invaded France (represented by the fleur-de-lis) in 1474, withdrawing after Louis XI ('*Lewis*') paid him a tribute of 75,000 crowns. Although often in league with Scotland (represented by the red or 'bloody' lion), France was not, in fact, 'hedged' or protected by Scotland at this time.
11: *witty*   crafty, cunning.
14:   in 1464 Edward secretly married Lady Elizabeth Grey while the Earl of Warwick (the 'king-maker') was negotiating a marriage for him in France. Warwick drove Edward into exile in 1470, although he was restored to the throne in 1471.

76

5: *Aurora*   see note to *OA* III.xix, line 1 (p. 195).

77

2: *whose lecture*   the reading or perusal of which.
8: *sublime*   extract, distil.

80

3: *stall*   seat of office or dignity.
6: *beautifier*   antedates *OED*, 1612.
8: *honour's grain*   scarlet or crimson.
12: *resty*   restive.

82

3: Narcissus drowned while gazing at his own reflection in a pool (Ovid, *Metamorphoses*, iii. 402–510).
4: Venus appeared naked before Paris.
6: *Hesperian taste* the golden apples guarded by the Hesperides (the daughters of Night and Darkness).

83

1: *Philip* Stella's sparrow, a bird traditionally associated with lechery.
3: *your cut to keep* to behave with propriety, modesty.

Third Song

4: *Amphion* see note to *AS* 68, line 6 (p. 208).
7–10: Thoas, an Arcadian youth, was rescued from bandits by a dragon to whom he had shown kindness; an eagle sacrificed itself in the funeral pyre of the maiden who had loved and nurtured it (Pliny, *Natural History*, viii. 61; x. 18).

85

6: *Not pointing to fit folks each undercharge* not delegating duties to the appropriate people.
13: *indentures* contracts.

Fourth Song

21: *hap* fortune.

86

3: *self-condemning* condemning myself (antedates *OED*, 1647).
4: *gripe* seize, grip.
5: *ermine* see note to *OA* III. xxiv, line 116 (p. 196).

Fifth Song

11: *lay* lyric, song.
26: *ambrosian* divinely fragrant (antedating *OED*, 1632).
36: *babies* dolls.
    shrewd mischievous, naughty.
62: *appeach* accuse, impeach.
68: *vagabonding*: vagrant-like (first citation in *OED*).
69: *son . . . mother* Cupid and Venus.
83: *refuse* refusal.
88: *froward* perverse, contrary.

Sixth Song

3 and 53: *whether* which.
25: *loft'ly* loftily (as 'loftly', the first citation in *OED*).

42: *exceptions*   legal objections.

Eighth Song

19: *arms crossed*   the traditional pose of the melancholic.
63: *witty*   endowed with reason.

Ninth Song

19: *persever*   persevere.
23: *caitiff*   wretched, miserable.
49: *blaying*   bleating.

87

8: *sadded*   saddened, made sorrowful.

88

3–4: *she | That to win me, oft shows a present pay*   another woman, whose presence (unlike Stella's absence) offers immediate satisfaction or contentment.
8: *cates*   dainties, delicacies.

90

8: *a poet's name*   'I will give you a nearer example of myself, who (I know not by what mischance) in these my not old years and idlest times having slipped into the title of a poet,' *Apology for Poetry*, p. 95.
10: *laud*   praise.

91

11: *wood-globes*   wooden globes showing the constellations.

92

1: *Indian ware*   exotic and precious material.
3: *cutted*   laconic, concise.
5: *total*   brief (only citation in *OED* in this sense).

Tenth Song

25: *grateful*   pleasing.
33: *lickerous*   salacious, lecherous.
43: *surcease*   put a stop to.

93

11: *'quit*   acquit.

94

3: *inbent*   directed inwards (first citation in *OED*).
10: *caitiff*   captive, prisoner, poor wretch.

96

2: *kind*   nature.
9: *mazeful*   bewildering, confounding (antedating *OED*, 1595).
11: *ghastliness*   horror, frightfulness (antedating *OED*, 1591).

97

1: *Dian*   goddess of the moon.
4: *standing*   a hunter's station or stand from which to shoot game.
8: *dight*   dress.

98

4: *lee*   sheltered from the wind.
7: *galled*   sore from chafing.

99

3: *mark-wanting*   lacking a target (not in *OED*).
9: *charm*   chirp, warble.

101

7: *inseparate*   inseparable (first citation in *OED*).
11: *prest*   ready, prompt.

102

5: *vade*   fade.
9: *Galen's adoptive sons*   doctors, followers of the Greek physician, Galen (AD 129–99).
10: *hackney on*   ride stumblingly, as on a worn-out horse.

103

9: *Aeol's youths*   breezes, sons of Aeolus, the god of winds.

Eleventh Song

37: *anger*   angry.
42: *Argus*   the herdsman transformed by Juno into a many-eyed dog and set to spy on Jove's mistress, Io (Ovid, *Metamorphoses*, i.622–746).

106

3: *Bare me in hand*   deceived, misled me.

107

7: *lieutenancy*   delegated authority or command.

Poems from *The Psalms of David*

Evidence suggests that Sidney's metaphrase of the Psalms was a late work, probably begun after *Astrophil and Stella* (Ringler, pp. 500–501). At the time of his death, Sidney had versified only the first forty-three, and these were then revised and the sequence as a whole completed by his sister, the Countess of Pembroke. Although circulated widely in manuscript, the text was not published until 1823. For an edition of the completed version, see J. C. A. Rathmell, ed., *The Psalms of Sir Philip Sidney and the Countess of Pembroke* (New York, 1963).

In his poem 'Upon the translation of the Psalms by Sir Philip Sidney and the Countess of Pembroke', John Donne wrote that 'They tell us why, they teach us how to sing.' It was the song-like quality of the biblical Psalms that Sidney most admired in his *Apology for Poetry*, and, drawing on one of his sources, *Les CL Pseaumes de David* (1562) by Clement Marot and Theodore Beza, but introducing many new forms of his own, Sidney presents the Psalms as an opportunity for metrical experiment and display. Each Psalm takes a different stanzaic form, the sheer diversity and variety of styles serving to set forth 'the inconceivable excellencics of God' (*Apology for Poetry*, p. 101). For a recent study, see Rivkah Zim, *English Metrical Psalms: Poetry as Praise and Prayer 1535–1601* (Cambridge, 1987).

Psalm XII

5: *abject*   degraded, despicable.
8: *cozening*   deceitful, fraudulent.
18: *Maugre*   in spite of, notwithstanding.
20: *throughly*   thoroughly.

Psalm XXII

3: *unhealthful*   unhealthy (first citation in *OED*).
10: *lauds*   praises.
14: *appalled*   dismayed, disappointed.
18: *mows*   grimaces.
20: *lust*   pleasure, delight.
27: *madded*   enraged (first citation in *OED*).
28: *Bashan*   a fertile region in Israel.
32: *wried*   twisted out of shape.
35: *potsherd*   fragment of pottery.
39: *bawling*   howling, yelping (antedates *OED*, 1594).
42: *rehearsed*   enumerated.
48: *desolated*   made desolate (first citation in *OED*).
    dogged   malicious, spiteful.

Psalm XXIII

13: *besett'st*   surround, encircle.

Psalm XXVIII

10: *'suing*   pursuing.
20: *guerdon*   reward, recompense.

Psalm XXXV

25 and 29: *bare*   bore.
30: *ware*   wore.
39: *abjects*   outcasts.
50: *fleer*   gibe, jeer.
53: *mowing*   grimacing.

Index of First Lines

A hateful cure with hate to heal 33
A strife is grown between Virtue and Love 125
Ah bed, the field where joy's peace some do see 164
Alas, have I not pain enough, my friend 106
Alas, whence came this change of looks? If I 147
All what you are still one, his own to find 52
And do I see some cause a hope to feed 133
Apollo great, whose beams the greater world do light 33
As good to write as for to lie and groan 119
As I my little flock on *Ister* bank 67
Aurora, now thou show'st thy blushing light 56

Be your words made (good sir) of Indian ware 160
Beauty hath force to catch the human sight 56
Because I breathe not love to every one 126
Because I oft, in dark abstracted guise 112

Come, *Dorus*, come, let songs thy sorrows signify 12
Come, *Espilus*, come now declare thy skill 3
Come, let me write. 'And to what end?' To ease 116
Come shepherd's weeds, become your master's mind 10
Come sleep, O sleep, the certain knot of peace 118
Cupid, because thou shin'st in *Stella*'s eyes 105

Dear, why make you more of a dog than me? 128
Desire, though thou my old companion art 136
Dian, that fain would cheer her friend the Night 164
Do not disdain, O straight upraised pine 51
Dorus, tell me, where is thy wonted motion 34
Doubt there hath been, when with his golden chain 128
Doubt you to whom my Muse these notes intendeth 131

Envious wits, what hath been mine offence 167

Fair eyes, sweet lips, dear heart, that foolish I 120
Fair rocks, goodly rivers, sweet woods, when shall I see peace? 37
Feed on my sheep; my charge, my comfort, feed 31
Fie, school of Patience, fie; your lesson is 127
Fly, fly, my friends, I have my death-wound, fly 109
Fortune, Nature, Love, long have contended about me 17

Get hence foul grief, the canker of the mind 57

Go, my flock, go get you hence 156
Good brother *Philip*, I have borne you long 143
Grief, find the words, for thou hast made my brain 162

Hark, plaintful ghosts! Infernal furies, hark 48
Have I caught my heav'nly jewel 136
Having this day my horse, my hand, my lance 119
Highway, since you my chief *Parnassus* be 144
His mother dear *Cupid* offended late 107
Hope, art thou true, or dost thou flatter me? 133
How is my sun, whose beams are shining bright 49

I cursed thee oft, I pity now thy case 122
I joy in grief, and do detest all joys 76
I might, unhappy word, O me, I might 115
I never drank of *Aganippe* well 138
I on my horse, and Love on me doth try 123
I see the house; my heart thyself contain 144
If mine eyes can speak to do hearty errand 18
If *Orpheus'* voice had force to breathe such music's love 143
In a grove most rich of shade 153
In highest way of heav'n the sun did ride 110
In martial sports I had my cunning tried 125
In nature apt to like when I did see 107
In truth, O Love, with what a boyish kind 104
In vain, mine eyes, you labour to amend 27
It is most true, that eyes are formed to serve 101

Lady, reserved by the heav'ns to do pastors' company honour 19
Late tired with woe, e'en ready for to pine 130
Leave me, O Love, which reachest but to dust 95
Leave off my sheep: it is no time to feed 32
Let dainty wits cry on the sisters nine 100
Let mother earth now deck herself in flowers 64
Let not old age disgrace my high desire 27
Like as the dove which seeled-up doth fly 93
Like diverse flowers, whose diverse beauties serve 52
Like some weak lords, neighboured by mighty kings 113
Lock up, fair lids, the treasures of my heart 53
Lord, help, it is high time for me to call 175
Love, born in *Greece*, of late fled from his native place 102
Love, by sure proof I may call thee unkind 132
Love still a boy, and oft a wanton is 137
Loved I am, and yet complain of love 30
Loving in truth, and fain in verse my love to show 99

Morpheus, the lively son of deadly sleep 115
Muses, I oft invoked your holy aid 126
My God, my God, why hast Thou me forsaken? 176
My lute, within thyself thy tunes enclose 55

My mouth doth water, and my breast doth swell 117
My Muse may well grudge at my heav'nly joy 135
My Muse what ails this ardour 40
My sheep are thoughts, which I both guide and serve 28
My true love hath my heart, and I have his 49
My words I know do well set forth my mind 121
My words, in hope to blaze my steadfast mind 29

No more, my dear, no more these counsels try 132
Not at first sight, nor with a dribbed shot 99
Now that of absence the most irksome night 158
Now was our heav'nly vault deprived of the light 79
Nymph of the garden where all beauties be 142

O absent presence, *Stella* is not here 170
O dear life, when shall it be 160
O eyes, which do the spheres of beauty move 120
O fate, O fault, O curse, child of my bliss 162
O grammar rules, O now your virtues show 130
O happy *Thames*, that didst my *Stella* bear 167
O how the pleasant airs of true love be 140
O joy, too high for my low style to show 134
O kiss, which dost those ruddy gems impart 142
O night, the ease of care, the pledge of pleasure 72
O stealing time, the subject of delay 54
O sweet woods, the delight of solitariness! 43
O tears, no tears, but rain from beauty's skies 165
O words which fall like summer dew on me 50
O you that hear this voice 150
Of all the kings that ever here did reign 138
Oft have I mused, but now at length I find 94
Oft with true sighs, oft with uncalled tears 129
On *Cupid*'s bow how are my heart-strings bent 108
Only joy, now here you are 145
Out, traitor absence: dar'st thou counsel me 158
Over these brooks trusting to ease mine eyes 30

Pardon mine ears; both I and they do pray 124
Phoebus farewell, a sweeter saint I serve 47
Phoebus was judge between *Jove*, *Mars*, and Love 105

Queen Virtue's court, which some call *Stella*'s face 103

Reason, in faith thou art well served, that still 104
Reason, tell me thy mind, if here be reason 42
Rich fools there be, whose base and filthy heart 111

She comes, and straight therewith her shining twins do move 139
Silvanus long in love, and long in vain 4
Since Nature's works be good, and death doth serve 88

Since, shunning pain, I ease can never find 91
Since so mine eyes are subject to your sight 28
Since that the stormy rage of passions dark 47
Since wailing is a bud of causeful sorrow 72
Some lovers speak, when they their Muses entertain 101
Soul's joy, bend not those morning stars from me 123
Speak Thou for me against wrong-speaking foes 182
Stella is sick, and in that sick-bed lies 166
Stella oft sees the very face of woe 121
Stella, since thou so right a princess art 170
Stella, the fullness of my thoughts of thee 124
Stella, the only planet of my light 134
Stella, think not that I by verse seek fame 159
Stella, whence doth this new assault arise 117
Stella, while now by honour's cruel might 159
Sweet glove, the witness of my secret bliss 45
Sweet kiss, thy sweets I fain would sweetly indite 141
Sweet swelling lip, well mayst thou swell in pride 141

The curious wits, seeing dull pensiveness 110
The Lord, the Lord my shepherd is 179
The love which is imprinted in my soul 58
The merchant man, whom gain doth teach the sea 45
The merchant man, whom many seas have taught 46
The scourge of life, and death's extreme disgrace 92
The wisest scholar of the wight most wise 111
This night, while sleep begins with heavy wings 118
Those looks, whose beams be joy, whose motion is delight 139
Thou blind man's mark, thou fool's self-chosen snare 94
Thou Pain, the only guest of loathed constraint 92
Though dusty wits dare scorn astrology 112
Thought, with good cause thou lik'st so well the night 163
Thy elder care shall from thy careful face 9
To one whose state is raised over all 3
To Thee, Lord, my cry I send 180
Transformed in show, but more transformed in mind 9

Unhappy sight, and hath she vanished by 169
Unto the caitiff wretch whom long affliction holdeth 84

Virtue, alas, now let me take some rest 100
Virtue, beauty, and speech, did strike, wound, charm 57

What, have I thus betrayed my liberty? 112
What length of verse can serve brave Mopsa's good to show 9
What may words say, or what may words not say 116
What tongue can her perfections tell 59
When far-spent night persuades each mortal eye 165
When I was forced from Stella ever dear 157
When Love, puffed up with rage of high disdain 91

When my good angel guides me to the place 129
When Nature made her chief work, *Stella*'s eyes 102
When sorrow (using mine own fire's might) 171
When two suns do appear 55
Where be those roses gone, which sweetened so our eyes? 166
Whether the Turkish new moon minded be 114
While favour fed my hope, delight with hope was brought 147
'Who is it that this dark night 168
Who will in fairest book of Nature know 135
Whose senses in so ill consort their step-dame Nature lays 152
Why dost thou haste away 53
With how sad steps, O Moon, thou climb'st the skies 114
With two strange fires of equal heat possessed 31
With what sharp checks I in myself am shent 108
Woe, having made with many fights his own 127

Ye goat-herd gods, that love the grassy mountains 74
Ye living powers enclosed in stately shrine 29
Yet sighs, dear sighs, indeed true friends you are 163
You better sure shall live, not evermore 93
You goodly pines, which still with brave ascent 51
You that do search for every purling spring 106
You that with allegory's curious frame 113
Your words my friend (right healthful caustics) blame 109

Discover more about our forthcoming books through Penguin's FREE newspaper...

READ MORE IN PENGUIN

In every corner of the world, on every subject under the sun, Penguin represents quality and variety – the very best in publishing today.

For complete information about books available from Penguin – including Puffins, Penguin Classics and Arkana – and how to order them, write to us at the appropriate address below. Please note that for copyright reasons the selection of books varies from country to country.

In the United Kingdom: Please write to *Dept. JC, Penguin Books Ltd, FREEPOST, West Drayton, Middlesex UB7 OBR*

If you have any difficulty in obtaining a title, please send your order with the correct money, plus ten per cent for postage and packaging, to *PO Box No. 11, West Drayton, Middlesex UB7 OBR*

In the United States: Please write to *Penguin USA Inc., 375 Hudson Street, New York, NY 10014*

In Canada: Please write to *Penguin Books Canada Ltd, 10 Alcorn Avenue, Suite 300, Toronto, Ontario M4V 3B2*

In Australia: Please write to *Penguin Books Australia Ltd, 487 Maroondah Highway, Ringwood, Victoria 3134*

In New Zealand: Please write to *Penguin Books (NZ) Ltd,182–190 Wairau Road, Private Bag, Takapuna, Auckland 9*

In India: Please write to *Penguin Books India Pvt Ltd, 706 Eros Apartments, 56 Nehru Place, New Delhi 110 019*

In the Netherlands: Please write to *Penguin Books Netherlands B.V., Keizersgracht 231 NL–1016 DV Amsterdam*

In Germany: Please write to *Penguin Books Deutschland GmbH, Friedrichstrasse 10–12, W–6000 Frankfurt/Main 1*

In Spain: Please write to *Penguin Books S. A., C. San Bernardo 117–6° E–28015 Madrid*

In Italy: Please write to *Penguin Italia s.r.l., Via Felice Casati 20, I–20124 Milano*

In France: Please write to *Penguin France S. A., 17 rue Lejeune, F–31000 Toulouse*

In Japan: Please write to *Penguin Books Japan, Ishikiribashi Building, 2–5–4, Suido, Tokyo 112*

In Greece: Please write to *Penguin Hellas Ltd, Dimocritou 3, GR–106 71 Athens*

In South Africa: Please write to *Longman Penguin Southern Africa (Pty) Ltd, Private Bag X08, Bertsham 2013*

READ MORE IN PENGUIN

A CHOICE OF CLASSICS

Netochka Nezvanova Fyodor Dostoyevsky

Dostoyevsky's first book tells the story of 'Nameless Nobody' and introduces many of the themes and issues which dominate his great masterpieces.

Selections from the Carmina Burana
A verse translation by David Parlett

The famous songs from the *Carmina Burana* (made into an oratorio by Carl Orff) tell of lecherous monks and corrupt clerics, drinkers and gamblers, and the fleeting pleasures of youth.

Fear and Trembling Søren Kierkegaard

A profound meditation on the nature of faith and submission to God's will, which examines with startling originality the story of Abraham and Isaac.

Selected Prose Charles Lamb

Lamb's famous essays (under the strange pseudonym of Elia) on anything and everything have long been celebrated for their apparently innocent charm. This major new edition allows readers to discover the darker and more interesting aspects of Lamb.

The Picture of Dorian Gray Oscar Wilde

Wilde's superb and macabre novel, one of his supreme works, is reprinted here with a masterly Introduction and valuable Notes by Peter Ackroyd.

Frankenstein Mary Shelley

In recounting this chilling tragedy Mary Shelley demonstrates both the corruption of an innocent creature by an immoral society and the dangers of playing God with science.

READ MORE IN PENGUIN

A CHOICE OF CLASSICS

The House of Ulloa   Emilia Pardo Bazán

The finest achievement of one of European literature's most dynamic and controversial figures – ardent feminist, traveller, intellectual – and one of the great nineteenth century Spanish novels, *The House of Ulloa* traces the decline of the old aristocracy at the time of the Glorious Revolution of 1868, while exposing the moral vacuum of the new democracy.

The Republic   Plato

The best-known of Plato's dialogues, *The Republic* is also one of the supreme masterpieces of Western philosophy, whose influence cannot be overestimated.

The Duel and Other Stories   Anton Chekhov

In these stories Chekhov deals with a variety of themes – religious fanaticism and sectarianism, megalomania, and scientific controversies of the time, as well as provincial life in all its tedium and philistinism.

Metamorphoses   Ovid

A golden treasury of myths and legends, which has proved a major influence on Western literature.

A Nietzsche Reader   Friedrich Nietzsche

A superb selection from all the major works of one of the greatest thinkers and writers in world literature, translated into clear, modern English.

Madame Bovary   Gustave Flaubert

With *Madame Bovary* Flaubert established the realistic novel in France while his central character of Emma Bovary, the bored wife of a provincial doctor, remains one of the great creations of modern literature.

READ MORE IN PENGUIN

A CHOICE OF CLASSICS

Aeschylus	**The Oresteian Trilogy**
	Prometheus Bound/The Suppliants/Seven Against Thebes/The Persians
Aesop	**Fables**
Ammianus Marcellinus	**The Later Roman Empire (AD 354–378)**
Apollonius of Rhodes	**The Voyage of Argo**
Apuleius	**The Golden Ass**
Aristophanes	**The Knights/Peace/The Birds/The Assemblywomen/Wealth**
	Lysistrata/The Acharnians/The Clouds
	The Wasps/The Poet and the Women/ The Frogs
Aristotle	**The Art of Rhetoric**
	The Athenian Constitution
	Ethics
	The Politics
	De Anima
Arrian	**The Campaigns of Alexander**
St Augustine	**City of God**
	Confessions
Boethius	**The Consolation of Philosophy**
Caesar	**The Civil War**
	The Conquest of Gaul
Catullus	**Poems**
Cicero	**The Murder Trials**
	The Nature of the Gods
	On the Good Life
	Selected Letters
	Selected Political Speeches
	Selected Works
Euripides	**Alcestis/Iphigenia in Tauris/Hippolytus**
	The Bacchae/Ion/The Women of Troy/ Helen
	Medea/Hecabe/Electra/Heracles
	Orestes/The Children of Heracles/ Andromache/The Suppliant Women/ The PhoenicianWomen/Iphigenia in Aulis

READ MORE IN PENGUIN

A CHOICE OF CLASSICS

Hesiod/Theognis	**Theogony and Works and Days/ Elegies**
Hippocrates	**Hippocratic Writings**
Homer	**The Iliad**
	The Odyssey
Horace	**Complete Odes and Epodes**
Horace/Persius	**Satires and Epistles**
Juvenal	**Sixteen Satires**
Livy	**The Early History of Rome**
	Rome and Italy
	Rome and the Mediterranean
	The War with Hannibal
Lucretius	**On the Nature of the Universe**
Marcus Aurelius	**Meditations**
Martial	**Epigrams**
Ovid	**The Erotic Poems**
	Heroides
	Metamorphoses
Pausanias	**Guide to Greece** (in two volumes)
Petronius/Seneca	**The Satyricon/The Apocolocyntosis**
Pindar	**The Odes**
Plato	**Early Socratic Dialogues**
	Gorgias
	The Last Days of Socrates (Euthyphro/ The Apology/Crito/Phaedo)
	The Laws
	Phaedrus and Letters VII and VIII
	Philebus
	Protagoras and Meno
	The Republic
	The Symposium
	Theaetetus
	Timaeus and Critias

READ MORE IN PENGUIN

A CHOICE OF CLASSICS

Plautus	**The Pot of Gold/The Prisoners/The Brothers Menaechmus/The Swaggering Soldier/Pseudolus**
	The Rope/Amphitryo/The Ghost/A Three-Dollar Day
Pliny	**The Letters of the Younger Pliny**
Pliny the Elder	**Natural History**
Plotinus	**The Enneads**
Plutarch	**The Age of Alexander** (Nine Greek Lives)
	The Fall of the Roman Republic (Six Lives)
	The Makers of Rome (Nine Lives)
	The Rise and Fall of Athens (Nine Greek Lives)
	Plutarch on Sparta
Polybius	**The Rise of the Roman Empire**
Procopius	**The Secret History**
Propertius	**The Poems**
Quintus Curtius Rufus	**The History of Alexander**
Sallust	**The Jugurthine War** and **The Conspiracy of Cataline**
Seneca	**Four Tragedies** and **Octavia**
	Letters from a Stoic
Sophocles	**Electra/Women of Trachis/Philoctetes/Ajax**
	The Theban Plays
Suetonius	**The Twelve Caesars**
Tacitus	**The Agricola** and **The Germania**
	The Annals of Imperial Rome
	The Histories
Terence	**The Comedies (The Girl from Andros/The Self-Tormentor/TheEunuch/Phormio/The Mother-in-Law/The Brothers)**
Thucydides	**The History of the Peloponnesian War**
Virgil	**The Aeneid**
	The Eclogues
	The Georgics
Xenophon	**Conversations of Socrates**
	A History of My Times
	The Persian Expedition

READ MORE IN PENGUIN

A CHOICE OF CLASSICS

St Anselm	**The Prayers and Meditations**
St Augustine	**The Confessions**
Bede	**Ecclesiastical History of the English People**
Geoffrey Chaucer	**The Canterbury Tales**
	Love Visions
	Troilus and Criseyde
Marie de France	**The Lais of Marie de France**
Jean Froissart	**The Chronicles**
Geoffrey of Monmouth	**The History of the Kings of Britain**
Gerald of Wales	**History and Topography of Ireland**
	The Journey through Wales and **The Description of Wales**
Gregory of Tours	**The History of the Franks**
Robert Henryson	**The Testament of Cresseid and Other Poems**
Walter Hilton	**The Ladder of Perfection**
Julian of Norwich	**Revelations of Divine Love**
Thomas à Kempis	**The Imitation of Christ**
William Langland	**Piers the Ploughman**
Sir John Mandeville	**The Travels of Sir John Mandeville**
Marguerite de Navarre	**The Heptameron**
Christine de Pisan	**The Treasure of the City of Ladies**
Chrétien de Troyes	**Arthurian Romances**
Marco Polo	**The Travels**
Richard Rolle	**The Fire of Love**
François Villon	**Selected Poems**

READ MORE IN PENGUIN

A CHOICE OF CLASSICS

John Aubrey	**Brief Lives**
Francis Bacon	**The Essays**
George Berkeley	**Principles of Human Knowledge** and **Three Dialogues between Hylas and Philonous**
James Boswell	**The Life of Johnson**
Sir Thomas Browne	**The Major Works**
John Bunyan	**The Pilgrim's Progress**
Edmund Burke	**Reflections on the Revolution in France**
Thomas de Quincey	**Confessions of an English Opium Eater**
	Recollections of the Lakes and the Lake Poets
Daniel Defoe	**A Journal of the Plague Year**
	Moll Flanders
	Robinson Crusoe
	Roxana
	A Tour through the Whole Island of Great Britain
Henry Fielding	**Amelia**
	Jonathan Wild
	Joseph Andrews
	Tom Jones
Oliver Goldsmith	**The Vicar of Wakefield**

READ MORE IN PENGUIN

A CHOICE OF CLASSICS

George Herbert	**The Complete English Poems**
Thomas Hobbes	**Leviathan**
Samuel Johnson/	
James Boswell	**A Journey to the Western Islands of Scotland** and **The Journal of a Tour to the Hebrides**
Charles Lamb	**Selected Prose**
Samuel Richardson	**Clarissa**
	Pamela
Richard Brinsley Sheridan	**The School for Scandal and Other Plays**
Christopher Smart	**Selected Poems**
Adam Smith	**The Wealth of Nations**
Tobias Smollett	**The Expedition of Humphrey Clinker**
Laurence Sterne	**The Life and Adventures of Sir Launcelot Greaves**
	A Sentimental Journey Through France and Italy
Jonathan Swift	**Gulliver's Travels**
Thomas Traherne	**Selected Poems and Prose**
Sir John Vanbrugh	**Four Comedies**

READ MORE IN PENGUIN

A CHOICE OF CLASSICS

Matthew Arnold	**Selected Prose**
Jane Austen	**Emma**
	Lady Susan/ The Watsons/ Sanditon
	Mansfield Park
	Northanger Abbey
	Persuasion
	Pride and Prejudice
	Sense and Sensibility
Anne Brontë	**Agnes Grey**
	The Tenant of Wildfell Hall
Charlotte Brontë	**Jane Eyre**
	Shirley
	Villette
Emily Brontë	**Wuthering Heights**
Samuel Butler	**Erewhon**
	The Way of All Flesh
Thomas Carlyle	**Selected Writings**
Arthur Hugh Clough	**Selected Poems**
Wilkie Collins	**The Moonstone**
	The Woman in White
Charles Darwin	**The Origin of Species**
	The Voyage of the Beagle
Benjamin Disraeli	**Sybil**
George Eliot	**Adam Bede**
	Daniel Deronda
	Felix Holt
	Middlemarch
	The Mill on the Floss
	Romola
	Scenes of Clerical Life
	Silas Marner
Elizabeth Gaskell	**Cranford and Cousin Phillis**
	The Life of Charlotte Brontë
	Mary Barton
	North and South
	Wives and Daughters

READ MORE IN PENGUIN

A CHOICE OF CLASSICS

Charles Dickens	**American Notes for General Circulation**
	Barnaby Rudge
	Bleak House
	The Christmas Books (in two volumes)
	David Copperfield
	Dombey and Son
	Great Expectations
	Hard Times
	Little Dorrit
	Martin Chuzzlewit
	The Mystery of Edwin Drood
	Nicholas Nickleby
	The Old Curiosity Shop
	Oliver Twist
	Our Mutual Friend
	The Pickwick Papers
	Selected Short Fiction
	A Tale of Two Cities
Edward Gibbon	**The Decline and Fall of the Roman Empire**
George Gissing	**New Grub Street**
William Godwin	**Caleb Williams**
Thomas Hardy	**The Distracted Preacher and Other Tales**
	Far from the Madding Crowd
	Jude the Obscure
	The Mayor of Casterbridge
	A Pair of Blue Eyes
	The Return of the Native
	Tess of the d'Urbervilles
	The Trumpet-Major
	Under the Greenwood Tree
	The Woodlanders

READ MORE IN PENGUIN

A CHOICE OF CLASSICS

Thomas Macaulay	**The History of England**
Henry Mayhew	**London Labour and the London Poor**
John Stuart Mill	**The Autobiography**
	On Liberty
William Morris	**News from Nowhere and Selected Writings and Designs**
Robert Owen	**A New View of Society and Other Writings**
Walter Pater	**Marius the Epicurean**
John Ruskin	**'Unto This Last' and Other Writings**
Walter Scott	**Ivanhoe**
Robert Louis Stevenson	**Dr Jekyll and Mr Hyde and Other Stories**
William Makepeace Thackeray	**The History of Henry Esmond**
	The History of Pendennis
	Vanity Fair
Anthony Trollope	**Barchester Towers**
	Can You Forgive Her?
	The Eustace Diamonds
	Framley Parsonage
	The Last Chronicle of Barset
	Phineas Finn
	The Small House at Allington
	The Warden
Mary Wollstonecraft	**A Vindication of the Rights of Woman**
Dorothy and William Wordsworth	**Home at Grasmere**